The Studio Sleuths

The Trio Of Fools

by

Barbara Melling

R BOOKS

This Edition
Rampart Books

ISBN 978-1-915778-45-1

Rampart Paperbacks

The Trio of Fools

1

Suddenly the man saw her. A shock went through him. Electricity pulsed and his heart pounded. *What the hell? It's her! I've found her, at last I've found her.*

Quickly he looked away. He didn't want her noticing him. Oh no, not when the fates had smiled on him and had at last handed her to him on a platter.

Later that day, when he'd found out where she was living, he sat in his sparsely furnished room and thought about the woman who had messed up his life. What bizarre set of circumstances had led him to her? What had been the chances of him finding her after all this time? He sat and thought and as he thought, the anger that he'd kept buried for years surfaced.

2

Monday September 3rd

Andrea Bailey walked the twenty metres from her cottage to her art studio and unlocked the door. The steady rain the night before had been heavy and kept her awake. Now she was worried about her students' work. Had it been damaged by the drips that came through the roof when the wind blew rain from the east? She entered the dark room and switched on the light. Her north facing studio needed the extra light even on the brightest of summer days, which this was not. Looking around, she breathed a sigh of relief. There was no damage this time, not even a puddle of rain-water on the red concrete floor. The wind must have come from the southeast last night, and she had got away with it again, but it was only a matter of time before she would have to bite the bullet and get someone to have a look at the roof.

'She came from Greece, she had a thirst for knowledge...' the voice of Jarvis Cocker came from her speakers as Andrea clicked the music on her phone to shuffle.

'She studied sculpture at Saint Martin's college, that's where I

caught her eye...' Andrea sang along. She was alone. No one could hear her.

Her studio was her pride and joy and had once been the old blacksmith's forge turning out horseshoes, fire grates and farming tools for a few hundred years, but which had lain unused for forty until she had moved in removing the extensive ivy and relocating a few birds and a million spiders. The earth floor had still exposed the shallow pit dug by long ago horses as they scuffed their hooves on the ground impatiently waiting to be shod, and the stone walls displayed their telltale scorch marks showing where once the blacksmith had sweated before the red-hot coals beating the white-hot iron into shape. It had been a place of industry and creativity, and the hub of the small hamlet in a time when horses were key to prosperity and an important part of the lives of everyone in this farming community.

A small grant from the Arts Council had allowed Andrea to patch up the roof, hang a wooden ceiling and lay a concrete floor. The broken windows were glazed, and a toilet installed, turning it back into a place of creativity and fun, restoring life and value to the building and halting nature's quest to reclaim it for a while longer. She offered art and craft classes and over the years when funds allowed had added heating and a tiny kitchen, and now her studio boasted a large room for her textile classes and a smaller room where her pottery lessons took place. A recent corridor along the outside allowed the potters direct access to their room, and a tiny stable attached to the side of the forge housed her kiln. It was small, but perfect.

'I wanna live like common people, I wanna do whatever common people do...' Andrea sang louder now. This was one of her favourites and she knew as the music sped up she would have to dance.

She lived next door to her studio in the small blacksmith's cottage with her cats Nonsuch and Mrs Tim, and it suited her well. Andrea had long ago retired from her work as an art psychotherapist, although she had kept going for a while after her husband Jack had died, leaving her to bring up their four children alone. He had been a fisherman and even now she sometimes relived the fateful night he had gone out aboard the fishing boat he part owned with his best friend and business partner Hayden into the North Sea and never returned. She had stayed in the area wanting to be close to the sea and her husband, and when one by one her three eldest children left home to go to university, she had moved into her present home with her youngest son and set up the studio. He too had left now, and she lived alone in the end cottage of a small row of six stone cottages down a secluded lane in a quiet hamlet by the river.

A few years after she moved in, the cottage at the far end of the row came up for sale and Jackie, Hayden's widow and her best friend of over thirty years, had bought it and now lived just five houses away. Their already deep friendship had been strengthened by their shared grief and together Jackie and Andrea had helped each other through the dark times and managed to emerge stronger and determined to enjoy life while it lasted.

'I took her to a supermarket. I don't know why. But I had to start it somewhere...'

It was Monday morning and unlike a lot of people Andrea liked them. She taught batik and felt-making in her Creative Textiles classes, holding one in the morning and one in the afternoon. Her evening classes had long ago ceased when she began to find it just too exhausting, and because there was no public transport nearby and the quiet country lanes around where she lived were narrow, unlit and without any pavements, there were not too many people who were brave enough to venture out on dark winter evenings especially with ice and snow on the road. So these days she held her classes during the day and now the people who came to her studio were usually retired or self-employed and able to choose their own hours.

'You'll never live like common people, you'll never do whatever common people do...' Andrea was bopping about now, her voice drowning out the song. No one could see or hear her, so what did it matter that a sixty-nine-year-old woman was dancing around enjoying herself?

The song finished and as the next one started, Andrea began to organise the studio ready for the morning class.

'I stay out too late. Got nothing in my brain. That's what people say, mmm mmm. That's what people say, mmm, mmm...' She was off again, accompanying Taylor Swift and dancing round the room. She had a lot of energy this morning and the relief of the rain not having come in had added to her good mood.

It was early September, the summer term had finished and the new autumn term was starting. There was to be a new woman joining the afternoon class that day. They were a happy crew, consisting of her best friend Jackie, Cora, Betty and Sal, and soon Kim would be welcomed to their number bringing the tally up to five and filling all the available places.

'Cause the players gonna play, play, play, play, play. And the haters gonna hate, hate, hate, hate, hate...' Andrea skipped and danced about as she sang at the top of her voice.

Most people had been coming for years, some since the beginning, and she was fond of them all. Everyone was welcomed and included into the groups. No one came who didn't fit in or who cast a shadow over the happy proceedings. There had been a woman once who had seemed to go out of her way to hurt people, saying unkind and unfeeling things and generally upsetting folk, so much so that eventually Andrea had to ask her to leave, a thing she had never had to do before and did not enjoy. Since that time she had suspended a red silk bag containing a mixture of dried herbs above the doorway which everyone who entered had to pass beneath, and there had been no repeat of the unfortunate episode.

'Baby, I'm just gonna shake, shake, shake, shake, shake. Shake it off, shake it off, hoo, hoo, hoo...' The music continued and Andrea danced and jigged about until the first people began to arrive for the class, then she turned the volume down and stopped dancing.

The morning class passed happily with the students working on their own individual felt work or batiks. Halfway through, Andrea put the kettle on in the tiny studio kitchen and made everyone a cup of something. She liked to cater for all tastes and offered a range of teas and coffee, even hot chocolate, and the students appreciated this and often brought in cakes or expensive biscuits to add to the usual varieties of custard creams and bourbons.

Between the classes there was a break of fifteen minutes during which Andrea put the unfinished work from the morning class to one side and set out the work in progress of the next group. She was expecting an early arrival from a new member, and true to form, Kim Merchant arrived ten minutes before the rest. This usually happened when a new person started, as they were often unsure where the studio was or how long it would take to drive there. A car drew into the tiny parking area outside and after a few minutes, Kim walked in. She was a woman in her mid-fifties dressed in jeans and a pale blue cotton jumper with her dark hair cut in a neat bob; she had a florid complexion and looked at Andrea with worried eyes.

'Hi, you must be Kim,' Andrea smiled as she ushered her through the door, 'you found it alright?'

'Yes, no problem, I've been here before,' Kim spoke in a rather husky voice as her eyes raked over Andrea, seeming to be searching for something. They saw a tallish woman, her once auburn hair now streaked with grey, pulled back into an untidy bun, and her slim body encased in old baggy jeans and a long tee shirt in faded green.

'Great, come in, come in. Have you come far?'

'Not really.' Kim offered no more information.

Andrea led her to one of the chairs set around a huge square table. 'When did you come here before?'

'I came to a one day felting workshop you did a few years ago. It was good. We all made felt mittens. I use mine quite a lot.' Kim's eyes continued to search Andrea, making her feel a little uncomfortable.

I wish she'd stop staring at me. It's like she's looking for something, thought Andrea. 'Oh yes, I remember you now. It's nice to see you again. How are you?'

They chatted for a while until the others drifted in.

'Afternoon, afternoon, afternoon,' a loud voice entered the studio, coming from a dark stocky woman in her late fifties with an engaging smile. Her hair was cut very short, and she wore loose fitting red and black cotton trousers and a red tee shirt bearing a stylised image of Che Guevara on the front that had been bleached by the sun over many summers.

She was followed by a fairer, thinner woman of around the same age, wearing faded baggy jeans and a short-sleeved lilac shirt with a purple stain shaped like a large beetle on the left sleeve.

'Hi there,' the fair woman smiled warmly at Andrea and Kim.

'Hi, it's nice to see you both.' Andrea did the introductions. 'Kim, this is Betty,' Kim nodded at the stocky woman, 'and this is Sal,' another nod to the fair woman.

'This your first day with us?' Betty asked, giving Kim a friendly smile. 'You'll be fine. We can be a bit odd but deep down we're darlings.' She burst out laughing.

'Hello all,' another voice sounded.

'Cora, hello,' Andrea, Betty and Sal chorused as Cora marched in and dumped her large bag on her chair. She beamed at Kim.

'Hi, I'm Cora, as no one seems to want to introduce us.'

'Give me a chance, I was just going to,' Andrea chuckled, 'Kim, this is Cora, Cora, this is Kim.'

Cora was in her early seventies, as sprightly as a sparrow and lots of fun. She, too, wore jeans and a cotton jumper, but hers was yellow and looked new.

'Goodness, you're being brave today,' Andrea laughed, 'wearing yellow?'

Betty and Sal also laughed and Andrea explained to Kim that batik involved using hot wax and fabric dyes, both of which could easily ruin clothes and that was why everyone with any sense came to the studio wearing old clothes.

'Rude,' laughed Cora, turning to Kim, 'they're laughing because I'm messy, I can't help it, it's my nature. You'd better not sit too near me unless you want to get splashed.' Then back to Andrea she explained, 'I know, but I need to go on somewhere after here. I'll put an apron on.'

'It probably would've been better to bring your yellow jumper in a bag and change before you leave Cora,' suggested Betty.

'Alright smart arse, I can't think of everything,' she and Betty laughed loudly together.

'Hello, hello,' another voice came from the doorway.

'How come you live the nearest and yet you're always the last to arrive?' Andrea asked the latest arrival.

'Just a skill I have, that's all.'

'This is Jackie. Jackie, meet Kim. It's her first time with us.'

Jackie stood in the doorway smiling round at the group, her smooth skin and short spikey grey hair belying her seventy years.

'Cora, why the hell are you wearing yellow?' everyone laughed, including Kim.

3

Monday September 3rd

Andrea's classes were perhaps not the usual type where the teacher would set the projects and everyone would do the same thing. Drawing on her art school and later her art therapy background, she encouraged her students to express themselves in their own style, giving them the confidence to have faith in their own abilities. She would set certain projects when people first began and were learning the various techniques, but when they felt comfortable in their skill, she would encourage them to have their own ideas of what they wanted to make and then help them to achieve them.

As Kim had done some wet felting at the workshop previously, she decided to continue with that and Andrea showed her where the coloured wools were kept and the various towels and tools needed to make a simple piece of wet felt. She reminded her of the correct way to lay out the wool fibres before soaking them with water and adding soap. She helped her to assemble the wet wool between pieces of bubble wrap and then begin the hard work of rubbing the fibres together. Having got her started, Andrea left her to check on the others. At the present time, the other four were all working on batiks although they often swapped around from one medium to the other, all that is apart from Sal, who didn't like felting and absolutely loved batik, so never did anything else.

Batik was Andrea's first love. She had studied fine art at art school and later taught herself the ancient technique. Now she made batik paintings on recycled cotton fabric, often using old bed sheets, although the technique could be used on any natural material. The method involved building up layers of wax and dyes on fabric. She would apply hot wax from one of her three electric wax pots, which were always set out on one of the large square tables. There were two large cast iron electric frying pans which were perfect for the job and one smaller plastic batik wax pot with a metal lining which someone had given her years ago, but she couldn't now remember who. When plugged in, the pots heated up and melted the wax, keeping it hot and perfect for working with. Wherever the wax was applied, the fabric would remain the original colour, resisting the dyes when they were added. When a new dye was painted on and had dried, more wax was added to areas that needed to remain that colour, and so on and so on. It sounded difficult and often took people a while to get the hang of it, having to basically think backwards as they had to work light to dark instead of the more usual dark to light, but when they eventually got it they were usually as hooked as Andrea was.

'If everyone's happy and I'm not needed for a bit, I'll go and put the kettle on,' Andrea said when everyone was settled into their work.

'Excellent idea,' agreed Betty, and the others nodded enthusiastically.

Andrea took the various orders for teas and coffees and retreated to the tiny kitchen just off the studio. Ten minutes later, she was back bearing a tray full of steaming mugs and a tin of biscuits.

'Your beverages ladies,' and she handed out the mugs with exaggerated politeness.

'Lovely, I'm gasping.' Sal took her tea and sat down with a biscuit.

Sometimes people stopped to have a drink and other times they worked on through. It depended on what stage they were at in their work. Today they all stopped, as they wanted to get to know Kim a little better.

'So have you come far, Kim?' asked Cora, dipping her biscuit in her tea.

'No, not really, a few miles, that's all.'

'Whereabouts do you live?' Betty liked to place people, not just out of interest, but as a very friendly and helpful person, she often gave lifts to people if they were stuck.

'I won't tell you if you don't mind,' Kim snapped. 'I don't like people to know where I live.'

'Oh, okay.' Betty was slightly taken aback, 'no problem, it's your business.' She looked at Sal and raised her eyebrows. Sal looked back and shrugged.

There was an awkward pause until Cora spoke. 'A van's just pulled up outside. Are you expecting a parcel?'

'Oh, great, it'll be my clay delivery. I was hoping it would come this week. I'm running very low.'

Andrea hurried out to meet the driver. She preferred her deliveries to arrive during classes. Often they came when she was in her cottage and by the time she'd searched for her shoes, located the studio keys and got the doors open, the delivery men weren't very happy. Worse still was if they arrived when she was out and she was left to bring in the heavy boxes which had been left outside and were sometimes wet with rain.

Andrea liked the clay to be put into the corridor outside

the larger studio, stacked against the wall out of the way until she was ready to lug it down to the little room used for the pottery classes.

'Please can you stack it here' she asked the driver with what she hoped was a winning smile.

'Yeah, no problem' the young man grinned at her.

He probably thinks I look too old to heave heavy boxes about. Although she preferred to believe it was her winning smile which made him so amenable. Even though she was quite fit through regular yoga and lots of walking, Andrea looked all of her sixty-nine years, with her fair share of wrinkles, especially around her chin for some annoying reason. But when her face began to sag with the years, she had still retained her dimples and with her mostly straight white teeth she relied on her smile to win people round.

The boxes were heavy and the delivery man carried them in one at a time, stacking them against the wall by the studio door. After he'd stacked all five boxes, he straightened up and rubbed his beard.

'Okay, all done. Can you stand there please, I'll need a picture.' He held up his phone and snapped Andrea standing by the pile of boxes as proof of delivery.

The door into the large studio was open and the delivery man had a good view of the women working, he looked around the room his eyes resting momentarily on each one and he smiled, 'you all look very busy ladies, I'd ask what you're doing but unfortunately I don't have time,' and with a cheery goodbye, he left.

'Don't anyone trip over the boxes in the corridor,' Andrea warned the class as she came back in.

'Oh shit!' cried Cora. 'Buggeration, I knew that would happen.'

She had knocked her mug over and although only half

full, the remaining tea began to seep along the table towards her.

'Hang on,' Andrea quickly pulled a piece of kitchen roll from the pocket of her jeans and mopped up the spillage before it got to the yellow jumper. 'Lucky there wasn't much left.' There was a tinkling sound on the concrete floor as something fell from her pocket. 'My tiger's eye crystal. Oh no, I hope it's not cracked.' Andrea dived under the table to retrieve it and studied it carefully. 'It's fine,' and she happily returned it to her pocket.

'You and your crystals,' Jackie shook her head. 'I swear you'd be a pound lighter if you didn't weigh yourself down with pockets full of them.'

Andrea grinned, 'I like them, you know I do.'

At this Kim perked up, 'Why do you have them? What do they do? Are they for protection?'

'People have used them for years and years and for many different reasons. Personally I carry them because I love them aesthetically and because I believe they help balance and support the body, working with its natural energies.'

'Interesting,' Kim looked at her thoughtfully, 'you believe in all that kind of stuff, don't you? I remember from when I came here before. I noticed you have a red bag hanging over the door. What's that for?'

Andrea explained about the red bag and they chatted about crystals for a while, while Kim showing a lot of interest became the most animated she'd been all afternoon. Then the conversation moved on to the latest studio competition.

Twice a year, Andrea would set a theme for a light-hearted competition and any students who wanted to participate could create something within the theme and enter it. The judging for the competitions always took place just before Christmas and around the beginning of June, when Andrea would set out the entries on a long table in the larger studio and everyone would vote for the winner. There would then be a lunchtime meal out, and Andrea would present the winner with a box of chocolates. The Much Coveted Box of Maltesers was highly prized and most people joined in the fun. The theme for the current competition was Blowing in the Wind and both the potters and the textile makers were busy either making their entries or planning what they were going to do.

Five minutes before the end of the class, everyone cleared up and put their materials away. Betty and Sal were the first to finish and the first to leave. They had lived together for nearly thirty years and between them they ran a successful boarding kennel. They always left the class promptly when it finished as they needed to get back to the dogs and the drive back to their home in a village about half an hour away was down thin bendy lanes full of potholes and constantly crossed by slow strutting pheasants who often changed their minds mid-crossing, darting back to the other side with loud shrieks and causing Betty to brake hard despite only ever driving at about 20 miles an hour.

Kim gathered up her few bits and pieces, ready to leave. 'Well, I'll be off now too', she said, making for the door.

'I hope you've enjoyed it Kim,' Andrea smiled at her, 'I hope we haven't put you off and you'll be back next week.'

'Yes, I'll definitely be back next week. Goodbye.' Kim left the building, got into her car and drove away.

Jackie and Cora were in the habit of hanging back a bit after the class had finished. The three of them were great friends and enjoyed a chat, but today Cora needed to get away on time.

'Well, what do you think of Kim?' asked Andrea. 'D'you think she liked it?'

Andrea always wanted new people to feel at home and

enjoy themselves. After all, it wasn't as if it was school. People chose to come along and were paying to do so.

'She seemed to like it,' said Jackie, 'although she didn't say much, did she?'

'Probably just a bit shy,' Cora gathered up her bag and walked towards the door.

'Yeah, I always think it must be hard coming into an already established group for the first time, and on her own, too. It takes some courage to do it.' Andrea was turning off the wax pots, unplugging them at the wall.

'Yeah, you're right. Maybe she's a bit shy,' agreed Jackie. 'She didn't want to say too much about herself though, did she?'

'Haha, she wasn't going to let Betty know where she lived, was she?' Cora laughed as she left the studio.

'Oh well, maybe she's waiting till she gets to know everyone a bit better.' Andrea waved goodbye to Cora. 'We'll see what she's like next week. If she comes back.'

4

Tuesday 4th and Wednesday 5th September

It was Tuesday and Andrea went into her studio to do a bit of work on the batik she was making for an exhibition in the early summer. She lit an incense stick and clicked the music on her phone to shuffle. She was working from a photograph she'd taken of the boats moored in the creek at a regular haunt of hers known as The Point. The creek was where Jack and Hayden had kept their fishing boat moored with the others, to floating jetties metres from the sea, where the catches were unloaded before being sold to local shops and restaurants. The Point was the name of the peninsular that projected into the North Sea. Most of the peninsular was a nature conservation area and the nesting place of many types of seabirds, both native and visiting, and the haunt of many bird watchers. There was a café situated not far from the creek and Andrea, Jackie and Cora would visit often, seating themselves by the large windows and gazing out over the salty marshland by the sea. It was a lovely spot and they would often walk for miles down the footpath to the shore and along the beach, looking out across The Wash to the distant Norfolk coast.

'Time flies by in the yellow and green, stick around and you'll see what I mean...' the dark brown voice of George Ezra filled the studio while she hummed along.

She studied her batik painting. The dye from the previous day had dried nicely and Andrea chose her favourite tjanting tool from the box and carefully added the hot wax to the areas she wanted to remain that colour. She had various tjantings and these traditional batik tools, about the length of a pencil, consisted of a metal bowl with a tiny spout coming from it, usually made of brass to retain the heat and attached to a wooden handle. The molten wax is held in the bowl and flows out through the pipe onto the material to create a line or a dot. Andrea always used tjanting tools for any detailed work. She put the tjanting into the hot wax and sang along with George as she waited for it to heat up.

'I'll be riding shotgun, underneath the hot sun, feeling like a someone, someone, someone...' Andrea was up and dancing about now. She liked to dance in the empty studio, unseen by the passing dog walkers unless they pressed their faces to the window. *'I'll be riding shotgun, underneath the hot sun...'*

When she had completed the waxing, she mixed her dyes and added another layer of colour. The painting was starting to appear, but she still had a long way to go and there was nothing more she could do now until it had completely dried, ready for more wax to be applied. She hung up her work to dry slowly, switched off at the wall the small electric wax pot she'd been using, turned off the lights and locked her studio. Back in her cottage she made herself a cup of tea and gave Nonsuch and Mrs Tim some lunch, then having put on her coat and walking boots, she grabbed her litter picking paraphernalia, phone and earphones and went out to get some fresh air to clear the wax fumes from her head.

Andrea loved the countryside around where she lived, the fields, the lanes and pathways. The river at the end of her road flowed from the Lincolnshire Wolds to the sea and would swell when the lush green limestone hills of the Wolds received their heavy rainfall, making the water fill and flow as it gathered volume, rising sometimes by three or four feet as it headed for the freedom of the sea.

Most days she went walking, managing if she could at least an hour if not two or more as she headed off around the country lanes, always armed with a litter picking stick and a plastic bag. She hated waste and hated litter. It was her soapbox and she would bore to tears anyone who was careless enough to ask her about it. It wasn't just about the mess, the laziness and the 'not my problem' attitudes that some people seemed to have nowadays. What annoyed her more than anything was the lack of thought or care for nature. *We share this space with the animals, birds and plants and they were here first. They don't destroy it, so why do we?*

She took her usual route down the narrow lane towards the river, there were no pavements and she walked on the road or the grass verges, on the way stamping flat and grabbing with her stick a discarded drink can and an empty cigarette carton and putting them in her plastic bag. The area where she lived was never really bad for litter unlike some towns and cities, but it was a popular dog walking area and there was usually a smattering of plastic bags, sweet wrappers and empty cans which if she didn't collect them regularly would build up.

This morning was a little different though. As she walked towards the red brick bridge that spanned the river, she spotted an old wooden bedstead leaning against the wall. *What on earth is that doing there?* Walking over, she inspected it and saw it was undamaged. *I wonder if it's been dumped or is someone going to pick it up later? I'll come this way tomorrow and see if it's still here.*

Continuing down the lane, picking up the odd stray crisp packet and cigarette end as she walked, she noticed a man walking towards her. He looked to be in his late sixties but could have been older, he wore a flat cap and carried a walking stick and had what she thought was a sprightly walk, very upright and a little regimental, swinging his stick out in front of him with every other step before putting it down again. He marched straight up to her and stared at her.

'I've seen you before,' the man stated as he continued to stare at her.

Oh? 'Yes, probably, I do a lot of walking.'

'You pick up litter?' the man studied her with amusement.

'Yes, I do.'

He reached out, grabbed the front of her bag and peered inside. 'What have you collected?'

Andrea wanted to stop him but could think of no reason why he shouldn't see the rubbish she'd collected that morning. 'Just the usual.'

The man smirked, and she pulled the bag back from his grasp.

His eyes landed on her litter picking stick. 'And you've got a special little stick to do it!' he threw back his head and laughed loudly.

I don't like you. Andrea replaced the earphones that she had removed out of politeness. 'Must get on. Goodbye,' and she walked away, leaving the man looking after her and still laughing.

The following day was Wednesday, her pottery day. Both her classes were full with five people in each. Pottery was very popular, and she was always getting enquiries, many more than for her textiles classes. Andrea believed it was because everyone knew what pottery was while fewer people knew about felt-making and hardly anyone knew batik even existed. She used the smaller studio room for the messy clay work, the area by the tiny kitchen and toilet for storing the clays, glazes and work in progress, and the tiny ramshackle stable attached to the forge—just enough room for one horse was perfect for keeping her kiln separated from everyone as it obviously became very hot when in use.

These days Andrea did little ceramic work herself, occasionally she'd get on the wheel and throw a pot or two, although she wasn't as good as she was because it required constant practice to retain the skill. Sometimes she would be inspired and hand build a dish or small sculpture, usually as a present for someone, but mostly she encouraged others to progress their talents.

Both pottery groups were loud with everyone talking and laughing together. Many people said they came for the social aspect just as much as for the teaching. They were good groups of people and Andrea enjoyed the classes, but there was more work for her to do than with the textiles classes and often by 2.30 on a Wednesday afternoon when everyone had gone and she had switched everything off and locked up, she was too tired to do very much else. She usually managed a short walk, but didn't go far. Today she would just go up to the bridge and check out the bedstead.

As she approached, she could see it was still there, leaning bizarrely against the wall of the bridge, but now it was wet from the overnight rain, and now she knew it had been dumped.

Honestly some people, lazy bastards, just take it to the tip if you don't want it. Andrea snapped a couple of pictures on her phone, then turned away to continue walking.

'What's all this?' said a voice. 'Someone left a bedstead?'

Andrea spun round. It was the flat cap man; she hadn't heard him approach and her heart sank.

'Yes, it looks like it.'

'And you're taking pictures. You really love rubbish don't you, collecting it and photographing it.' Again he threw back his head and laughed loudly.

Andrea stood and looked at him. *What an obnoxious man you are.* She stayed looking at him, hoping to shame him into an apology or at least get him to stop laughing, but he continued to laugh and laugh until tears formed in his eyes and he fished in his pocket for a tissue. Having wiped his eyes, he screwed up the offending paper into a ball and dropped it onto the grass verge.

'What on earth are you doing?' Andrea couldn't help herself. 'You can see I'm picking up litter and you purposely go and drop your tissue on the verge. If you don't want it, take it home and dispose of it properly.'

'But you enjoy picking it up so much I thought I'd give you a treat.' The man laughed some more.

Andrea picked it up with her litter picker and put it into her rubbish bag, then turned on her heel and walked away from the horrible man, his mocking laughter following her down the lane.

When Andrea got home, she reported the dumped bedstead, complete with photos, to Fix My Street, a useful council website. Within the week, it was gone.

5

I'm watching you. I've found you now and I'm watching you.

As the weeks passed, the man kept an eye on the woman. Discreetly. Quietly. She would have no idea until he was ready. Already he knew her weekly routine, where she went and who came to visit. He was learning how she lived.

As he watched, an idea occurred to him and from the idea came a plan.

6

Monday 23rd September

Autumn was coming. The leaves of the Horse Chestnut trees in the lane were among the first to change into their seasonal colours and the spiked green fruits were growing plumper each day and would soon fall and split revealing their fat brown bellies to the dog walkers as they silently passed by.

At the studio, the autumn term continued with no dramas or upsets. And in the afternoon the textiles class students happily chatted as they worked on their projects under the guidance of Andrea. Jackie had finished her batik and was about to begin work on a long-felted scarf made of dove grey Marino wool with a large dandelion clock at one end and the fluffy seeds blowing away down the length. It would take her about three or four weeks and lots of physical work, but it would be worth it, she'd not only have a beautiful warm scarf ready in time for the winter but would also have an interesting piece for her entry into the current competition Blowing in the Wind.

The wet felting work was done on the other large table as felting and batik did not mix, so Jackie joined Kim, and having set out her towels and bubble wrap, began to sort out her wool from the boxes of different coloured fibres. Cora immediately expanded into Jackie's previous space, spreading out her trays of dyes and various paint brushes.

'Ha, you didn't hang about taking over my place, Cora.'

'It's only while you're felting. Don't panic,' Cora chuckled. 'I just thought I'd take advantage of your temporary absence.'

'Trying to pick up some of my artistic vibes more like, it's too late, the *Maltesers* are mine!'

'No chance,' Betty joined in, 'they've got my name on 'em.'

'They're mine this time,' said Sal with a giggle. 'I deserve a win after coming second in the last two competitions.'

'Bad luck then,' Cora grinned round the room. 'They'll be coming to me; I can feel it in my bones.'

There was always a lot of good-humoured banter in the group and Kim was beginning to relax more, but it was not until now in her fourth week that she began to open up.

'Where did you move from?' asked Cora later on when they were having their tea.

'Grantham.' This was the first thing Kim had told the group about herself, and everyone's ears pricked up.

'How long have you been here?' Cora continued, 'I expect you notice the difference, living here in the country to life in a city.'

'Grantham's not a city, it's a town,' Kim corrected and there the conversation ended.

Betty, never one to let a silence continue for long, embarked on a long story about a Jack Russel puppy that had come to their kennels and enjoyed his stay with them so much he hadn't wanted to go home when his owner came to collect him, and the owner was so furious she had demanded her money back.

'You didn't give it to her—did you?' asked Jackie, looking up from her felting.

'No, I bloody didn't, silly woman,' Betty roared with laughter. 'As if.'

Everyone was working on something for the competition and Betty had nearly completed her large picture of a hot air ballon. She had batiked a piece of material for the background sky and had made some wet felted pieces which she had cut into shapes for the coloured panels of the balloon, the envelope as she had proudly informed everyone it was called, and she was in the process of needle felting all the pieces together onto the cotton fabric sky. She stabbed through the felted wool and into the cloth using special barbed felting needles and a felting brush and planned to needle felt more details and use stitching for the ropes which attached the envelope to the basket or gondola.

'You've got the terminology down to a tee,' said Jackie as she carefully teased out the wool fibres for her scarf. 'I'm impressed. Have you ever been up in one?'

'Haha,' laughed Sal, 'she's been boning up on it, looking at pictures online when she's supposed to be on kennel cleaning duty.'

A small domestic squabble broke out between Betty and Sal, not unknown in the studio, and the others, having heard many similar disagreements before, all laughed. They knew these little spats were nothing serious and that Betty and Sal absolutely adored each other, but it was funny listening to them.

The conversation moved on and the women began to discuss the spate of robberies that had been taking place in the surrounding areas for some months now.

'I hear there's been another robbery,' Sal said as she mixed yellow dye powder with water. 'Round Spilsby way now. They seem to be getting nearer.'

'Yeah, it's worrying isn't it?' Cora looked up. 'Bit too close to home for my peace of mind.'

Betty sat back from needle felting her balloon and stretched her back, 'I wouldn't worry too much Cora, it's probably only the rich people in the big houses that get burgled. Why would they risk small houses?'

'Yeah, I suppose so, although it said on the news they seem to be targeting randomly. There's no real pattern, big houses and small, in busy towns and in remote rural locations.'

'Well just make sure your doors and windows are locked at night and when you're out, you'll be fine.' advised Betty as she returned to her felting needles.

Towards the end of the class, Andrea tried her luck with Kim. 'Were you working in Grantham?'

'Yes, I worked for Avere, the big canning company there. I was in H.R., you know, Human Resources. I was there for over thirty years.'

Kim looked too young to have retired, but Andrea didn't want to ask why she'd left, although she was keen to know.

'What made you move over here?' she asked instead.

'I've got no ties, my son Kevin is grown up and has his own life and my husband and I parted company some years back, he was drinking and it was difficult, so I bought a few acres of land and put some sheep on it.'

'Ooh lovely, so you've got a little smallholding.'

'Not really, my land isn't near my house,' Kim was opening up a bit more. 'I live about eight miles away from it.'

'That's a bit of an odd setup, isn't it?' Jackie joined in the conversation.

'Well, I bought the land a few years before I moved here, when I was still working in Grantham. I was reading the paper one day, and I saw a package of land up for sale. I decided to be impulsive and bought it. It was about ten acres in all, with a rundown building on it. I couldn't resist.'

'What a great thing to do,' said Andrea.

'I had an idea of getting a little small holding going and doing up the building, maybe planting a small copse of trees so I could be more self-sufficient and live by my little woodland in my retirement, but the best laid plans etcetera, etcetera.'

'What happened?' asked Cora. 'sounds like something went wrong.'

'Well, to begin with, I need a change of use for the land as it's currently farmland and I'm not allowed to garden it. Then I've discovered it's not that easy to plant a woodland, even a small copse like I wanted, it's expensive and although the forestry commission will help a bit there's a lot of hurdles to jump first and you need various permissions from lots of different agencies, I'm still wading through it all. And finally, I discovered the building was an animal shelter and I can't get planning permission to live there.'

Andrea looked at Kim. She saw a tired woman, worn out with bureaucracy and thwarted plans.

'Everything I try to do gets disallowed,' Kim went on. 'it's exhausting, so I've temporarily put some sheep on the land to keep the grass down and I'll have to see what happens.'

Betty was sympathetic 'That's a shame. Sounds like you had a good plan. Bloody bureaucracy.' And everyone agreed it could be a nightmare at times.

'Oh, I didn't tell you did I,' Andrea changed the subject, 'a few weeks ago I met this horrible man as I was out walking,' and she told them about her two meetings with the flat cap man.

'What a dreadful man,' Sal looked up at Andrea, 'some people are really ignorant.'

'Best to avoid him, just wants to get a rise out of you.'

Betty stabbed her needle through the wool a little harder than necessary. 'Obviously a complete arse.'

The others laughed at Betty's indignation, and she laughed too, but all the same they warned Andrea to keep out of his way.

The class came to an end with expressions of sympathy and a couple of 'chin up's' for Kim, and everyone drifted off home. As usual, Jackie and Cora remained behind for a while.

'It's an odd set up that Kim's got, isn't it?' Andrea mused as she tidied the work away and turned off the wax pots, 'what with living eight miles away from her land and everything. How does she keep an eye on it?'

'I know,' agreed Cora, 'and she can't really enjoy her land, can she? If I was her, I'd sell it and buy somewhere else. There's got to be plenty of suitable places around.'

'Anyone up for a coffee date this week?' Andrea asked. 'The Point?'

'Definitely.' said Jackie, 'but I can only manage Friday. Any good?'

'Fine by me,' said Andrea. 'I've got nothing planned, just working on my batik. I'm a regular Billy-no-mates.' She laughed.

'Well, I'm extremely popular as you might expect,' Cora grinned, 'so unfortunately I can't make it.'

'What's it like to have a life?' asked Jackie with a wry smile. 'I really can't imagine it.'

'Actually, I'm off to my sister's on Thursday for a long weekend,' Cora explained. 'she's got an appointment at the hospital and she wants me to go with her, and we're going to the cinema too.'

They chatted for a while about what film Cora and her sister were to see and then with a cheery wave Cora left to go home.

Cora didn't live far, about a five-minute drive away. She had a bungalow on the other side of Drayflot, their local town. She had divorced many years ago and now lived happily with her cats, Ollie and Milton. She had no children but was very close to her older sister, who lived in sheltered accommodation on the outskirts of Cambridge. Every four weeks or so Cora would drive over and stay for a few days. She enjoyed staying with her sister, being in a city with shops and nice restaurants. They always had fun and usually went to the cinema or to the theatre to see a play or a show.

'Well, I must be off too,' Jackie picked up her bag. 'See you Friday, I'll drive. Usual time at mine. I hope you don't meet the flat cap man again.' And with that, she began the short walk back to her cottage.

7

Monday 30th September and Thursday 3rd October

The following Monday, Kim arrived at the class looking very flustered and a little teary. The others were already there, and realising something was wrong, immediately stopped organising themselves and gathered round to find out what it was.

'Hi Kim, are you okay?' Andrea asked with her usual greeting.

'Not really, no,' Kim stared round at the others, 'I'm a bit upset, actually.'

'What's happened?' Cora was immediately sympathetic.

'I don't know where to begin,' the woman looked at breaking point. 'I really don't, and it all sounds so mad.'

Andrea took charge. 'Right then, sit down and tell us what's wrong.'

Kim slumped down into a chair, leant on the table and put her head in her hands.

'I don't think they like me,' she began. 'I think they're trying to frighten me.'

'Who's trying to frighten you?' asked Jackie.

'I don't know. That's the problem.'

'Well, why do you think whoever it is doesn't like you?' Jackie persisted.

'I don't know that either, but I think it's something to do with my land.'

'Right, well that's something,' Jackie walked over to her felt work and started to set it out. It wasn't that she'd lost patience or interest, it was only that she felt it might take a while to prize whatever was going on out of Kim, and she decided she may as well continue with her work while she listened.

'Maybe start from the beginning,' Andrea suggested. 'Take a deep breath and just tell us what's been going on.'

Kim took a deep breath and seemed to regain a little composure. She lifted her head from her hands and took another deep breath.

'As I think I've told you, about seven years ago, I saw an advert in the paper for a land auction. I was working in Grantham and thought it would be a good plan for my retirement. Build a little house, grow my own vegetables, plant some trees and live there quietly. I went to the auction and after a tussle with a couple of farmers who also wanted the land, I won it. I suspect I paid over the odds, but I didn't mind as I had my dream. Well, to cut a long story short, it wasn't as simple as I'd thought. What, with all the permissions and land change of use and so on, and then the building having no planning permission bombshell, but as I told you I bought some sheep to keep the land from becoming overgrown, and everything was going Ok. Then three years ago the company I worked for amalgamated with another larger company and I was offered a hefty lump sum if I took early retirement. It was too good an offer to refuse, and I decided to take it and move up here. Obviously,

I couldn't move into my dream cottage as it didn't exist, so I bought a small house about eight miles from my land. It's nothing special, but it's fine while I fight for planning permission.'

Andrea sat and listened, eager to know what had happened. Cora and Sal had abandoned any pretence of working and sat taking in every word, while Jackie and Betty, although obviously intent on hearing Kim's story, were continuing with theirs. No one said anything as no one wanted to interrupt Kim's flow and risk her clamming up as she had done before.

'It wasn't too long after I moved odd things began to happen.'

'What kind of things?' Andrea couldn't help herself.

The others looked at her with warning eyes and she shut up.

'I would go and walk the land, walking the boundaries and checking the sheep and I began to notice piles of mud and weeds from the ditches all lined up along my side of the ditch on my land. Then one time I actually saw the next-door farmer dumping the stuff on my land!'

'Well, that's just the farmer clearing out the ditches for drainage. They do it every year,' Jackie knew about these things.

'Why would he put it on Kim's side?' Sal asked.

'Probably just easier. I can't see that being very sinister.'

'Then I noticed clumps of long grass bundled together like sheaves of wheat and dotted about the field.' Kim went on.

'What—actually tied in bundles?'

'Well, sort of wound round with grass and placed around the perimeter of the field.'

'Ooh er, that's weird.' Sal made a face.

'Anything else happened you think is odd?' asked Jackie.

Kim looked round at the faces. 'I know there's nothing there, and it all sounds ridiculous, but I'm sure there's something going on.'

Secretly neither Jackie nor Betty thought there was anything to Kim's worries, she was making a mountain out of a molehill, and Andrea and Sal were also beginning to wonder what the fuss was about, but no one voiced their thoughts as they could see how upset Kim was.

Andrea decided to change tack.

'So, who do you think is doing these things? Your neighbour? Who owns the adjoining land?'

'Three separate farmers, one on either side and one on the back. Between them, they own all the surrounding land.'

'Hmm, sometimes landowners can be a bit funny, especially round here,' Andrea said, 'they often don't take well to incomers.'

'So, do you think it could be one of the farmers?' Jackie asked.

'I don't know who it is, but the farmers don't like me, that's for certain. They think I'm a newcomer playing at farming, and I'm not even farming. I want a small holding and tiny deciduous woodland. The sheep are only there to keep the grass down.' Kim's voice had gone into a whine and Betty having had enough changed the subject.

'A woman came into the kennels at the weekend wanting to board her dog, Flossie, a long-haired retriever. She'd rung us months ago and booked Flossie in for a fortnight while she went on holiday. Fine, you might think, what's wrong with that? Well, I'll tell you what's wrong with that. She only bloody turned up with Flossie and her five two-month-old puppies!' Betty roared with laughter. 'What a bloody cheek. She hadn't even told me. I mean, who goes away when their dog's had puppies anyway? She said the holiday was booked before they knew about them, and it was too expensive to cancel. So, we had six dogs to board. You should have seen Sal's face. It was a picture.' Betty roared again.

'Imagine,' said Sal, 'we had a nice cosy kennel set up for Flossie but there was no room for another five in there too, not comfortably anyway. We had to rush round like mad women to accommodate the six of them together. We managed it though. Luckily, it's not peak season, and we had room.'

'The bloody woman said it had never occurred to her to let me know as they would all be together anyway,' Betty continued, 'honestly people have no idea. Luckily our kennels are designed to be adaptable to accommodate more than one dog. We have adjustable walls, but that's not the point. And to top it all, she only wanted to pay for one dog as she said the puppies were still on mum's milk. I ask you, not a thought for the amount of shit being produced.' Another roar of laughter, and this time everyone joined in.

'There's something else.' Kim's voice had lost its whine and was more of a whisper now. 'I'm sorry to squash the mood, but I have to tell someone. I'm so worried.'

The laughter stopped.

'Go on,' said Cora, 'tell us what else is worrying you.'

'I went to the land at the weekend and there was a dead crow pinned to the broken animal shelter.' Kim looked round at everyone, her eyes full of tears. 'Nailed to a beam. That can't be explained away, can it? Someone is trying to get rid of me and I think they're using black magic to do it.'

They all stared at Kim. Was she really frightened or just barmy? It was hard to tell.

During the week, Andrea, Jackie, and Cora met up again at The Point. They walked down to the sea and along the shoreline. The tide was quite far out, and they wandered over the wet sand kicking at clumps of seaweed, chatting and laughing and enjoying the fresh air despite the cold wind. The east coast was flat, there were no interesting rock pools full of crabs and sea anemones, or cliffs full of fossils like there were on the south coast or in Wales. Further up the country to Yorkshire and Northumberland, the coastline became more rugged, but their bit was flat and open and they could see for miles and miles.

Andrea bent down and picked something up.

'What've you got there, a shell?' asked Cora.

'No, it's a Hag stone.' Andrea held out a white stone about the size of a large egg with a perfect hole though the middle of it.

'What on earth's a Hag stone? I've never heard of one before.' Jackie came over to have a closer look.

'It's a stone with a naturally made hole running through it. They're thought to bring good fortune, protection, healing and knowledge.' Andrea turned it over in her hand looking very pleased with herself.

Jackie began to search around. 'I want one.'

'It's said that you don't find a Hag stone, a Hag stone finds you.' Andrea explained, and she put it in her pocket.

Jackie was still searching. 'What do you have to do with them?'

'You can wear them round your neck, but this one's too heavy for that, so I'll keep it at home for good luck. Or you can nail it to your barn door to stop the witches from taking your horses for a gallop in the night.' She laughed.

'You two actually believe all this, don't you,' Cora grinned, 'what a load of folklore rubbish.'

'I love a bit of natural magic, as you know, but I'm not sure Jackie's as immersed as I am.'

'I'm a curious sceptic,' Jackie was turning over a piece of driftwood with her foot, 'although to be honest, more sceptic than curious.'

Cora was a regular churchgoer, and this kind of thing wasn't for her. She did a lot for the church and played a large part in the church community, running the monthly lunch club and helping with the Christian book group. She was responsible for her own window in the church, which she decorated each week with flowers and beautiful special arrangements for festivals. Despite her strong faith, she was completely tolerant of the beliefs of others and never dismissed them. Andrea knew she wasn't mocking her, it was only their normal good humoured teasing.

'Oh, look at this one I've found,' Jackie picked up a grey stone, 'it's got a white stripe running across it.'

'That's a Wishing Stone,' said Andrea, 'an excellent find, well done.'

'A Wishing Stone, what do I do with it... just make a wish?'

'You trace your finger round the white line, close your eyes, make a wish, then throw it as far as you can into the sea. Then your wish will come true.' Andrea smiled, she wasn't much of a believer in wishes and spells and the like but she enjoyed folklore and ancient customs and beliefs, and she did believe in the natural magic of the planet and the well-being people could get from communing with natural things including rocks and stones, hence the crystals she always carried in her pocket.

'But the sea's miles out. I can't throw it that far,' Jackie said.

'Or you can give it to someone else. Your wish will still come true.'

Jackie traced the line with her finger and made a wish. 'Here you are Cora, this is for you,' and she gave the Wishing Stone to Cora, who took it with a laugh.

'Thank you very much. I will treasure it always.' She put the stone in her pocket then turned away and raised her eyes up to heaven.

8

Monday 14th, Tuesday 15th and Friday 18th October

October progressed, and the leaves had all changed colour now and many had fallen coating the lanes and filling the ditches. The conkers too lay on the ground shining up, begging to be noticed. Andrea came back from her regular walks with pockets full of them and put them in bowls around her house. She didn't believe they had any special powers. She just liked them with their deep rich colour and the way they felt in her hand, although it was said that they deterred spiders, something to do with a chemical they give off.

It was Monday afternoon, and Kim arrived at the class in a state of near collapse.

'I've had a huge shock.' She went over to her chair, sat down, and put her head in her hands.

Andrea noticed Betty arch an eyebrow and rolled her eyes. Although very kind and someone who would do anything for anyone, Betty was straight talking and called a spade a spade. She had no time for all the drama and what she regarded as overacting.

'Go on then, tell us what's happened,' said Jackie settling

down to hear the latest while she did the monotonous soapy rubbing of the wool between the layers of bubble wrap.

'I went to my land on the weekend, and it was awful. There were hundreds of black feathers all over the big field.' Kim's voice wobbled as she described what she'd seen. 'They were all stuck in the ground in rows. It was terrifying, I can't tell you. It was black magic, I'm sure of it. I didn't know what to do. I panicked and then began collecting them up. I couldn't leave them there. I just needed to get rid of them. I had some large supermarket carrier bags in my car, so I grabbed them and started stuffing them full of feathers. I collected four full bags and there were still thousands left.'

A weird noise came from Betty, somewhere between a sigh and a cough, with a bit of a tut in there somewhere too, but Kim was too deep in her recall to notice.

'I took them home and put them in my rainwater barrel to purify them. I drove back the next day and collected the rest, another six bin bags and two big Bags for Life absolutely stuffed full. There were millions. It killed my back, but I had to get rid of them. I wasn't going to let whoever did it win. I took them home and washed them all in the rainwater butt. I had to cleanse them, then I dug some holes in my garden and buried them. It took me all day and well into the evening. I was still burying them in the dark, but I needed them gone.' She put her hands to her face and began to sob.

Andrea gazed at the broken woman in front of her. She couldn't think of anything to say.

Cora looked up from her work. 'What an odd thing to have happened. What d'you think had gone on? A hawk perhaps, or a kestrel killed a group of blackbirds?'

'It wasn't a bird. There were far too many, and they were sticking up out of the grass, not in piles like when a hawk has made a kill. Someone or more likely a group of people, maybe a coven had put them there on purpose to frighten me off my land.'

'If they were all stuck in the ground, it must have taken whoever did it ages and why on earth would anyone bother?' Jackie asked as she straightened up, giving her back a rest from the rubbing.

'To frighten me, I tell you. They want my land.' Kim had raised her head from her hands and was staring at the group, her eyes wide.

Andrea looked at her. She's certainly very scared but I don't know how we can help, she thought. 'What a shame you didn't think to take some photos. We might have had a few ideas, but it's certainly a mystery.'

'If you're worried, why not go to the police?' Betty suggested.

'I did, but they aren't interested. They say there's nothing they can do.'

'Well, I don't suppose there is, really. No witnesses or even photos of the crime, if it even is a crime.'

'Why don't you just sell up?' suggested Cora. 'You'd save yourself a lot of worry and you could get some land somewhere else with proper planning permission for a house.'

'Yes, you could have your dream,' agreed Andrea.

'It's certainly the most sensible solution,' Jackie joined in. 'You wouldn't even have to bother with an estate agent. Just ask the neighbouring farmers to make you an offer and take the highest.'

'I'm not going,' said Kim emphatically. 'They're not driving me off my land. I'll get my small holding, and I'll get my house. I won't be beaten by them.'

There was no arguing with Kim, so no one tried, but everyone secretly thought it was a silly way to go on and that Kim would make herself ill. She should sell up and move on.

The next day was beautiful, one of those magical autumn days when the sun shines and the leaves glow golden in its light. Andrea needed to be outside. She put on her boots, grabbed her litter stick and bag, told Nonsuch and Mrs Tim that she wouldn't be long and off she went. It was lovely being in the fresh air, and Andrea smiled as she held her face up to the sun. After a while, she plugged her earphones into her phone and continued to listen to her audiobook. It was "The count of Monte Cristo by Alexandre Dumas". She loved the classics, and this was one of her favourites. Due to her dyslexia, Andrea found it much easier to listen to the unabridged audio books she could access on her phone, especially the long epic tales.

She was striding out, heading towards the river, enjoying the sunshine, the countryside and her book when she passed the layby that the fishermen sometimes used and was caught up short by the sight that greeted her. A mountain of mattresses, broken beds and chairs had just been dumped there. This was a new low, she'd seen fly tipping and indeed kept her eyes open for it, but this was not the usual bin liners or maybe old settee that someone couldn't be bothered to dispose of properly, this was on another level entirely. There were loads of it. Someone had loaded up a large trailer or a van and driven out here specifically to dump it, possibly more than once, by the size of the pile. What the hell is this? Andrea took photos from all sides of the pile. This may be too much even for Fix My Street, but they'll know what to do anyway. I just can't believe some people. How can they be such absolute bastards?

'I thought I'd find you photographing the rubbish. I know it's your hobby.'

Andrea turned round to see the obnoxious flat cap man

standing behind her grinning. She decided not to engage with him.

'Excuse me,' and she walked away.

'Aren't you going to introduce yourself, Andrea Bailey?' The man called after her.

A shock went through her. He knows my name. Andrea turned round.

'It seems I don't need to, although it's no secret.' She turned to walk away again.

'My name is Ernest. How do you do Andrea Bailey? I'm very pleased to meet you.' Ernest, still grinning, stepped towards her with his right hand outstretched.

He wants me to shake his hand, no bloody chance the man's a creep. Turning her back on him, she walked away.

'I hope we can be friends, Andrea Bailey,' Ernest called after her and then threw back his head and laughed.

Later that week over coffee at The Point, Andrea told Cora and Jackie about Ernest.

'I know this is a silly question, what with your background and all, but there's no chance he's got special needs, is there? Maybe he doesn't understand social niceties, boundaries and such?' asked Jackie.

'No way, I worked in mental health for years and years and recognise people with difficulties or different ways of communicating. No, Ernest knows exactly what he's doing and saying and he's going out of his way to be unpleasant.'

'Wow, what a creepy man,' Cora said, then she sipped her cappuccino.

'Sounds like you should really keep out of his way then Andrea,' Jackie stirred her latte thoughtfully, 'seriously I mean it, he sounds unhinged, could be dangerous.'

‘Don’t worry, I’m going to avoid him as much as I can. Although it’s easier said than done, he seems to appear from nowhere a lot of the time.’

‘How does he know your name, though?’ asked Cora.

‘I think he must have either asked someone, a dog walker or someone, or seen that I have the studio and looked it up online and found it out that way.’

‘Just keep out of his way Andrea, that’s all, keep well away from him,’

9

Nearly every night, the man would sit alone and plan. There was a lot of preparation to do. He would take his time and do it properly. Everything had to be in place for his plan to work. He made lists and began buying the things he needed. He had to think it through from every angle. He would have one chance and only one. He must not mess it up.

10

Monday 21st & 28th October 4^{th,} 11th & 18th & Tuesday 19th November

Kim arrived the following Monday afternoon with the next instalment of her life. Something seemed to be happening to her each week, and now it was becoming a bit of a soap opera. Now Kim had been to a witchcraft shop in a nearby town. She had visited it before, and this time had told the owner about the feathers in the hope he might help her or at least give her some advice. He told her that black feathers were not the omens of doom that Kim had imagined, but represented a shift or a need for change. This did nothing to ease Kim's fears that she was being driven from her land. To her mind, this was further proof. She was now absolutely convinced witchcraft was being used to oust her. How else would they know to use black feathers to bring about a change?

'So, what are you going to do?' asked Sal. 'Did he give you any advice?'

'He was very nice and seemed interested. He told me about a book he had for sale about protection spells and rituals. He said that might help, but I've got something similar already that I bought from him a while ago.'

Betty made one of her noises and Cora rolled her eyes, but Kim didn't notice.

'You have to do something,' said Andrea, 'you're going to make yourself ill. If you really won't sell up, then you have to take measures, put up CCTV cameras or something. You can't rely on magic and spells, you need to be proactive. Can you go round to talk to the neighbours, try to reason with them?'

'I'm surprised at you, Andrea,' Kim looked at Andrea, genuinely puzzled. 'I should've thought you, of all people, would understand about spells.'

'What? Why? I don't dabble in witchcraft.'

'You have a red silk bag full of herbs over your doorway, you have crystals in your pockets, and I believe you hang bells in your oak tree.'

Jackie laughed. 'Banged to rights there Andrea.'

Andrea laughed too. 'You're right Kim, I do all of those things, but in your position, I would sell up, no question. My thoughts on the subject of magic, natural and otherwise, are different to yours and it would take too long to explain them even if I wanted to, but let me just say this, if I were ill, I wouldn't sit at home drinking potions and chanting spells, I would go to see a doctor.'

'Andrea's right, you need to be sensible,' Betty joined in. 'Get some cameras up and talk to your neighbours. There's no point just moaning about things. You need to help yourself. Take the initiative.'

Kim was quiet after this. The class continued with the usual joking and stories from Betty. No one knew whether Kim was thinking about what had been said or had taken offence, but they knew if she had been offended she'd soon get over it.

The following week, Kim reported that she'd put a CCTV camera up on her run-down croft and two security lights that went on if someone trespassed at night. She had also put a camera above her front door. It seemed she had listened after all and everyone agreed this had been a sensible thing to do, although secretly they all hoped she would calm down a bit now as to be honest, they were finding it a little exhausting.

There was no chance of that however as the next week she came to the class saying lots of small holes had been dug in the flower beds in her front garden and as if that wasn't crazy enough, she now believed naked people were walking past her house at night.

'Oh, come on now,' Betty couldn't help herself, 'naked people? It's bloody November!' and she roared with laughter.

'I know it's hard to believe, but I managed to get some photos.' Kim got her phone out. 'They're not very good, I'm afraid, but they're something.' She scrolled through her photos. 'These are the holes.'

Everyone crowded round her phone and peered at the photos. The holes in the garden were clear enough, but they were only pictures of a few small, fairly shallow holes dug in the soil of the flowerbed, about the size a gardener would dig to plant a bulb or a small plant.

'And these are the people, the naked people.'

The photographs of the people were taken in the dark through a window and without a flash. The grey, grainy pictures showed a blurred shape which could have been a figure walking past, possibly two walking abreast, if you squinted. There was absolutely no indication that they were naked.

'What makes you think they were naked, Kim?' asked Jackie as she peered at the phone.

'I know the photos aren't very good, but honestly when I looked through the window, it looked like they didn't have any clothes on. There was no collar or hat. Look at the photos, the shape is very smooth—there's no outline of clothing.'

'They could just have been wearing a smooth jacket,' Cora said. 'Sorry Kim, but it doesn't look very sinister to me.'

'Me neither, I'm afraid,' agreed Jackie. 'Just someone going for a walk.'

Kim looked dejected. She was trying hard to get people to believe her and take her worries seriously, but no one would and now, when she thought she had photographic proof it had been useless.

'I'm sorry Kim,' Andrea moved away, ready to make the tea, 'we can see how worried you are, but do you think you might be making a mountain out of a molehill?'

'I know it all sounds mad. I know I sound mad, but I don't know what to do to make people believe me. You all think I'm crazy...'

'We don't think you're crazy,' Cora said gently. 'We can all see how worried you are. We're just concerned you're getting it all out of proportion and you're making yourself ill.'

'The police think I'm crazy,' continued Kim as if she hadn't heard Cora speak. 'I'm at my wit's end. Maybe I am crazy.'

'If you won't sell up, why don't you go away somewhere? Have a little holiday, get away somewhere nice, right away from everything,' Sal suggested. 'You're bound to feel better when you come back.'

'Maybe,' said Kim quietly.

The class continued in a more subdued mood than

usual, and even the arrival of tea and biscuits didn't lift the atmosphere. Everyone got on with their work, but there were no jokes, no laughing. Even Betty didn't have a story to liven the atmosphere.

Kim had finished making her wet felted piece and had decided to turn it into a cushion cover, so for the last week or so she had been patiently needle felting a neat row of tiny red and blue flowers onto it.

'That's so pretty Kim, well done,' Andrea said as she looked at the work. 'How about needle felting some unattached petals or making the flower heads into a sort of cascade from the corner? It would look great, and you could enter it into the competition if you wanted to. Blowing in the Wind, it would be perfect.'

'Hmm, I might, I'll see. I'm not really in the mood this week. I think I might go home. It's only twenty minutes early. Sorry.'

When Kim had left, the mood in the studio lightened. It was like a heavy blanket had been lifted and within minutes the good-natured banter and laughter had returned and Betty took the opportunity to regale them all with another tale from their kennels.

'We had a little Cocker Spaniel, Rusty, in last week,' she told them. 'She was such a sweet little thing, very good natured, but very, very old.'

'Oh no Betty, don't tell them that please,' Sal laughed as she looked at her partner.

Ignoring her, Betty continued, 'Her owner, a Mrs Knoblett, had booked her in overnight while she went to London for a theatre trip. Well, Rusty hadn't wanted her dinner despite us obeying every one of Mrs Knoblett's detailed instructions of what to give her. Sal was a bit worried, but Rusty seemed okay, so we put it down to her being away from home and not having much of an appetite.

Anyway, that night at about two in the morning I heard an almighty wailing coming from the kennels, so I ran down thinking it was one of the dogs, but no it was Sal in floods of tears. She was crying so much she couldn't speak and just pointed to Rusty, who was lying in her bed, on her back with her tongue lolling out.'

'Oh no, poor Rusty,' said Jackie.

Again, Betty ignored the interruption and continued. 'Well, after telling Sal to stop crying and to get a bloody grip, I went into Rusty's pen and gently stroked her. She immediately woke up and was as happy as anything, tail wagging and everything. Turned out Rusty liked to sleep in that position and Mrs Knoblett had forgotten to mention it. She'd also forgotten to tell us her dog was bloody deaf! Poor Sal, thought she'd died whilst in our care!' Betty hooted with laughter and Sal grinned sheepishly.

'It was a perfectly reasonable assumption to make,'

'Not without checking first it wasn't, you dozy article,' Betty laughed some more, but then looking affectionately at Sal, she said, 'but I wouldn't have you any other way.'

'There's never a dull moment with you two is there,' Andrea laughed. 'Anyway, it's time to finish now, I'm afraid. Have a good week everyone, and I'll see you next Monday.'

And on that note, they tidied up and left.

The following week, Kim arrived at the studio with the news that her sheep were ill. She had gone to the police with another accusation that she was being victimised, but they weren't interested as there was no crime and no proof of a crime. They had told her sheep get ill occasionally, especially if they're not being looked after properly and advised her to call the vet. She'd done so, and he had given them something, and now she was waiting to see if they would recover.

Kim was in the middle of telling them about this latest problem when Betty said, 'There's someone looking in the front window.'

This wasn't unusual as passing walkers, seeing the lights on, now and again peered in to see what was happening, but when Andrea looked up, she saw Ernest's face pressed up against the glass, hand shielding the light, scanning the room. She pretended not to notice and casually wandered to the door and locked it. She didn't want him coming in and trying to join them—no way. But he wandered off without trying the door and Andrea breathed a sigh of relief.

Kim was now coming every week with a tale of something bad having happened in her life. The next Monday, Kim told them one of her security lights attached to the rundown building on her land had been smashed and some of the bricks had been taken out of the wall and left on the ground. To her, this was yet more proof of regular black magic rituals taking place on her land. She was convinced a sinister coven was meeting in the small building and when the others asked why anyone would meet there as it sounded like it didn't even have a roof, Kim told them she believed it might be a sacred site or a crossing of ley lines. They pointed out that if the building was run down and a virtual a ruin, then naturally bricks would fall out of the walls, especially in the strong easterly gales they had been experiencing lately. But Kim had gone to the police and surprise, surprise, they were not interested—no crime and no proof of a crime.

By now, Betty had completely lost interest. She thought

Kim was batty and ignored her tales of persecution. Jackie just switched off and got on with her work, not engaging with the madness of her stories. Cora also thought she was a bit odd but felt sorry for her and was sympathetic up to a point. Even Sal was beginning to lose patience with her, although she was still keen to hear updates. Only Andrea was gripped. Oh yes, she too thought Kim was losing her hold on reality, but she loved a mystery and was fascinated by how it would pan out, if indeed it ever did.

Andrea was very interested in why people behaved as they did. Functioning people usually had a reason to explain their weird behaviour and Andrea, her psychotherapy background never far from the surface, was interested in understanding what made Kim tick.

The next day, Andrea went out walking as usual. She took the lane down to the river and then followed the smaller lane alongside the riverbank. She watched the ducks and moorhens swim out from the sheltering reeds to the safety of the middle of the river as she approached. She always felt bad when they did this, as she didn't want to disturb them, but it was better they were scared of her than risk being caught by someone else after a free dinner.

Andrea couldn't concentrate on her audiobook today, she kept thinking about Kim. She couldn't help worrying that something was wrong, but whether it was real or in Kim's mind, she couldn't tell. She did not want to become too involved; she knew about the importance of keeping boundaries and the difficulties that could arise if they were crossed. She was Kim's art teacher, that was all. She wasn't her therapist; she wasn't even her friend. She was just pondering this when her thoughts were interrupted as she approached the second layby that the fishermen used. There in front of her, virtually filling the small layby, was another mountain of dumped rubbish. *What the hell's been happening here?*

There were two double mattresses, boxes and bin liners full of old junk, electrical waste, broken tiles, jagged pieces of metal, and a couple of large pieces of what looked like asbestos. *Oh god, this is appalling. This isn't just dropped litter or even some lazy git dumping an old settee because he can't be bothered to take it to the tip, this is commercial fly tipping. It's serious. I need to photograph it and report it. I'm furious. If bloody Ernest comes along now laughing and trying to be funny, I shan't be responsible for my actions.*

Luckily for him, Ernest didn't come along, but a few days later the council did and within the week the dumped rubbish was gone.

11

Monday 25th November. 2nd December & Thursday 12th December.

It was late November, a busy time for the studio. The competition entries had been set up and displayed for a fortnight to allow everyone to vote, and plans for the Christmas lunch were well underway. The competition prize giving was always a fun event and at Christmas, Andrea tied it in with the Christmas lunch, which was usually held at the café at The Point. She had been collecting names, deposits and menu choices for a week or two now and most of the people who came to the studio were coming.

At the afternoon textiles class, Kim arrived with the latest instalment of the seemingly endless saga of her life, or 'Kimanation Street' as Sal had dubbed it. This time it seemed her house had been broken into. There were no signs of forced entry, but she knew someone had been in. There was nothing on the CCTV, but she was positive that someone had gone in and drawn magical signs on the walls and ceiling. She had photos on her phone, but the so-called drawings were so faint they could hardly be seen and could easily have been only hairline cracks in the plaster. Kim had been to the police but again with no sign of forced entry and nothing taken, there was no crime. She was now even more worried because the Winter Solstice was not far off, the longest night, and Kim was convinced something bad was going to happen on the night of the twenty-first of December.

Then there were mysterious magical scratches on her car. Kim arrived at the studio and announced that here was the proof at last. They didn't need to just take her word for it or look at bad photographs. Here at last was tangible evidence that all she had told them was true. Her car doors had been scratched with occult symbols, proof that she was being hexed.

Everyone stopped what they were doing and trouped outside to look at Kim's car. It was freezing in the little car park as they all stood round the red Astra. Kim looked so triumphant that no one said what they really thought, even Betty held her tongue, but the tiny scratches to the paintwork at the base of the two doors on the driver's side had, to everyone's eyes, quite obviously been made by foliage. It looked like the doors had been opened against a prickly bush and a little bit of scratch remover from any car accessory shop would get them looking good as new. They all made commiserating noises and tutted and then trouped back inside to get warm. This is how they were with Kim now, making the responses they thought she wanted and then moving on.

'The votes have been counted and we have a winner for the competition Blowing in the Wind,' announced Andrea, 'please go and have a look.'

There had been twenty-one entries in the competition, an excellent amount, and they had all been arranged anonymously on a long table by the window, each with their printed title below them. They were numbered and everyone could vote for as many as they liked, although only once per entry. As usual, it was a good display with a mixture of batiks, felted work and ceramics. It was always interesting looking at what had been made in the other classes and everyone enjoyed seeing the creative ways people interpreted the different themes.

'Oooh I got first prize!' Jackie was delighted, 'the Much-Coveted Box of Maltesers is mine!'

'Well done, Jackie,' Cora grinned at her, 'your Dandelion scarf was beautiful, a well-deserved win.'

'Oh, my goodness,' squealed Kim, 'I can't believe it. I've got third place! My felted cushion cover came third. That's brilliant.' Kim beamed round the studio and looked the happiest she had looked for weeks.

The others smiled at her; it was nice to see her looking so pleased; they congratulated her and complimented her on her work.

'Congratulations,' said Andrea smiling at her, 'well deserved, it's a lovely piece of felting.'

There had been two second places, a cleverly detailed miniature ceramic guitar with a photo of Bob Dylan in the centre and a batik picture of a yacht in full sail, and two third places, the other one being a set of ceramic wind chimes, beautifully glazed in rainbow colours.

The day of the Christmas lunch came and at 1.30 pm, sixteen women could all be found seated along a beautifully set table in the café at The Point. A handful of people including the two male members of the pottery classes had not been able to come, but those that had were all dressed in their best Christmas jumpers or sparkly tops, some had Santa hats on and one woman was wearing reindeer earrings which played Jingle Bells at random and very soon became so annoying she had to take them off and put them in her bag.

Before the food arrived, Andrea announced the prize winners.

'We have two third prizes. The first goes to Sita for her wonderful ceramic wind chimes,' everyone clapped, 'and the other third prize goes to Kim for her pretty felted cushion. Well done everyone.' More clapping as Andrea handed Sita and Kim their prizes of mini bags of Maltesers.

Andrea announced the second prize winners and handed them each their prize of a slightly larger bag of the same sweets. Again everyone clapped and cheered.

'And the first prize goes to Jackie,' everyone clapped, 'with her gorgeous felted Dandelion scarf.' Andrea handed over a box of Maltesers with exaggerated pomp and Jackie stood up and accepted them with great dignity. The clapping and cheering continued with much congratulating and complimenting each other until the waitresses began to arrive with the first course.

Andrea watched Kim as she chatted and laughed. She was sitting a few seats away from her with Cora and Sal nearby and two people from the pottery class that she had just met that day. She seemed to be having a great time, getting on well with everyone, joining in the talk and laughing and joking. As usual, the food was delicious and there was plenty of it, with the lovely staff offering seconds and sometimes thirds. They had the traditional turkey with all the trimmings, including the ever-popular pigs in blankets, and for the vegetarians there was a tasty and beautifully presented sweet potato and chestnut tart with cranberries. There were Christmas crackers and those not driving had wine. Everyone was having fun. Between the courses, Andrea passed round pieces of paper with the dates for the start of the new term in January and the title of the next competition theme. Musicals.

Christmas pudding or white chocolate cheesecake came next, and the mood round the table was perfect. When they had finished and were on coffee or for some - more wine, Andrea announced the Secret Santa. Everyone had been asked to bring a present costing no more than three pounds and wrapped anonymously. It was purely for fun, hence the low price and people were encouraged to be silly if they wanted to. They jumbled them up, then each took one and when Andrea gave the word began to pass them round the table, one neighbour to another, until at random Andrea said stop. Having made sure no one had their own original parcel, they all opened them at once.

'HAHAHAHA' the roar of laughter came from Betty, then as people realised what she had opened, the whole table erupted in laughter. Betty had unwrapped a miniature Blow Up Boyfriend. It turned out that one of the potters had found it in one of the cheap novelty shops in Skegness and brought it along. It was harmless enough, as when fully inflated, it was about fifteen inches high and showed a comic muscle man in tiny trunks with his arms up flexing his biceps. But this didn't stop Betty,

'Bloody wasted on me,' she laughed. 'A blow-up doll and a man at that!' she looked over at Sal who was wiping tears of laughter from her eyes.

'If you really don't want it, I'll swap with you, you can

have my golden chocolates,' said Sita, the potter who had come joint third with Kim, 'I don't eat chocolate, and I could do with a boyfriend.' Everyone laughed as Sita had recently celebrated her seventy-eighth birthday, 'I haven't had one for ages now and he looks like he'll be perfect for me, not too demanding and I can let the air out when I've had enough of him.' The laughter and good natured joking continued until eventually the lovely staff at The Point began clearing away and the party broke up.

Kim came up to Andrea, who stood talking to Jackie, Sita, and another potter.

'This has been great fun. Thanks for organising it, Andrea,' she said, 'I've already got an idea for my entry for the next competition. I'm going to think about it properly over the Christmas holidays.'

'Well, you've got plenty of time,' laughed Andrea. 'It won't be judged until the end of June.'

'Anyway, I'm off now, thanks again, it's been fun. Have a lovely Christmas and I'll see you all in January.' Kim looked round at the remaining group and waved goodbye. They waved back, wishing her a merry Christmas.

12

The time was right, everything was in place. The man could make his move now.

Today's the day. This is the perfect opportunity. I'd be a fool to miss it.

Later that day, he pushed the bolt across, removed his balaclava and surgical gloves and leant back against the door, ignoring the muted noises coming from the other side.

Well, that wasn't too hard.

13

Monday 6th & 20th and Thursday 23rd January.

Andrea had enjoyed Christmas, she had gone to stay with her eldest son and his family. Her other children and their families had all either stayed at her son's house too or had joined them for Christmas Day. It had been lovely with all the family together and she'd enjoyed it immensely. She stayed on for a few days after Christmas to spend more time with her grandchildren and after a week she returned home, and she went out walking.

It was good to be back and Mrs Tim and Nonsuch were pleased to see her despite having been well looked after by Verity who lived in the cottage next door and popped in to feed the cats when Jackie was otherwise engaged. Andrea walked down to the river, following her usual route along the riverbank next to the lane. She was heading for the fishermen's lay-by to check that it was still free from rubbish and as she approached; she realised that sadly it wasn't.

A pile of broken office equipment stood proudly in the centre of the pull in. A fortress of filing cabinets, computer tables and ancient computers, skirted by a moat of spilt and overflowing bin bags. *For god's sake, what is wrong with people?* Andrea took her phone from her pocket and began taking pictures. She was just finishing when she heard laughing.

'And here you are again, Andrea Bailey, adding to your photographic collection.' It was Ernest. Of course, it was Ernest. Turning up like a bad smell.

Andrea decided to take a different tack this time and smiled at him. 'Happy New Year Ernest,' she said.

'A very happy New Year to you too, Andrea Bailey. More rubbish for you to enjoy, you must be delighted.' The man laughed in her face.

Andrea looked at him and waited for him to stop, and when he did, she said, 'I wonder if you can tell me what you find so funny. I'd love to join in on the joke. I like to think I've got a good sense of humour, but I honestly can't see the funny side of this sort of thing.' She gestured towards the pile.

'But it doesn't matter, Andrea Bailey, that's the joke. It's only unwanted stuff. It really doesn't matter.'

'Of course it matters. It's dangerous, and it's wrong and whoever keeps doing it is breaking the law.'

Ernest stopped smiling. 'Breaking the law, you say. So, you're a pillar of the community, are you Andrea Bailey? Never broken the law yourself. Never got a parking ticket. What must it be like to be so perfect?' He burst out laughing again. 'Carry on with your photography Andrea Bailey, don't let me put you off.'

'You don't put me off,' said Andrea trying to keep a pleasant smile on her face, 'and for your information I don't pick up the bits of dropped litter and report all of this fly tipping because I'm some sort of vigilante, I do it because I have respect for nature and the countryside and believe it should be cared for and not polluted by lazy people.'

'Saint Andrea Bailey, how lucky we are to have such a saint in our midst.'

'Goodbye, Ernest.'

Andrea walked away, she continued down the lane and turned along the little road that ran back over the river further north. That road, though used by tractors and a few folk as a cut through, was not used enough to prevent grass growing down the centre and as she walked the length of it, she came across three other sites of fly-tipping. These were not as large as the first one, but she could see they were commercial rubbish, building debris from house renovations and repairs. *There's something going on round here and it can't continue. I'm going to find out who's responsible and do something about it.*

The beginning of the new term was always an interesting class, with everyone full of stories and anecdotes about their Christmases. Spirits were high, and they were all pleased to be back. Jackie had gone to her sister-in-law's for the festivities. She had always got on well with Hayden's sister, Goldie, and spent some much-needed family time with her nieces and nephew. Cora and her sister always spent Christmas together, alternating between their homes, and this year it had been Cora's turn to go to her. They had attended the cathedral for the Christmas Day service and had been invited to join friends for dinner, this together with a visit to the pantomime, had made for one of the best Christmases Cora had had for years. Betty and Sal were of course, full of stories about the dogs that had boarded with them for the holidays. It was always a busy time for them, and they loved it.

'No Kim then?' asked Sal.

‘No, I’m surprised she’s not here,’ said Andrea, ‘maybe she’s ill although she hasn’t let me know.’

‘Or maybe something happened to her on the twenty-first,’ laughed Betty. ‘Perhaps she’s been turned into a frog!’

‘Probably just too much overindulgence over Christmas and New Year and she needs longer to recover,’ Jackie chuckled.

They settled down to the class. The new theme of Musicals had spiked an interest, and ideas were being bandied about. Sal was still working on a batik she had started in November, but had one or two ideas for her next project. Betty wanted to do some wet felting for a change and was having a think about what to attempt next, so was doing some preliminary sketching. Cora went straight into a batik picture of a man, arms spread apart, wearing a colourful coat for Joseph and the Amazing Technicolour Dream Coat, and Jackie although busy on another project, had brought along a photograph of a print she’d found online of stylised chess pieces. Jackie loved anything Art déco or Art nouveau and the chess pieces picture was perfect for her.

‘It’s weird without Kim,’ said Cora after a while. ‘Does anyone else miss her? I know she’s as crazy as a box of frogs, but I feel like she’s part of the class now.’

‘I know what you mean,’ Jackie agreed. ‘When she’s not banging on about being persecuted by witches, she’s actually okay.’

‘She had a good time at the Christmas lunch. She was chatting to everyone like she didn’t have a care in the world,’ Betty joined in. ‘Hopefully she’ll have got everything back into perspective and have calmed down by next week.’

‘I’ve never understood why the measurement of craziness is a box of frogs,’ Sal said. ‘I mean, has anyone ever seen a box of frogs? They may all just go to sleep.’

Betty raised her eyes to heaven, and everyone laughed, and for the moment, Kim was forgotten.

January was cold, they had no snow, but the temperature dropped below freezing and the countryside turned white and sharp. The roads were treacherous with icy patches where the watery sun couldn't reach, and the cars crawled along the ungritted roads. Andrea had been out walking and had found and reported more fly-tipping, but so far had been unsuccessful in tracking down the culprit. And Kim had missed three classes.

'I've emailed Kim,' Andrea told the Monday afternoon class. 'I don't usually follow up if people stop coming. Sometimes people decide they want to stop and for one reason or another don't want to tell me, fair enough I say and I don't chase them for their reasons but with Kim it's different, she went out of her way at the Christmas lunch to come and tell me she was coming back this term and how much she was enjoying it. She even had an idea for the new competition. Why would she do that if she was planning on leaving?'

'Maybe she's ill or there's a family crisis or something,' suggested Cora.

'Yes, of course, I think that's probably it, so that's why I've emailed her, just to check she's okay. She may have tried to let me know and got my email address wrong or something. Anyway, I've sent a message and I'll see what she says.'

The class ended, and as usual, Jackie and Cora hung around after Betty and Sal had left.

'Anyone up for a walk and a coffee at The Point?' asked Jackie.

'Definitely. When?' Andrea looked round questioningly.

'I'm free Thursday,' Cora grinned.

So, Thursday morning found the three of them in the warm café at The Point removing coats, hats and scarves and rubbing their hands together having walked down to the sea and along the beach in the teeth of a freezing north easterly wind that had obviously come all the way from Siberia solely to meet them. When they were settled with their cradled coffee cups slowly bringing the feeling back to their numb hands, the conversation got round to Kim.

'Andrea, did you get a reply from your email to Kim?' asked Jackie.

'No, I didn't. It's weird. I really thought she'd get back to me.'

'How odd.' Jackie sipped her coffee and smiled. 'Mmm, the coffee here is delicious.'

'I wonder if something's happened to her?' Cora grinned. 'Maybe the witches have got her after all.'

'Yes, maybe Betty's right and she's been turned into a frog,' laughed Jackie. 'Frogs can't reply to emails, Andrea, so that's your mystery solved.'

Andrea laughed too. 'But it is a mystery, and I'd like to know what's happened.'

They finished their coffees, and Andrea went to the counter and ordered seconds for them all, this time including a large slice of passionfruit sponge cake, a fruit flapjack and a piece of Lincolnshire plum bread.

When they were settled again, Cora put down her half-eaten flapjack and looked at Jackie and Andrea. 'Right, I know this is a weird idea, but hear me out.'

Andrea and Jackie smiled encouragingly.

'It's winter and none of us have too many commitments. We all like puzzles, we all like trips out, and we all like nice lunches.'

'Agreed,' said Andrea, finishing her plum bread, and Jackie nodded.

'So how about we try to look into the mystery of Kim's disappearance?' Cora made exaggerated hand gestures of quotation marks when she said disappearance.

'I'm up for that. It sounds interesting and if there are nice lunches involved, so much the better,' said Jackie, 'but where do we start? We don't even know where she lives. Do you know Andrea?'

'No, people don't give me their addresses, just a contact number or an email address. And remember when Betty asked her? She wouldn't even give a clue to where she lives.'

'Well, we do know that her piece of land is in East Kime. How about we have a drive out and see if we can spot it. It'll be fun, a nice ride out and we can find somewhere good for lunch,' suggested Cora. 'what d'you think?'

Andrea nodded, 'Yeah, why not. It'll be interesting to see if we can spot her strip of land and you never know she may even be there tending her sheep or something.'

And so it was agreed. They would go on Saturday and Jackie would drive.

14

The man quietly pulled back the bolt and carefully opened the door. The woman sat upright on the bed, legs stretched out, looking at him. He put the mug of tea and bowl of cereal on the wooden chair. He said nothing. He left the room and bolted the door. He grinned to himself as he removed his balaclava.

It's working. Not long now.

15

Saturday 25th January

Andrea arrived last, Cora and Jackie were already sitting in Jackie's car, ready to go. She ran up and jumped in the back.

'Morning girls, wow you two are keen this cold and frosty morning.'

'Good morning, yes Cora was here at quarter to.' Jackie started the engine.

'Once I'm ready, I've got to go,' Cora explained, as if they didn't already know what she was like.

They knew roughly where they were going, they knew where East Kime was, and Jackie said she used to work round there years ago when she was a community carer making home visits and knew it a bit so they were quite hopeful.

'What'll we do if we can't find it?' Andrea asked.

'Find somewhere for coffee, of course.' Jackie said with a giggle.

'And what'll we do if we do find it, but there's nothing to see and no one to talk to?' Andrea persisted.

'We'll go and find some coffee.' Jackie and Cora spoke together and they laughed again.

About half an hour later, they found themselves peering out through the windows of the car as they slowly crawled round the lanes of East Kime, trying to locate two specific fields amongst a sea of other fields. They were looking for a slight pull in by a wooden gate, just beyond which would be a run-down stone building with a security light and CCTV camera, and they knew there were some sheep in one of the fields. How hard could it be?

'Look that's—oh no, there's a herd of cows in the far corner.' Andrea trailed off as she spotted the far off herd.

Jackie pulled into a gateway to a field, mud carved up by tractor wheels. 'This one? It looks a possibility. Maybe we need to get out and look.'

'I don't think so. Why would there be tractor tracks and where's the rundown building?' Cora asked.

Jackie had eased herself out and was standing looking around. 'Needle in a haystack comes to mind,' she said with a sardonic smile.

'Is the coffee calling yet?' asked Cora hopefully.

'Let's give it a bit longer. We haven't been down that lane on the left yet.' Jackie got back in the car.

'East Kime isn't very big,' said Andrea as she stared out of the window at the passing fields. 'I don't understand why we can't find it. D'you think it might be near a farmhouse? We've just been looking at open fields, but she's got neighbours.'

'Yeah, maybe,' Jackie turned the car left into the last untried lane.

'That's it!' Cora pointed, 'Look, that has to be it, the gateway, the broken building, the sheep, it's got to be, hasn't it?'

Jackie pulled the car off the road, and they all got out.

They leant on the closed wooden gate and surveyed the scene. Just ahead of them, down a little track, was the small rundown building. They could see piles of rubble stacked up against the wall and the roof, such as it was, sagged dangerously.

'That's quite obviously an old animal shelter,' Andrea shielded her eyes from the weak sunlight. 'I wonder why she thought she'd get planning permission for that.'

'I don't think she came to see it before buying it. I think she just bought it in an online auction, sight unseen.' Cora said.

'Ridiculous.' snorted Jackie.

They stood looking at the scene, not wanting to open the gate and wander about. They didn't think they should trespass. After all, if there was a mystery, it was only in their heads at the moment. The morning was cold, but the early frost had gone, and a pale sun shone on the glistening green fields making them glow. A few sheep chewed the grass surrounding the building, and the fields stretched away to more fields in the distance, broken only by a thin strip of bony trees dark against the sky. The Lincolnshire Wolds at their best.

'It's a lovely spot, I can see why she wanted it,' Jackie said as she gazed at the view, 'but I can't see any feathers, stacks of grasses or piles of muck. It looks lovely.'

'I can't see a CCTV camera either.' Andrea was squinting at the dilapidated shelter.

'Me neither,' agreed Cora.

'There's one there. I can see it on the corner.' Jackie was the only one of the three who didn't need glasses, so was often relied on for distant details.

Andrea pointed to the right. 'There's a house over there.' Beyond the adjacent field stood a large square farmhouse typical of the area, with a small crew yard to the side. 'Should we go round and do some investigating?'

‘Why not? We’ll be the Studio Sleuths.’ Cora grinned, ‘what have we got to lose?’

‘We’ve come this far. We should find out what we can—come on.’ And Jackie got back in the car and started the engine.

As they drew into the crew yard next to the farmhouse, they saw a man walking towards them. Tall and overweight, he had a red face, balding head and wore an old wax jacket with the right-hand pocket hanging off. An ancient looking brown spaniel padded along beside him. Jackie stopped the car, and they got out.

‘Morning ladies, can I help you?’ barked the farmer, looking like the last thing he wanted to do was help them.

‘Good morning,’ they chorused.

‘We were wondering if you could help us. We’re trying to locate the woman who owns those couple of fields over there.’ Cora pointed towards Kim’s land.

‘Oh, were you, well I don’t know anything about the damn woman, so if you don’t mind,’ and he turned away.

Jackie loved dogs. She was between pets at the moment and missed her recently departed old friend of fifteen years.

‘Hello,’ she said, tickling the elderly spaniel behind his long soft ears, ‘you’re a lovely old fellow, aren’t you. What’s your name then?’ The dog made no effort to follow the farmer and sat enjoying the attention, rubbing his grey muzzle against Jackie’s hands.

The farmer stopped walking and turned to them.

‘Bloody Nigel, silly sod, he’ll let you do that all day. He’s as soft as toffee.’

Toffee’s not always soft, thought Andrea, *sticky, but not soft,* but she decided not to say anything and leave it to Jackie to butter up the farmer.

Jackie chatted about Nigel for a minute or two and then asked about Kim again. ‘The thing is, we know her and haven't seen her for a while. We know she has this strip of land, but we don't know her address. We're trying to find it out so we can go and check on her.'

The farmer looked at them. He saw three elderly women wrapped up against the freezing January weather and he thawed. 'Hmmmm. Friends, eh?'

'Well, sort of. I run art classes at my studio, and she's been coming for a while and then she suddenly stopped,' Andrea explained, 'It's a bit of a mystery, really.'

'We were just passing this way and thought we'd see if she was about,' Cora added, 'then we noticed your farm and thought we might as well ask. You never know.'

'Hmm, I've probably got her address at the house. Come up and I'll look.' The farmer turned and walked off across the yard.

Jackie, Cora and Andrea looked at each other, grinned and followed, with Nigel walking happily at Jackie's side.

In the house they stood in a large square hallway full of coats and muddy boots and watched as the farmer rummaged in the drawer of a huge dark wood dresser. 'MONICA!' he turned and bellowed, 'MONICA WHERE'S THAT BLOODY WOMAN'S ADDRESS?'

A tall, well-built woman with an enormous bosom desperate to escape from the valiant clutches of a hand knitted cardigan appeared. She looked to be in her fifties and spoke in a very loud voice.

'Which bloody woman is that, John?' then she stopped and seemed to notice the three women for the first time. 'Hello, who are these people?'

'They're friends of the damned woman next door and they want her address. I can't find it. I thought it was in here, d'you know where the bloody thing is?'

At the mention of Kim's name, Monica's eyes narrowed. 'I'm not sure we've still got it,' she snapped.

'We're not exactly friends,' Andrea said quickly. 'she used to come to my art classes and we're trying to get in touch with her. We wondered if you could help us.' The winning smile appeared, but it was the mention of art classes that seemed to melt Monica.

'Art classes, eh? I do a bit of painting myself, dogs and stuff, you know. I'm not much good but I enjoy it. That's one of mine on the wall there.' Monica proudly pointed to a small painting of a dog's head.

Goodness me, pity the poor dog if it looked like that, thought Andrea, looking at the pushed in snout, different length ears and squinting eyes, but then she noticed the title and date in the corner and took a chance. 'Well, I never, is that Nigel?' she said

'Oh, you recognise him. I'm quite pleased with it. I had to do it from a photograph of course. He won't ever sit still.'

They all looked down at Nigel, who was sprawled on the doormat, exhausted from the short walk to the yard and back.

'I recognised him straight away. It's a very good likeness, well done.' The winning smile again.

Jackie and Cora joined in with praise for the awful painting and soon Monica, having pushed John aside, was sorting through the drawer and located the address. She copied it onto a Post It note and handed it to Andrea.

'Thanks. Can I ask when you last saw her?'

'I don't go out of my way to see her you know,' Monica's eyes had narrowed again, 'she's an unpleasant woman and as mad as a hatter. I'm sorry if she's a friend of yours, but ...'

'Oh, she's not really a friend. We just know her through the art classes and need to get in touch about something,' Jackie explained.

'Bloody woman's got a screw loose, if you ask me.' John boomed, 'I tried to clear her ditches, and she went completely mad. Started shouting and carrying on, got a bloody screw loose.'

'She shouldn't have land,' Monica joined in. 'can't look after it. The ditches were filling up with mud and the fields weren't draining properly. She was obviously not going to do anything about it, so John kindly did hers when he did ours. She came out shouting and screaming at him, saying he was deliberately dumping rubbish on her land. He was putting the scooped spoil on her side of the ditch. It's common practice to put the spoil on the side belonging to the owner so it can drain. I was inside the house, but I could hear her ranting, so I came out to see what was going on. She was screaming at John so I told her to shut up and gave her a few home truths about how she shouldn't be here, she can't be trusted to manage land and also how she shouldn't be allowed livestock either, she hasn't a clue how to look after sheep, I said to her why don't you just leave? No one likes you, you're not wanted here, bugger off back to wherever you came from and let someone who knows what they're doing have the land, I said...' Monica was getting more and more agitated and going red in the face, and the heroic cardigan looked like it would soon concede defeat and unleash untold terrors, so they decided it might be a good time to leave.

'Well, thanks for the address. We must be off now. Goodbye.' Cora took charge and so with a few more goodbyes and a final tickle of Nigel's ears, they left.

Back in the car, they gathered themselves together.

'What now?' Jackie knew she didn't need to ask.

'Coffee.' Andrea and Cora said together.

They drove to West Kime about three miles away from the farm where they found Flour Power, a nice little bakery with a small café attached. They took a cappuccino, two lattes and a lunch menu to a table by the window and settled themselves down.

'Wow. Well, that was unexpected.' Andrea said, grinning at the other two.

'I know, weren't we good? Are we proper sleuths now?' Jackie laughed, and Cora and Andrea grinned. 'The Studio Sleuths are officially launched.' They clicked their coffee cups together in a toast. 'Three regular Miss Marples.'

'As long as we're not Hercule Poirots,' Cora chuckled, 'I know I'm getting old but I haven't got a moustache yet.' They laughed so loudly the two other customers in the cafe turned to look at them.

'I genuinely thought we'd leave with nothing, but thanks to Nigel, we've got an address.' Andrea fished in the pocket of her jeans and pulled out the Post It note.

'17, Conkers Lane, Stickville,' she read, 'should be Bonkers Lane. She sounds worse than we thought.'

'Yeah, although Moniker was beginning to sound a little deranged herself. Good job we left when we did. She was starting to hit her stride.' Jackie laughed.

'OK, who's up for a trip to Bonkers Land, then?' asked Andrea, 'Cora will be busy Sunday. I know and the class is on Monday. How about next Tuesday?'

'Tuesday's good for me,' Jackie said.

'I can do Tuesday,' Cora checked her diary. 'what time and where?'

Andrea said she'd drive next time, so they arranged to meet at hers. Then the conversation switched to the important business of what was on the lunch menu.

16

The man shut the door and pushed the bolt across. It was all working exactly to plan. He pulled off his balaclava, but kept his surgical gloves on. He took the bucket away and emptied it.

Not long now.

17

Tuesday 28th January

The following Tuesday was another cold morning, but the roads were ice-free which was lucky for Andrea. She hated driving on icy roads. Stickville was either a large village or a small town it was difficult to tell, it had a church at one end with a small hall next to it which displayed a large sign saying God Welcomes You and one underneath saying Come to Knit and Knatter, Fridays at 10. Some local joker had crossed out the word Come.

The High Street stretched out down the hill and they could tell they were in the Wolds. There were no hills where they lived. There was a small Co-op supermarket, a petrol garage, a men's barber shop named Jack the Clipper, a small police station, a little bakery rejoicing in the title Florrie's Floury Baps, two charity shops and a hardware shop called Nailed it! with spades and large bags of dog biscuits stacked outside. There were also two pubs, one of which was boarded up, but the other The Trio of Fools looked healthy enough. One or two little roads led off the High Street, with a few more shops and businesses, but unfortunately there was no café.

‘Shame, there’s nowhere to get a coffee.’ Cora looked around as they drove through.

‘Yeah.’ Andrea agreed, ‘there doesn’t seem to be a café or anything.’

‘We’ll try the pub later. I’m sure they’ll have a coffee machine,’ suggested Jackie from the back seat, ‘but we’re too early. They’re not open yet.’

They found Conkers Road on the edge of the village. The houses were only on one side of the street and looked out across open fields. They were numbered consecutively and number 17 was easy to find. It was in the middle of a row of small semi-detached houses.

‘Is her car anywhere about?’ Jackie asked. ‘I think she drives an Astra.’

‘I wouldn’t know,’ Andrea had no idea about cars, ‘I don’t notice makes of cars, I only know she’s got a red one.’

They had a look around, but from the cars parked on the road, only two were red and neither was an Astra. They parked outside number 17 and walked up to the front door, Jackie looking carefully at the row of wintering plants that slept in the straight flower bed that edged the path. Cora rang the bell, and they stood waiting. Nothing happened. She tried the bell again and Jackie knocked with her knuckles. Still nothing. Stooping down, Cora peered through the letterbox.

‘Can you see anything?’ Andrea asked.

‘No, just an empty hallway, no sign of life. Well, she’s obviously not home. Time to go?’ Cora straightened up and looked at the other two, but Jackie was knocking at the house next door.

The houses were such that the front doors were next to each other with a shared alleyway between them leading to their back gardens and Jackie had stepped round a large potted shrub and was waiting on the step of Kim's next-door neighbour.

'I think someone's coming,' she said.

The door was opened by a woman in her early forties, her hair hidden beneath a woollen hat and wearing bright red leggings and a purple anorak.

'Hello?' the woman looked a little surprised to see three mature ladies standing on her doorstep, all muffled up against the cold.

Probably thinks we're Jehovah's Witnesses or selling something, thought Andrea.

'Oh hello, sorry to disturb you,' Jackie smiled. 'We were knocking next door and there's no reply. We wondered if you'd seen Kim at all? We've arranged to meet her today.'

'No sorry, I haven't seen her for a while. I can't help you.' The neighbour went to close to the door.

'Only it's odd her not being here,' Jackie persisted, 'what with our arrangement to come today.'

'Doesn't surprise me,' said the neighbour, opening the door again. 'She's a bit odd all round, if you ask me. Sorry if she's your friend, sorry.'

'She's not really what you'd call our friend. She comes to my art classes, and we know her through them.' Andrea explained.

'We've known her a few months, but only as a classmate.' Cora added.

'Oh, I see, well I still can't help you. I've not seen her for a while. If I see her, I'll tell her you called, shall I? What are your names?'

'Yes please, we're Andrea, Jackie and Cora from the art studio. Sorry to disturb you.' Andrea turned away and Cora went to follow, but they heard Jackie continue talking.

'I know it's a nuisance, but the thing is she promised me some cuttings from her rose bush, and if I don't take them today, I'll miss the right time to plant them up. D'you think we can pop into her back garden and take a few? I know she won't mind.'

'Hmmm,' the neighbour looked at them and saw three elderly ladies wrapped up in coats and scarves who had come especially for cuttings from a rosebush. 'OK, come with me. I'm Erin, by the way.'

She led the way down the tiny alleyway and opened the door to Kim's back garden. It hadn't been locked, but it was a tall wooden gate and looked like it might have been. Once inside, Jackie looked round for a rosebush. Luckily there were two. She went to the furthest one over by the back fence. Erin stood at the gate, watching them. She obviously wasn't going to leave them alone. They might look harmless, but she still didn't know them from Adam. Andrea and Cora gazed with admiration as Jackie extracted a small plastic bag, a remnant from her dog walking days, and a pearl handled penknife from her bag. Of course she'd have the equipment. A true gardener was never off duty.

'I wonder if you'd hold the bag for me, please Erin?' Jackie called to the neighbour as she fumbled about, pretending to have trouble opening the plastic bag.

Erin left her vigil by the door and went to help Jackie, and Cora and Andrea immediately began to look around.

'I know she's a funny woman, but she won't mind my taking the cuttings.' said Jackie as Erin held the bag for her.

'Funny woman is right,' agreed Erin, 'she complains about my ciggy ends. They're not even in her garden. She says I shouldn't leave them all over the place, but I like to have a smoke on my front step in the evening, looking over the fields you know, and it's none of her business if I leave them on my path or flick them in my flower bed. I collect them up now and again when they get noticeable.'

Jackie smiled to herself, but she said, 'Yes, she can be quite odd, can't she.'

'Odd, I can tell you things—' Erin was getting going now, maybe because she was talking only to Jackie, and it felt more like a chat. 'A few weeks before Christmas, I looked out my back bedroom window and guess what I saw.' She didn't wait for Jackie to guess but continued, 'she was in her back garden in the pitch-dark digging holes. Digging holes! In the dark! Madness. She was burying stuff, I couldn't see what, but it looked like piles of black stuff. I mean, what's that all about?'

Obviously the feathers, thought Jackie, but she said, 'Goodness, what an odd thing to do, but maybe she was gardening, enriching her soil with manure or something.'

'Yes perhaps, but why in the dark? I don't know. Anyway, have you got your cuttings? I need to go out now. I've got to go to work. I was just on my way out when you rang the bell.'

'Yes, thanks Erin, we'll get off, sorry to hold you up.' Jackie stuffed her bag of cuttings into her shoulder bag and Erin ushered them towards the gate, then with a chorus of goodbyes, they left.

———

As Jackie had predicted, The Trio of Fools was open when they got there and as soon as they were settled with two lattes and a cappuccino in a corner of an otherwise empty bar, they began to laugh.

'My god you were good Jackie,' Andrea said between giggles.

'Absolutely inspired,' agreed Cora.

'Haha, it was lucky she had some rose bushes, although

I had dogwood and honeysuckle as a backup. Most people have at least one of those.' They laughed some more and sipped their coffee.

'Well, while you were busy with Erin, I had a peep in the rainwater butt and there were still a few black feathers floating there and I also noticed some mounds of earth which could be feather burials,' said Andrea. 'The feathers were big, I'd had an idea they were little fluffy ones, but they were long, like wing feathers.'

'Interesting,' Jackie nodded her head. 'Yes, Erin told me she'd seen Kim burying them.'

'Not as interesting as what I found,' Cora raised an eyebrow. 'By the back door was a stone frog, and I had a peep at it as my sister has a similar one. There's a little door in the base and people keep spare keys in them. I didn't open it, of course. There wasn't the time, but what say we go back for a proper nosey?'

'You clever old bird,' said Andrea admiringly. 'I'm up for another visit.'

'Erin said she was going to work, so how about we go back when we've finished our coffee?' Cora suggested.

'Good idea,' Jackie sipped her latte, 'If she comes back and spots us we can say we dropped something, my penknife or something.'

So, they were all decided and an hour later, refreshed with coffee and a trip to the pub loo, they found themselves safely in Kim's back garden. They had parked a little further down the road to avoid Erin noticing a strange car if she came back and were now standing watching Cora as she slid open the secret door in the base of the stone frog to reveal a key.

'Yay, well done Cora, chief sleuth of the morning, I'll make you a badge,' Andrea laughed.

'Don't do that. I need to keep incognito for my sleuthing skills to flourish,' said Cora with a grin. 'Shhh, keep the noise down a bit. We don't want to be found in here if we can help it. Is it a back door key? It looks like one to me.'

18

Tuesday 28th January

Within seconds, they were inside Kim's kitchen. It was small, cluttered, and smelt appalling.

'Oh my god, what's that terrible smell?' Jackie started to gag and put her hand over her nose and mouth. 'Smells like someone's died.'

'Don't say that! I never thought of that!' Andrea was horrified at the idea. 'What if she died and is lying here—Dead?'

They looked about them. There were dirty dishes in the sink with old, dried food stuck to them, the counter was cluttered with dirty saucepans, and the smell was horrific, like something rotting.

'URGH, it looks like no one's been here for a while.' Cora poked at half a mouldy loaf in its plastic bag. 'That smell is really awful. I can almost taste it.' She made a face and pulled her scarf over her mouth and nose.

'This isn't good,' Jackie was looking worried. 'not good at all, but let's have a look round now we're here.'

'Do you think we should? Shouldn't we just call the police?' Andrea suggested.

Suddenly things had become serious. No one actually said it, but they were all thinking the same thing. What if they found Kim's body?

'We'll stay together and have a quick look round, then we'll call the police, depending on what we find.' Jackie had taken charge.

'Okay, but it's so hot in here I need to take my coat off first,' Cora began removing her thick winter coat, although she kept her scarf over her face, Jackie followed suit and not wanting to disturb anything they left them in a heap on the floor by the door. Andrea, although also hot, somehow felt protected in hers, so she kept it on. Then leaving the kitchen together, they cautiously went out into the hallway.

'We'll look upstairs first,' said Jackie as she started up the stairs. 'We should check the bedroom.'

'Oh god is this where we find a month-old body?' Andrea's voice was husky, her throat seemed to have contracted.

Cora nodded, unable to speak.

The house was silent and stifling and they found themselves tiptoeing and whispering, it didn't seem right to make any noise. They slowly climbed the stairs keeping close together and at the top found themselves on a small landing with a large blanket chest by the banister and three doors leading off. They pushed open the first door and peered into a small bathroom. There was a towel draped over the rim of the bath and various bottles lined up around the sink. It was a bit untidy but there was nobody in there. Slowly they backed out and quietly opened the next door.

'The spare bedroom,' whispered Cora. Her voice had come back but sounded higher.

'More of a dumping ground,' Andrea whispered back.

The room contained a single bed piled high with fabrics which on closer inspection, turned out to be sheets, duvet covers and a few coats. There was a chest of drawers with a mirror on top and a small wardrobe. They looked at each other and shrugged, then Jackie tiptoed across to the wardrobe and carefully opened the door. They all held their breath. It was full of clothes. A collective sigh of relief escaped them all.

We've all been watching too many murder mysteries on the telly. Why the hell would there be a body in the wardrobe? Andrea let out an involuntary snort of laughter, and Jackie and Cora stared at her questioningly. She raised her shoulders in an apologetic manner and they continued on their mission.

The third door opened into Kim's bedroom. Bigger than the other room, it faced the road and had a lovely view across the farmland. Still huddled together, the three women peered cautiously round the door, but Jackie, who was in front, quickly drew back, almost knocking Cora and Andrea over.

'What is it?' whispered Andrea. 'What's the matter?'

'Is she in there?' asked Cora, forgetting to whisper. 'Don't say there's a body in there, please don't.'

'I don't know. I saw a lump in the bed,' whispered Jackie.

'Bloody hell,' Cora's voice trembled.

'Come on, we have to look, we have to.'

They were all trembling now, frightened at what they might find. Jackie pushed the door open again, and they tiptoed in terrified of what was in the room. Sure enough, there was a lump in the bed about the size of a person, a hunched shape with the duvet carelessly thrown over it. Keeping very close together, they approached the bed.

'Kim,' Andrea called softly, 'Kim, is that you? Are you asleep?'

'It's us Kim. Cora, Andrea and Jackie from the class,' Cora spoke gently as she put out her hand to the lump. Her hand sank into the duvet and down into the lump. Quickly she pulled it away and drew back the duvet revealing a long bolster pillow.

'What the hell?' Andrea gasped.

'Thank goodness, it's only a pillow. I thought we'd found her.'

'It's a weird pillow. Why's it so long?' Andrea was still whispered.

'It's an orthopaedic support pillow,' explained Jackie in a low voice. 'People have them to support dodgy hips or bad backs. Kim said she'd hurt her back picking up all the feathers, remember?'

'Thank goodness it's not her, but she may still be here. That smell is awful.' Cora's voice was muffled through her scarf, which was still pulled up over her nose.

They looked round the room. There was a slightly larger wardrobe to the one next door, another chest of drawers with a mirror on top, a small armchair and a double bed flanked either side by matching bedside cabinets. Once more, Jackie went over to the wardrobe and looked inside. That too was full of clothes. She began to rummage about.

'What are you doing?' asked Cora, 'looking for Narnia?'.

'Just trying to get an idea of whether she's gone away, taken her clothes, that sort of thing.'

'Ahh, I see, good idea. Well, it doesn't look like it to me.'

They tiptoed back out onto the landing, where they stopped and stared at the blanket chest.

'Oh no, she can't be in there. It's like an Agatha Christie plot. People don't die in blanket chests.' Cora looked at the other two.

'There's a lot of bedding on the spare bed. I would've thought she'd keep that in the chest.' Andrea whispered.

'If Kim's body is in there, it means someone must have put her in there. This is too much. I didn't bargain for murder when we broke in and contaminated a crime scene.' Cora's muffled voice wobbled.

'You've been watching too many detective stories on the telly. Calm down, let's just look inside before we start panicking.' Jackie slowly opened the heavy lid of the chest.

The women hung onto each other as they gazed inside, each fully expecting to see the rictus grin of Kim's folded dead body staring up at them. A collective sigh of relief escaped them when they saw only folded curtains, shoe boxes, and some old toys.

'Thank God. Come on, we've still got the downstairs to do yet.' Jackie gently closed the lid and led the way quietly downstairs. It still seemed wrong to make a noise. They crept downstairs again, still keeping close together as they tiptoed into the sitting room. The large L shaped room was a sitting room in the larger part of the L, and a dining room in the smaller part. Like the spare bedroom and the kitchen, it looked a mess. Papers, bills, a passport, books, newspapers, scissors and a scrap book were all jumbled untidily on the dining room table. The books and scrapbook on closer inspection proved to be all about black magic and the occult. Cushions were heaped on the sofa, a small footstool was upside down on an armchair, and a vacuum cleaner stood in the middle of the floor, still plugged into the wall. But there was no body.

'Well, we haven't found a body, thank god,' Jackie said, relieved.

'What is that horrendous smell then? And where's it coming from?' Andrea walked back into the kitchen determined to find out.

The stench turned out to be coming from the kitchen bin, which was nearly full and contained a large piece of putrid raw meat, unwrapped, grey and slimy. Andrea gagged as she pulled out the bin liner and tied a knot at the top. She opened the back door, put the bag in the dustbin and then left the door open to try to get rid of the smell.

'Were you two thinking what I was thinking?' asked Andrea returned to the sitting room.

'That we'd a find a body? Yes absolutely, I'm still a bit shaky, I need to sit down.' Jackie flopped down into the only empty armchair in the small sitting room.

Cora moved the footstool from the other armchair and sat down too. She removed the scarf from her face. 'Thank goodness we didn't. I don't know what we would have done. As it is, we have to tell the police she's missing. She obviously hasn't been here for weeks.'

'You're right,' Jackie agreed, 'but maybe we should have a nosey around a bit first, seeing as we're here and everything.'

'Yeah, once the police get involved we won't be able to, and I want to know what's going on.' Andrea was already shuffling amongst the pile of books and newspapers on the table. 'There's an old passport here. It ran out in November, oh she's got the renewal forms here too. She must have been about to get a new passport. I wonder why she didn't do it online? Anyway if she's away on holiday, she hasn't gone abroad. Ooh look, here's an address book, looks a bit old, I guess she's got all her contacts on her phone now, but you never know. Talking of which is her phone here? Or her handbag?'

They began searching again. The room was a mess with shoes everywhere and more books and newspapers on the floor; it wasn't easy to know where to look. On the plus side, no one would know they'd been there.

'Kim must hate housework,' Jackie moved an armchair revealing a dirty mug and a small plate which had been underneath. 'There's stuff everywhere.'

Andrea began looking around on the floor for a bag. 'I don't blame her.'

'I think she was about to do some when she stopped.' Cora said, 'the vacuum's out and plugged in. The footstool was up on a chair with the cushions. I think she was about to start cleaning up.'

'There's a handbag here,' Jackie dug out a brown leather bag from beneath a cushion and waved it at the other two. 'should we look inside?'

'We've come this far,' said Andrea coming over for a closer look.

Jackie opened the bag and took out a hairbrush, a few crumpled tissues, a pen, a lipstick and a small purse containing some coins, a ten pound note, two bank cards and a Tesco Club card.

'Looks like this is the bag she uses. It's got her bank cards in. Why would she have gone without it? She wouldn't just go away without her bag.'

'If she's got her phone with her, she might not need her bag,' Andrea pointed out. 'Her bank cards could be on her phone.'

'True and she never brought a handbag to the class that I noticed,' added Cora 'although she could have left it in her car I suppose.'

'Her car keys!' Andrea shouted, making the others jump, 'I'm sorry, I'm getting overexcited, but they're not in her bag, are they? And what about her house keys? They're not here either.'

'Well, they could be anywhere in this mess.' Jackie pointed out.

'Have you noticed something else?' Cora asked, 'It's so hot in here. The heating's on. Why would she leave the heating on if she's gone away? She wouldn't, no one would.'

They continued searching but finding nothing that could shed any light on where Kim might have got to; they decided it was probably time to go. Jackie and Cora collected up their coats, and they all moved out into the garden. Cora was just replacing the back door key in the stone frog when Andrea noticed a small trowel balanced on the outside kitchen window ledge. Picking it up, she began to dig down into a raised mound of earth by the side fence where she thought some feathers might be buried. The ground was hard with the frost, but luckily she didn't have to go very deep before she found some. Andrea found three more feather pits and although she didn't dig deep, it was clear to them all that there were hundreds buried if not thousands.

'These are definitely wing or tail feathers, maybe from crows. Look how stiff the quill bits are even now after they've been buried for weeks.'

'Quill bits, ha, you mean the shaft, and your shaft would be stiff too if you'd been buried in this freezing ground,' said Jackie with a grin.

'Yeah, I suppose, but you'd think they wouldn't stay so stiff after all this time.'

'Can you both stop talking about stiff shafts please,' Cora giggled. 'How can I continue to hone my sleuthing skills if you keep making me laugh?'

And they all laughed.

'Shhhh.' Andrea put her finger to her lips.

But they continued to laugh, they couldn't stop. They laughed real rib aching, tears falling laughter, because stiff shafts were funny and because they'd been terrified.

19

Tuesday 28th January

Back at The Trio of Fools, they ordered their food at the bar. The landlord asked them to sit down and said it would be brought over to them. The pub was not very busy and there was a free table by the log fire near the bar. They grabbed it, sat down and looked around. They hadn't properly noticed the pub earlier when they'd been in, but now they saw a cosy pub with a curved bar, an open fire and comfortable chairs around heavy oak tables. A few tables were already taken and a couple of locals were seated on stools at the bar. The friendly atmosphere was perfect. Calming and reassuring.

The three women were all thinking the same thing, with the state the house had been left in and the buried feathers in the garden. Maybe there was something in what Kim had told them. Maybe there was some truth behind her worries after all. It was beginning to look that way. They settled down to review what they knew.

'Right, I'm going to write down what we know,' Jackie said, taking a notebook from her bag and starting to jot down some notes.

. . .

1. *Kim has not been at her house for some weeks – unknown how many.*
2. *She seems to have her phone and keys with her.*
3. *She seems to have her car with her.*
4. *She has not gone abroad on holiday.*

5.Her story of the feathers is true.

6.Her neighbours (house and land) think she's odd/mad even.

The waitress came over with a tray.

'Two tomato and basil soups with homemade bread and a fisherman's pie. Three pots of tea.' She unloaded the tray and after they had thanked her, she left them to it.

'Two soups,' said Andrea, and they all laughed.

It was hard for people of their generation to hear that phrase without thinking of the hilarious Victoria Wood TV sketch where Julie Walters, playing the elderly and very wobbly waitress, brought two empty soup bowls to a couple in a restaurant having shaken it all out as she walked from the kitchen.

'What now?' asked Cora, diving into her fish pie. 'Do we tell the police she's missing? And if so, do we also tell them we broke into her house?'

Andrea put down her soup spoon. 'I don't think we actually broke in, but it's a moot point. We were there without permission. I vote we go to the police and say she's missing, but don't mention that we've been inside her house. They'll know we've been round there if they follow it up as they'll probably speak to Erin, but no one knows we've been inside and I think that's probably for the best.'

Cora nodded, 'Agreed. We really should tell someone.'

'True,' said Jackie, buttering her bread, 'how about we pop into the local police station after we finish here.'

The food was delicious, and they took their time, enjoying their cosy new surroundings and their lunch and delaying as long as possible talking to the police.

Nearly two hours later, the three women trouped into the local police station. Stickville was lucky to have its own police station. Most small towns didn't have one anymore and people had to either travel to a larger town, phone, or go online if they wanted to report anything. Stickville police station was very small and had only two policemen on duty at a time. One of them was behind the desk as they entered.

'Now then ladies, what can we do for you?' a large policeman in his late forties smiled at them from behind a plastic screen.

'Good afternoon Sergeant, eh?' Jackie waited for the policeman to give his name. *It's always best to have a name to refer to should it be necessary.*

'Sergeant Potts.'

'Ah, good afternoon Sergeant Potts, I'm Mrs Hardy and my friends here are Mrs Bailey and Mrs Cromwell.'

'Good afternoon, ladies,' said the sergeant with a bemused smile. 'How can I help you?'

'We think our friend is missing,' Cora jumped straight in.

'She's not really our friend. We know her through art classes,' Andrea added a little unnecessarily.

'We haven't seen her for some weeks and are not sure whether to be worried or not,' continued Jackie.

Sergeant Potts smiled as he looked at the three women standing before him. All wrapped up in their hats and gloves, he could only see their eyes and even those not very clearly as two of them wore glasses.

Here we go, three old dears wanting a bit of attention. Prob-

ably been reading too many Miss Marple books. Ah well, we're not really busy today. May as well find out what they want.

'What makes you think she's missing?' he asked, smiling round at the three eager faces.

'She hasn't been back to the art classes, despite saying she was coming back for the new term in January,' Andrea explained.

Ahh, I was right. They just want a bit of attention. 'Maybe she just changed her mind.'

'She was really keen when we saw her at Christmas,' said Cora, removing her scarf to speak clearer.

'Is that all you've got, ladies? She's given up her art class? I'm sorry but it's not enough, I'm afraid.'

'We've been to her house a couple of times,' Cora ignored a warning glance from Jackie, 'and there's no answer. Her neighbour hasn't seen her either.'

'Is she elderly? Your sort of ag...,' he trailed off, 'how old is she?'

'She's 56 and in good health, as far as we know.'

Probably not dead in her sleep then. 'What's her name?' Sergeant Potts sighed and turned to a computer screen.

'Kim Merchant, Mrs Kim Merchant. She lives here in Stickville.' Jackie told him.

'Mrs Kim Merchant.' *Hmm I know that name.* 'Mrs eh? has she a husband d'you know?'

'She's divorced,' said Cora, 'lives alone here in Stickville.' *Sod it we've literally just told him that, he'll think I'm senile.*

The sergeant looked at the screen for a few minutes and Kim's recent reports came up.

Mrs Kim Merchant.

17, Conkers Road, Stickville, Lincolnshire.

D.O.B. 15-05-1967

. . .

18th October 2022 – Mrs Merchant reports a dead bird nailed to an old building on farmland she owns. Mrs Merchant believes it is a sign of black magic being performed on her land.

No action taken.

26th October 2022 – Mrs Merchant reports a large quantity of feathers have been dumped in her field by person or persons unknown. Mrs Merchant believes they were put there to frighten her and are connected with black magic rituals.

No action taken.

4th November 2022 – Mrs Merchant reports small holes dug in her front garden by person or persons unknown. Mrs Merchant believes a vendetta is taking place against her and that black magic is involved.

Action – advised CCTV cameras to be installed.

10th November 2022 – Mrs Merchant believes she sees naked people walking up and down past her house at night. Mrs merchant believes this is connected to black magic rituals.

No action taken.

21st November 2022 – Mrs Merchant believes someone has poisoned her sheep. No fatalities. Mrs Merchant believes this is due to black magic practices taking place on her land.

Action - Checked due to possibility of foot and mouth.

Vet reports Orf virus infection (scabby mouth), common in sheep usually due to unvaccinated flock or grazing on course pasture/thistles. Advised vaccination.

7th December 2022 – Mrs Merchant reports her house has been broken into. Mrs Merchant reports occult symbols scratched on her ceilings.

Action - Police attended scene. No sign of break in, nothing reported missing, no evidence of symbols on the ceilings.

No Further Action

13th December 2022 – Mrs Merchant reports occult symbols have been scratched on her car.

Action – Constable viewed car in police car park. Feint scratches on both lower driver side doors, probably due to opening them near brambles.

Mrs Kim Merchant lives alone and shows signs of being lonely and a possible fantasist. No more action advisable.

Oh no, it's the bloody mad woman. I don't need any more of her. I might have guessed these three would be friends of hers.

'Well ladies, there's nothing we can do at the moment. Just because she's given up art classes and wasn't home when you called doesn't mean anything. But as you've taken the trouble to pop in, I'll make a note of your worries. What name was it please? I only need one of you,' he added hurriedly.

'Cora Cromwell, Mrs.'

'Address and contact number, please.'

Cora dutifully supplied the information and the policeman made a note.

'I'm sure she's fine, probably just gone away for a few weeks, that's all.'

Any minute he's gonna said, 'Ahh Bless' thought Andrea and she turned to leave. Jackie and Cora also realised he wasn't interested and with a half-hearted, 'thank you officer,' they all left the police station.

Sergeant Potts turned back to his computer screen and updated Kim's file.

28th January 2023 – Mrs Cora Cromwell reported Mrs Kim Merchant had not attended art classes since Christmas.

No action taken.

There was nothing else they could do, and it was beginning to get dark, so they piled into Andrea's car and she drove them all back to her house.

'Coming in for a cup of tea?' she asked.

'Go on then, but I need to get back fairly soon. Ollie and Milton are very good, but I don't want them to worry.' Cora laughed, but she wasn't entirely joked.

They were sitting in Andrea's cosy front room drinking tea, relieved to be away from Kim's house and the unhelpful policeman. The room was comfortably furnished and on the window ledge Andrea had put a few pieces of pottery she'd made over the years, now filled with dried grasses and seed heads, and one or two small framed batiks were hung on the wall.

Jackie leant back in her armchair and said, 'Damn, we

forgot to look at the ceiling. Kim told us there were signs scratched into the ceiling, symbols. We didn't look.'

'Hardly surprising when we were expecting to be greeted with a body any minute,' Cora pointed out, then after a while she added quietly, 'I think that was the most frightened I've ever been in my life.'

'It was frightening.' Jackie said and Andrea agreed, but both women had experienced fear before, and that fear was stronger and more terrifying than anything experienced today. Neither would ever forget the horror of the night all those years ago when they had both waited, clinging to each other, gripped by paralysing fear and filled with cold terror as they waited in the coastguard's office, listening to the rain as it lashed furiously at the black windows, waiting to hear if the fishing boat that held the happiness of both their lives in the safety of its grasp had lost its fight against the storm that had blown in from nowhere.

20

Checking his balaclava and surgical gloves were in place, the man gently pulled back the bolt and opened the door carefully. The woman was lying on the bed staring vacantly at the ceiling. He put the mug of tea and sandwich down on the chair next to her. She made no move.

'Sit up and drink your tea. There's food there if you want it.'

Slowly she swung her legs down to the floor and picked up the mug.

21

Saturday 1st & Sunday 2nd February

It was the weekend and Jackie was busy; she had a trip planned with her neighbour. Ruby was in her eighties and lived with her son in the cottage next door to Jackie. Ruby and Jackie shared an interest in gardening and Jackie would pop round to study seed catalogues in the winter and talk cuttings and dividing shrubs the rest of the year. They would regularly go off to the large garden centre at Woodcroft where they could potter around for hours, occasionally buy a plant or two and always have a nice lunch.

Jackie also helped out with the town's primary school gardening project. Some years ago, an enthusiastic teacher had set up a small allotment at the school where during term times, the children could plant fruit and vegetables, tend them and reap the harvest. There were also a few chickens kept there, too. Volunteers from the town would step in during the holidays and outside school hours to help and Jackie did her share. On Sunday she was down on the rota to let the chickens out in the morning, help with a bonfire in the afternoon and then shut the chickens up again around half past four when dusk began to fall. If there were any eggs, she was allowed to take them, but this time of the year there wasn't much daylight and the eggs were few and far between.

Cora too had a full weekend planned. She was visiting her sister again. It was to be a fun few days and she was looking forward to it. They had tickets for the theatre to see a play about mistaken identity, a comedy, and they had also booked a table at a posh seafood restaurant that Cora loved. She would stay as long as she could, making the most of the visit, and drive back on Monday morning, going straight to the studio for her art class.

Andrea had no plans and so took advantage of the dry weather to hang out some washing and think about cleaning out the fridge. Deciding to save that job for a more miserable day, she tidied round a bit and ate a bowl of soup. Afterwards she put on her walking boots, grabbed her litter stick and said goodbye to Nonsuch and Mrs Tim who ignored her, sleeping as usual curled up together in the armchair by the window in a weak sunbeam, and set out for an extra-long walk. She would walk into the town today and then back round the fields by the river, about seven miles altogether and if she set off now, she'd be back long before dark.

She walked into Drayflot, picking up rubbish with her trusty litter picker as she went. This was her fourth and longest lasting litter picker. She had paid more for the Streetmaster Pro than her previous pickers, and it had paid off. She'd had it five years now, and it showed no signs of aging. It had a strong steel rod and could grab anything with its two pincers, making short work of the discarded cigarette packets, old tissues and drink cans that she came across on her journey.

The council had done a good job clearing away the huge pile of dumped rubbish from the fishermen's layby, but there had obviously been a tournament in the past few days and Andrea spent some time collecting up their empty sandwich boxes, cigarette butts and plastic bottles. Generally, the local fishermen were very good and rarely left any rubbish behind, but perhaps this had been a larger contest and had brought in fishermen from other towns who were not quite so careful. She slithered down the bank hanging onto a strong-looking tussock of grass and reached with her litter stick out into the river to grab a plastic bag which floated there ready to trap an unwary duck or a fish.

Oooh grass, please don't break, please don't break. Just a bit more—Got it! Yes, well done me. And she scrambled back up the bank on her hands and knees and continued down the lane.

On the way into town, there was a litter bin. They were few and far between around there, where she could empty her plastic bag, which she then folded up and put in her pocket. She didn't pick up the litter in the town, only in the countryside. She did it for the animals and birds that lived in the landscape, not the people in the town who were quite capable of gathering up their own mess, or better still, not dropping it in the first place.

Sometimes in the lanes people saw her collecting the litter and stopped to thank her or shouted their thanks from bicycles or car windows. She would nod and smile and accept their thanks politely, but she didn't do it for them. She hated the rubbish, especially on the tracks and footpaths near her home. She hated that people just threw it anywhere without a thought for anyone or anything else. *Just take it home.*

She did it for the animals and birds that lived there. She picked up plastic and bits of wire from the fields for the elusive brown hares that ran across them. Camouflaged in the winter against the bare earth of the land until she got a little too near and made them break cover. Streaking away over the empty ground to a safe enough distance before stopping to look back. *That's thanks enough for me.*

She collected crisp packets, plastic bottles and tin cans from the grass verges, ditches and bushes that bordered the lanes. The little muntjac deer, the rabbits and rodents didn't want the waste from thoughtless humans spoiling and blocking their established runs and paths. *That's why I do it.*

She gathered up cigarette boxes and cigarette ends, empty sandwich packets and lidded coffee cups from down by the river and like today, often slithered down the bank when feeling brave and fished plastic bags from the river, scrambling back up on all fours. She enjoyed doing it, feeling she was making a difference, albeit a small one, and whilst doing so had discovered where the swans nested each year and seen their grey cygnets, newly hatched and swimming. She had watched the coots and moorhens bringing up their gangly young. She noticed kingfishers swoop past in a flash of electric blue or sit stock still on a low branch waiting for their dinner to swim to them, and occasionally she spotted the cormorant dive and surface seconds later with his fish supper, silhouetted against the glare of the water. *That's my reward.*

Once and only once she watched an otter stalk and catch a water vole and take it back to his underground holt. Tracking the scent along the waterline where the water voles live. Sleek, long and dangerous he ducked in and out of the river cutting through the water one minute and running along the mud bank the next, turning back on himself and then darting forward again until he disappeared into the undergrowth only to return seconds later with the hapless vole hanging from his jaws Later that same day as she sat in the little room at the front of her cottage with the window wide, she watched a stag, antlers high and heavy, trot past busily engaged on a mission of importance. What a magical day. *That's all the thanks I want.*

Oh yes, and once she had found a tightly folded twenty-pound note, that was nice too.

Drayflot was an old market town and in its heyday had been a flourishing town full of shops and pubs and noisy with the hustle and bustle of busy life, but nowadays it was a shadow of its former self, although evidence of its previous glory could still be found in the town's museum, tucked away down a side street. Since they'd built the by-pass, the town had died and now despite the railway station and free parking in the market square it boasted only a pub The Dray, a Co-op, a small garage, a pet shop, a wool shop and a post office that was only open mornings. Andrea didn't go into the Co-op as there was nothing she needed and also her jeans were covered in mud from her riverbank escapade, although that wouldn't have mattered at all as no one would have given her a second glance in this farming community.

'Andrea, hey Andrea,' a voice called her name.

Turning, she saw a small woman being dragged along by a large dog.

'Teddy, stop Teddy. Hi Andrea, how are you? Haven't seen you for ages. You okay?'

'Oh, hello Netty,' Andrea said with a smile, 'yes I'm fine thanks, you okay? And Teddy?'

Netty always looked immaculate, neatly dressed and hair always perfectly styled, and today was no different. They had first met years ago when Netty had joined Andrea's art classes to try pottery. They had got on well, although Netty had left after a few weeks as her reluctance to cut her beautifully manicured and elegantly long fingernails prevented her from working successfully with the clay. But they had remained friends and often bumped into each other when out and about.

'How is everything? I'll tell you what, let's have a cup of tea in The Dray and catch up? We can sit outside with Teddy and I can have a ciggy.' Netty wasn't one to hang about and she was heading into the pub before waiting for a reply.

'Alright, but we definitely need to sit outside. I'm covered in mud.'

They settled themselves in the so-called Beer Garden amid the metal kegs stacked against the wall and chatted and drank tea and Netty happily smoked her cigarettes, elegantly held between her exquisite fingers. It was fun, and both women enjoyed the chance meeting and subsequent catch up. There was much to say, and it was an hour and a half and another cup of tea later when they left the pub and Andrea continued on her way through the town and out the other side. *I should have gone back the way I came, not carried on the long way round,* she thought. Now *it'll be dark by the time I get home.*

She continued walking, taking the rarely used footpath between the road and the river. She didn't come this way very often, and it was interesting to view the river from this side. It was lovely, and she was enjoying the fresh air. She had her audiobook, unabridged of course, Daphney Du Maurier's Jamaica Inn one of her favourites, playing in her earphones and the time passed in an enjoyable dream of watching the swans and ducks on the river, peering down at the lumbering slugs and occasional busy beetle as they crossed her path, whilst being caught up in a thrilling tale of smugglers and wreckers on the Cornish coast.

After a while, she became aware the light was fading. *Oh, bloody hell, I'm gonna have to get a move on or it'll be pitch dark and I haven't got a torch with me.* Andrea always forgot there was a torch on her phone, but had she remembered it was doubtful she'd know how to find it. The ducks were settling down in the reeds for the night and the swans had disappeared. She quickened her pace. Eventually she reached the end of the footpath where she climbed over the wooden stile, and turning the corner was back on the road. *At least I'm on the road now and won't fall in the river in the dark.*

She crossed the bridge and began the last mile and a half to her home. It was dark now and a fine drizzle began falling. *Oh no, my washing's out. If I'd got back sooner, I could have saved it.* She pulled up her hood and tightening it against the increasing rain as she continued walking. The time was actually only about six thirty, and in a town or city with lots of people about it would just be a very wet early evening, but here in the midst of the country with very little traffic on this single-track lane, with no pavements and no street lighting it was as if it was midnight.

She walked on, head bent against the rain. Suddenly she noticed a large black shape in the distance and as she approached, she realised it was a van. *What's that van doing just parked there? No lights, just pulled up on the verge by the field.* She crossed over the road to avoid the parked van, and as she passed, she saw a man taking something out of the rear doors. He was so intent on what he was doing he failed to notice the dark figure passing silently by on the grass verge across the road. She slowed down a little, watching him. *What the—he's dumping rubbish! He's the bastard that has been dumping all the bloody rubbish. What a scumbag!* She tiptoed past not wanting to confront him, alone as she was in the dark. *I can't make out the reg number, but it's a big van with a squarish shape, no windows in the back and it's a dark colour.* She was further away now, looking back at the front of the van. *There's nothing I can do, I can't even take a photo it's too dark and if I use a flash he'll see, as it is I'm pretty sure he hasn't seen me and I don't want a confrontation in the dark.*

Forty minutes later Andrea was back inside her cosy cottage, her wet coat dripping by the door, her muddy jeans in the laundry basket and Nonsuch and Mrs Tim curling round her legs letting her know they were starving and could possibly die if not fed immediately.

The next day the rain had stopped and having put the washing machine on again, Andrea decided to go and see exactly how much rubbish had been dumped by the mysterious van man. Her coat was still wet from yesterday, so she put on the jacket she'd worn when they'd gone to Stickville and grabbing her litter stick set off back to where she'd seen the van. As she walked, she saw a can had been thrown into the long grass. She fished it out, stamped it flat, then reached into her pocket for the plastic bag she'd carefully folded up the day before. *Oh no, I've got a different coat on, damn I've got no bag.* She searched her pockets just in case a spare bag was lurking somewhere. There was no bag, but there was something. Her hand closed round a small fat book, and she pulled it out. *Oh, my goodness, it's Kim's old address book! I found it when we were in her house. I must've just slipped it in my pocket when we began searching for her phone.* The bag was forgotten as Andrea quickly flicked through the alphabetised pages. *M... M... Merchant... Maybe her husband or son are in here.* But she was out of luck only Maud Epstein, Mark Dongle and Mechanic – Tom, were listed. *Damn, she lists them by first names or professions.*

Returning it to her pocket until later, Andrea continued her walking until she came to the place she'd seen the van the previous night. There was a hedge with a closed gate and a farm track leading into a ploughed field. By the hedge on the verge by the side of the road was a broken settee, an old fridge and four full black bin liners, one of which had split open spilling out old electrical wiring, bits of plaster, rusty nails and other bits of rubble. She took out her phone and photographed the mess, then went home reported it to Fix My Street and returned in her car with a plastic bag to collect up what she could of the spilt wiring and rusty nails in case an innocent creature walked this way in the dark and hurt themselves.

22

Monday 3rd & Tuesday 4th February

The Monday morning textiles class passed agonisingly slowly for Andrea. Eventually, however, with cheery calls of 'goodbye' and 'see you next week', the studio emptied and Andrea removed their work to the safety of the shelf and got out the work in progress belonging to the later class. Cora arrived first, her journey back from her sister's having been quicker than she had expected. Yes she'd had a lovely time thanks and the seafood restaurant had been wonderful. Next Betty and Sal arrived full of smiles and cheery greetings, and finally Jackie came, standing in the doorway and beaming round at everyone as she always did.

They settled down to their work. Cora was well underway with her latest batik. Having finished Joseph and his Technicolour Dreamcoat, and made a good job of it too, she had moved on to Priscilla Queen of the Desert and had a photograph of a camel in full festival regalia with a colourful saddle or Mahawi on its back. She was starting with the background, and as Andrea pointed out was making good progress. When the background was completed, she would wax over the areas she wanted to keep and make a start on the camel, but that was a few weeks away yet.

Sal had brought along a small wooden box about the size of a bread bin, with four little drawers in it. She had bought it online, and it had arrived in the post that morning. It was made from a light untreated wood, possibly pine, and was perfect for batiking on to. Sal was delighted as Andrea explained how she could batik the raw wood, and at the end of the process, polish the wax into it to protect it and keep the colours waterproof.

'What are you going to use it for, Sal?' asked Jackie.

'Well, you know I collect postcards, don't you? I thought I'd keep my collection in here. They're all over the place at the moment. The drawers are just the right size to take them standing upright so I can pull open a drawer and flip through them. I'll get some pretty ceramic knobs instead of these boring little wooden ones and it'll look lovely.' Sal looked happily at her new acquisition and began to think about designs.

When the tea and biscuits arrived, Betty and Sal stopped working and waited expectantly to hear the next instalment of 'Kimanation Street'. The others had kept them up to date with their findings, their sleuthing as Cora insisted on calling it, and now Betty and Sal were keen to know how they had fared at Kim's house the previous Tuesday. Between them, Jackie, Andrea and Cora updated them and Betty and Sal were duly impressed with their courage at entering Kim's house and looking round. When Jackie described how they'd gone to the police and how Sergeant Potts wasn't interested and believed nothing was wrong, Betty said that she wasn't surprised as there was no proof that Kim hadn't just gone away on holiday.

'But the house was a mess, the heating was left on, and

the rubbish hadn't been taken out. She's obviously not gone on holiday,' Cora pointed out.

'I agree,' said Betty, 'but the police don't know that, as you couldn't tell them you'd been inside snooping around.'

'Well,' said Andrea, 'I've made a find which might throw some light onto the mystery.' And she told of her unexpected discovery of Kim's address book and how she must have dropped the book into her pocket without thinking.

'Anyway, the thing is I trawled through it last night and found a Kevin Merchant living in Sleaford and a Charlie Merchant living in Grantham.'

'I think Kevin must be Kim's son. I think I remember her saying he's called Kevin,' said Sal.

'So Charlie must be her ex-husband. I wonder if he knows where she is.' Andrea sipped her tea thoughtfully.

'He may do or may not. She told us their marriage had broken down due to his drinking, so we don't know if they're still in touch or not.' Jackie said.

'How about a trip to Grantham? We could pop in and see if Charlie's in and have a chat.' Cora suggested.

'Maybe we should ring first,' wondered Jackie. 'We can't really just turn up.'

'Why not?' asked Andrea.

'Well, what if he's not in for a start?'

'Okay, maybe you're right. Who fancies ringing him?'

'I'll do it,' Jackie picked up her phone. 'what shall I say if he answers?'

'Well, just ask him if he knows where Kim is and take it from there,' Betty suggested.

Jackie entered the number into her phone, and they all waited silently. Then she made a face and then hung up. 'Unobtainable. Looks like we'll be having a trip to Grantham after all.'

'If he's not there, we'll have had a nice day out in Grantham anyway,' Andrea grinned and the others agreed.

With the tea and biscuits finished, the class continued and whilst they were working, Andrea told them of her evening encounter with the fly-tipper.

'So now that I know he drives a big square van and dumps his crap after dark, I know when to go and look for him.'

'Be careful,' warned Sal, 'if he's dumping commercial rubbish, it means he's got a business and won't take kindly to you interfering.'

'I'll be careful, but I need to get proof.'

They had decided to go to Grantham by train and at 8.40 the next day Andrea, Jackie and Cora were on the platform at Drayflot railway station waiting for the tiny train consisting of just three carriages to open its doors. An hour and a half later they disembarked at Grantham station, walked immediately to the nearest coffee shop and after two lattes, a cappuccino, and a toasted teacake each, they were off walking to the address in Kim's book. Not wanting to arrive empty-handed, they had bought a bag of Danish pastries from the coffee shop and were taking it as a gift.

After walking through the busy town to less a sought-after area, they found the slightly shabby street. Numerous coloured bins were lined up outside the once lovely houses, three stories high and paint peeling. They no longer housed well-to-do families with perhaps a live-in maid. These days, the sea of bells by the front doors indicated at least six dwellings in each building. At number 8 they searched the bells for flat number 4 and rang it, it was marked Merchant, at least it looked like Merchant, but it really could have said anything. They waited for an answer. There was none. They rang again, still nothing, but then a thin girl in a huge coat came out of the front door and told them Charlie was usually home at this time and to go on up, number four, first floor.

The outside belied the inside, which was actually fine. The stairs were carpeted in a durable rush matting, slightly stained but clean, and the place smelt pleasantly of air freshener and cooking. At Charlie's door, they rang the bell and waited, looking at each other questioningly. The door opened and Charlie Merchant stood looking at them through red-rimmed eyes. He was a tall man, possibly only in his early sixties, but looking much older. He wore baggy black jogging pants and an old green jumper and was holding an open can of larger.

'Now then, who are you?' he asked, studying them suspiciously.

'We're friends of Kim,' said Jackie, taking charge and reverting to her days when she was a carer for the elderly, working in the community, helping them remain at home for as long as possible. 'You must be Mr Merchant, Charlie Merchant. Can we call you Charlie?' Jackie put out her hand to shake Charlie's. Mesmerised by the friendly, capable woman who stood in front of him, he shook it. 'We've come to see how you're getting on,' Jackie continued. 'My name is Jackie, and these two ladies are Cora and Andrea. Can we come in, please?'

Charlie opened the door wide and stood back. In his slightly befuddled state, he was no match for Jackie in full flow.

Jackie led the way and Cora and Andrea followed smiling at Charlie as they passed him. They stood in the middle of the large room, looking round. The flat was small and smelled of stale beer. There was a wooden table with two upright dining chairs next to the window, which was hung with a net curtain. An armchair that looked reasonably new but was very stained and had a pizza box and two empty lager cans under it. It stood in the middle of the room, facing an electric fire and a large TV screen. The TV, which also looked quite new, was on and a game show was blaring out as the audience cheered the contestants. The other side of the room housed a small kitchen area with a cooker and a small fridge. A sink and worktop were cluttered with dirty cups, plates, cutlery and a few more takeaway cartons and boxes flowed from the overfull bin. Two more doors, both open, led to an untidy bedroom and a tiny bathroom.

The three women stood in the middle of the room, looking round.

'We've brought you some Danish pastries,' Cora waved the bag. 'I hope you like them. Shall we have some tea?'

'Who did you say you were? Friends of Kim?' Charlie was bemused. Who were these three elderly ladies who had come to visit? Why him? They looked quite friendly though, and it was always nice to have visitors and they'd brought him breakfast too. He smiled. Charlie had a nice smile despite having a few teeth missing. His blue eyes crinkled, and he chuckled. 'Sit down ladies, take your coats off and sit down, make yourselves at home.'

No one really wanted to sit. The place was so messy, so again Jackie took charge.

'We haven't come to sit about. We've come to give you a hand. You sit down and we'll make ourselves useful. Have you tea and milk?'

'Got tea bags, but the milk's all gone.' Charlie opened the fridge revealing three cans of lager and a virtually empty plastic milk bottle. 'Need to get some from the corner shop.'

'Don't worry, I'll go,' said Andrea, making for the door, keen to get some fresh air.

When Andrea returned twenty minutes later having bought milk, instant coffee, two packets of biscuits, a bag of sugar, a bottle of washing up liquid and a roll of black bin liners, she found Cora at the sink making good headway into the mess on the worktop and Jackie pushing a small vacuum cleaner round the floor, having piled up the empty cans and food boxes in one place for want of a bin bag. Thankfully, the TV had been turned down so they could sit and talk.

'Here Jackie,' Andrea handed her the bin bags, 'I bought a few bits and pieces. Shall I put the kettle on?'

Charlie was sitting in his armchair, gazing happily at the team of ladies that had arrived out of the blue. He watched them with a contented smile on his face. In his hazed state, he wasn't absolutely sure what was going on, but he was pleased it was.

Ten minutes later, the washing up was finished, and the tea had been made. The takeaway food detritus had been bagged and removed together with the contents from the overflowing bin, and the window had been opened despite the cold weather. Jackie turned up the electric fire, having first checked with Charlie that his electric bill was paid. Yes, it was paid, Kim saw to all that, paid his rent and his bills. She was a good woman, an angel. At last, they sat down, Jackie and Cora on the dining chairs at the table by the window and Andrea on a chair she'd found in the bedroom and brought through. Sitting with their tea and Danish pastries, they made an odd group, three older women and a bemused alcoholic man sitting in a tiny room chatting amicably.

'So, have you seen Kim lately?' Andrea asked casually, 'does she come and visit?' It seemed perfectly obvious to her she didn't by the state of the place. *Surely if she visited, the place wouldn't be in this mess.*

'She comes over sometimes, regularly I think,' Chalie slurped his tea.

'Do you know when she last came?' asked Cora.

'Couldn't tell ya, me duck,' he said, 'I'm not good with dates.' Charlie had a Nottinghamshire burr and sounded like he'd been born and bred there.

'Ahh, no it can be difficult to keep track sometimes,' Jackie nodded, 'we haven't seen her for a little while ourselves. We wondered if she was on holiday.'

'Dunno me duck.' Charlie wasn't a great talker, but he smiled round at the women and seemed pleased to have their company.

'Do you ever go and visit her?' asked Cora. 'Do you go to her house at all?'

'Nah,' he chuckled, 'she comes here to see me.'

'I know she's got some lovely sheep. Have you been to see Kim's sheep?' Andrea changed tack.

'No time for sheep, really,' said Charlie, picking the remaining pastry crumbs from his jumper and licking his fingers. 'didn't know she had any, she might've told me, I forget stuff sometimes. She comes here sometimes, she pays me rent and me bills and stuff, she's a good girl.' Charlie laughed, 'you her friends then?'

'Yes, we met her at art classes,' said Cora.

'Yes, she's a good girl. Pays for me rent, you know. I don't want for much, she pays me bills too.' He laughed again. For all his alcohol problems and shambolic lifestyle, Charlie Merchant seemed happy enough.

They knew they were not going to get anything more from Charlie and so after they'd washed up the mugs and tidied round a bit more; they said goodbye and went off in search of some lunch. After they had left him, Charlie

Merchant went to his fridge and took out a can of larger, sat down, turned up the sound on the TV, opened the can, chuckled and promptly forgot they'd been.

Cora, Andrea, and Jackie walked back to the centre of the town pleased to be out in the fresh air. They soon found a nice-looking café where they ordered some food at the counter and took their teas to a table in a corner at the back.

'So that was Charlie,' said Cora, removing her coat. 'he was more or less what I was expecting.'

'He was happy to see us and seemed pleased we came.' Andrea took hers off too and hung it over the back of her chair. 'We didn't get anything useful out of him though, did we? He hasn't even been to Kim's house before, let alone know where she might be.'

'No, and he doesn't know she's got some land,' Jackie said. 'There was no way he was going to be able to suggest where she could have got to.'

'Two sundried tomato and goat's cheese quiches' the waitress arrived and placed them in front of Jackie and Andrea. 'Chips are coming.'

'Well, it hasn't been an entirely wasted day. These look delicious.' Andrea picked up her knife and fork and dived in.

The waitress returned, 'One hot pork roll with stuffing and here's your large bowl of chips.'

They tucked in to their respective lunches, sharing the chips between them and when they'd finished and were sipping their tea, they decided what to do next.

Their train home wasn't until half-past five, so they spent a very pleasant afternoon mooching about Grantham, enjoying just wandering around. They visited St Wulfram's church, known for its very tall spire and had afternoon tea in a beautiful hotel said to be England's oldest coaching inn, dating back to the thirteenth century and visited over the years by seven kings and queens. They looked at the statue of Margaret Thatcher, explored the shops and the Guildhall, peered up at the beehive high in the branches of the tree outside the Beehive pub, one of the oldest pubs in Grantham and where, since at least 1830 there had been a hive of bees in the lime tree above the pub sign. They had a lovely time and completely forgot about Kim.

On the train going home, Andrea asked, 'should we just give up looking for Kim. I mean, we've got nothing to go on and the police aren't interested. I don't really know what we can do.'

'We haven't seen her son yet. How about we go and see Kevin. Perhaps he'll know something?' Jackie said.

'Oh lovely, a day out in Sleaford. I'm game,' Cora grinned.

23

The man took the mug and empty plate away to wash and bolted the door behind him. So far, everything was going to plan.

Don't get overconfident, I've got a long way to go yet.

24

Wednesday 5th February

The pottery classes had finished early. The numbers were down due to seasonal colds and flu and Andrea had contacted the few potters who were coming and combined both classes together in the morning. Now she had most of the afternoon free and decided to take advantage of it and go for a walk. She locked the studio, fed Nonsuch and Mrs Tim and put on her stout walking boots and coat, then with her litter stick in hand, she set off down the lane. It was dry and bright, early signs of spring were beginning to show and despite the biting cold wind that the east coast seemed to welcome, the green shoots of future daffodils were beginning to push their way through the drifts of snowdrops that clung to the banks of the drainage channels which cut through the landscape.

Andrea walked, enjoying being outside and feeling the cold wind on her cheeks, and as she walked, she thought about her latest batik painting. She was still working on it and had quite a way to go before it was finished. She needed to get a move on as the summer exhibition was getting ever nearer and she had committed to putting at least three pieces in. She was a member of the Lincolnshire Artists Group, affectionally known as the LAGs, and twice a year they put on an exhibition of members work, once in a gallery in the grounds of Massey Hall, a beautiful Lincolnshire Heritage Trust property not too far away from where she lived, and once in the chapter house of Lincoln cathedral. The summer exhibition was at the Massey Hall and the quality of the work would, as usual, be high. Andrea always sold her work, most of it anyway, with even her smallest pieces fetching healthy three figure sums.

She shouldn't really be out spending hours wandering around the countryside. She had to get her batik finished. Apart from having to finish her third piece, they still all needed to be framed. She had a lot of work to do and the deadline was getting nearer. She was off to Sleaford on Saturday with Jackie and Cora to try to find Kim's son. Another day out of her studio, she really should prioritise her time better. But she was looking forward to Saturday. She enjoyed being out with Jackie and Cora, chatting and laughing and discovering new places to eat, and the mystery that they had built up around Kim was the perfect excuse for their trips.

As she walked, she wondered why they had latched onto Kim; she knew they didn't need an excuse to go out together, but all three had jumped at the chance to find out what they could about a woman they had only known for a few months. Andrea couldn't speak for the others, but she had been touched by Kim's despair, the way she had looked when all those weeks ago in the studio she had told them of her perceived persecution, Andrea had seen a broken woman totally aware no one believed her and most people thought she was mad.

Andrea was so deep in her thoughts she did not notice the lane ahead and it was only when she heard his voice that she realised Ernest was walking towards her, unmistakably, with his upright military gait and swinging his stick.

'Good afternoon, Andrea Bailey.'

Oh no, it's flat cap man, and it's too late to avoid him, damn.

'This isn't your usual time for being out walking, is it?'

What's it got to do with you when I go out? 'No, I'm not usually out around this time.'

'Still picking up litter I see. You really do love the stuff, don't you, Andrea Bailey?' Ernest laughed heartily and wiped his eyes.

Honestly, why is that funny? Just go away and leave me alone. 'Yes, most days, as you know,'

'I don't know how you find any to pick up. There's never any round here.'

Maybe that's because I pick it all up. 'Oh well, I must be off now, don't want to be late back.' Andrea began to walk away.

'How far do you walk, Andrea Bailey? Where do you go? Do you have a route, Andrea Bailey? A litter spotting route?' Ernest was roaring with laughter now, but he wasn't giving up.

'Oh here and there, you know, I must go now, bye,' and she continued on her way. *That man, he's a pain in the arse. Why is he so interested in my actions? He doesn't know me and I've never given him any encouragement. Anyone else would just say hello and walk on by.*

Having shaken Ernest off, Andrea climbed over the wooden stile onto the track which stretched along the top of the riverbank. Today she was back on her usual side of the river looking at the familiar view of the flat landscape. She watched the ducks, soon they would begin searching for partners and in a few weeks, they would be pairing off ready for nest building, the green-headed drakes, three or four to one female, angrily squabbling and chasing each other away with much splashing and loud quacking. This afternoon though, they swam contentedly together, the calm before the storm. At the end of the riverbank, a small lane crossed over the river and Andrea climbed over another stile and leant on the red brick bridge, looking back at the way she'd just come. She saw the river spread out before her, a rippled silver band cutting through the land, she saw the path she had just walked like a green thread high on the riverbank In the distance she saw the ducks gliding on the surface ignoring the wind, and looking down into the water. Below her, she saw her reflection dark against the sky looking up at her. She smiled to herself; it was a wonderful place, and she loved it.

She had intended to cross the lane, climb the next stile and continue along the further stretch of riverbank, but as she turned to continue her walk, she glanced down the usually empty lane to her right and she saw a dark brown van parked up on the verge. *Is that the van I saw the other day? Could be - large, squarish, no windows. What's he up to, I wonder? Maybe I'll walk that way and see what's going on. It's off my route home, but I can cut round by the railway to get back.* So Andrea set off towards the parked van.

It was parked on the verge on the wrong side of the road facing her and as she neared it, she could see a man standing on the grass by the door on the passenger's side. It was Ernest; she knew that upright stature and flat cap anywhere. He was talking to the driver through the open window. *Oh no, not bloody Ernest again. How'd he get round here so quickly? I must have taken longer than I realised, standing watching the ducks.* Andrea stayed on the opposite side of the lane to the van and tried to walk past unnoticed, but she was out of luck.

'We meet again, Andrea Bailey!' shouted Ernest.

Andrea nodded and raised her litter stick in acknowledgment, but kept on walking. The person in the driving seat turned and looked at her, but in the shadow of the van she couldn't make out the face. As she passed, she heard Ernest's voice and picked up the words 'Andrea Bailey' and 'art studio'. When she had passed by and was hidden from view by the van itself, she turned, grabbed her phone, and quickly took a photo of the back of the van with the registration number. Then she carried on walking to cut back round by the railway, then went home.

25

Saturday 8th February

The three friends had decided to go to Sleaford on Saturday because they thought it could be a good day to catch Kevin at home. They had agreed it was best not to phone first in case he put them off or just wanted to talk to them on the phone and they thought they might get more of an idea if they met him face to face. They also wanted a day out.

They got off the train at Sleaford station and walked through the town to The Hub. Once an old seed warehouse, The Hub was now a centre for craft and design. They had been before to view interesting exhibitions and buy unusual gifts from the little shop, and Andrea had done a couple of felting workshops there many years ago. The atmosphere was busy and since the café had been upgraded, there was now even more space to sit and look at the river, which was lucky as this Saturday morning it was heaving with people. An hour later invigorated by two lattes, a cappuccino and a flap jack each for Jackie and Cora, they set off walking to Kevin's house and twenty minutes after that; they turned into a quiet road near the castle ruins. Small stone cottages with small neat front gardens ran down both sides of the road and they found Kevin's house easily. There was no car outside, but they knocked on the door anyway and waited. A pretty young woman in a peach-coloured track suit opened the door. Her blonde hair was pulled back in a ponytail and she wore no make-up.

'Hi, can I help you?' she spoke with a soft Australian accent and looked enquiringly at the three older women who stood muffled up against the cold on her doorstep.

'Hello, yes, I'm Jackie Hardy and these ladies are Cora Cromwell and Andrea Bailey.' Jackie smiled and waved an arm at the other two. 'Are you Mrs Merchant?'

'Yes, I am,' the blonde woman was wary. What *on earth do these three want?* 'What can I do for you?'

'Well, we're actually looking for your husband, Mr Kevin Merchant. We're friends of his mother, Kim.'

'Is everything alright?'

'Oh yes, fine, we just wanted to pop by and have a word with your husband,' Jackie continued. *Damn, that sounds really suspicious.*

'Oh, I see. Well, Kevin's out at the moment. He takes the girls to swimming lessons on Saturday mornings, but he'll be back quite soon. Do you want to come in and wait?' *They look quite harmless and friendly enough.*

'That's very kind of you.' Jackie strode past Mrs Merchant with Cora and Andrea following.

They were ushered into a pretty sitting room, invited to take off their coats and sit down, and offered tea, which they gratefully accepted. The room was bright and spotless, the pink and white floral three-piece suite which they settled into was soft and comfortable and as they looked around them at the polished coffee table and breathed the fresh scent of lavender all three of them were thinking the same, *What a difference from Charlie's home.*

'Here's the tea, help yourselves to sugar. My name's Carol, by the way.' Carol introduced herself as she came in the room holding a tray with four mugs of tea, a bowl of sugar and a small plate of custard creams.

'This is very kind of you, Carol.' Andrea helped herself to a pretty china mug from the tray, now set down on the polished coffee table.

'Have you come far? You're friends of Kim, you say.'

'Drayflot, not too far.' Andrea replied.

'We came on the train,' added Cora unnecessarily. *Why the hell did I say that?*

'We're not really close friends of Kim. She comes to my art classes, and we know her through those,' continued Andrea. 'She's been coming for some months now, and she's quite good, actually.'

'Oh really, I had no idea she was artistic.' Carol was sitting now, cupping her mug of tea in her hands and looking with interest at the three unknown women in her sitting room.

'Has she never shown you anything she's done?' Jackie asked.

'I don't see her very often.' Carol's mouth tightened. 'She's quite a difficult woman to get to know. She came for Christmas day, of course, brought the girls some presents, and Kevin goes to see her probably every couple of months, but she doesn't often come over here to see us. I wish she would. I'd like the girls to see more of their grandmother and I know Kevin would as well, but there you are. Everyone's different, I suppose.'

'Yes, indeed,' agreed Jackie. 'Do you know when—'

'Oh—that sounds like Kevin and the girls now.' Carol jumped up as a car drew up outside and two little girls of about five and seven with wet hair came running up the front path.

From the sitting room they could hear Carol open the front door and greet the children in the hallway asking how the lesson had been, and the children laughing and telling her what they'd been doing this week before running upstairs to put their empty swimming bags away and to dry off their hair a bit more. Then they heard muffled talking between Carol and Kevin and shortly afterwards, the door opened and Carol returned clutching an armful of wet towels, followed by Kevin.

'Kevin, this is Jackie, Cora and Andrea, friends of your mum. Ladies, this is my husband Kevin. Please excuse me, I must deal with this wet swimming stuff and see to the girls.'

Carol left the room and Kevin stood looking down at the three strange women seated comfortably in his sitting room drinking tea. He was a tall man like his dad and with the same blue eyes. His dark hair was cut short, as was his stubble beard, and he wore blue tracksuit bottoms and an unzipped grey hoodie over a black T-shirt. He looked athletic and handsome.

'Well, this is unexpected,' he smiled at them as he took a seat in the spare armchair recently vacated by his wife. 'So, you're friends of mum, are you?' *Didn't know she had any.*

'Hello Kevin, it's lovely to meet you,' Cora began. 'Your wife's been very kind and given us tea despite us turning up out of the blue.'

'Yes, we must apologise for dropping in uninvited,' added Jackie. 'We were in Sleaford and thought we'd pop by on the off chance.'

Ha where did that come from? thought Andrea, glancing at Cora and raising an eyebrow.

'So how can I help you?'

'We just wondered if Kim was away on holiday,' Jackie continued. 'We need to get in touch about something and can't get hold of her.'

'Not as far as I know. What d'you need to see her about? It must be important if you've come over here to ask me.'

'Oh no, it's nothing important,' Jackie assured him in her best soothing voice. 'Nothing to concern yourself with. It's just that we were passing anyway.'

'She's been coming to my art classes for a few months now and really enjoys it. She's very good, you know,' Andrea explained. 'She was keen to join up for the next term but hasn't been back. I've emailed her but got no reply. I need to know whether to save her place or not. I don't want to give it away if she's just gone off on holiday.'

'Yes, we thought you might know,' Cora added.

'No, I've no idea, but I wouldn't worry about her, she does this you know, goes off for a few weeks without telling anyone, then she comes back, assuming everyone had known she was going and wondering why we were worried.' Kevin smiled round at the women.

'We aren't really worried but maybe a little concerned. You see, she told us she felt someone was trying to get her to give up her piece of land, you know, the bit she keeps her sheep on.' Jackie said.

Kevin straightened up and his blue eyes hardened. 'What did she tell you?'

'Someone had nailed a dead bird up and was leaving weird little piles of grass about the place and loads of black feathers. She thought it might have something to do with black magic, or maybe a witch's coven was using her land.'

'Oh no, not that again,' Kevin said tightly, 'she's obsessed with witchcraft.'

'She seemed quite concerned about it.'

'She told me about the incidents with her land and how she believes people want her off it. I said if she was that worried, why not sell it and be done with it, but she was having none of it—she's a stubborn woman.'

'So you think there's nothing to be worried about. We know she's been to the police, and they aren't concerned at all.'

Kevin stood up suddenly.

'Why the hell are the police involved? Wasting police time, typical. My advice is give her place away if someone else wants it, she can be very unreliable. She's always believing there are conspiracies or plots against her. It's just rubbish. No one wants her silly strip of land. Now if you don't mind, we have things to do.' He held open the sitting-room door. 'Thank you for your concern, ladies, but I'm sure my mother has just taken it into her head to go away for a few weeks and not bothered to let anyone know. It's as simple as that.'

Jackie, Andrea and Cora replaced their china mugs on the tray, gathered their coats and bags and made for the front door.

'Thank you so much for putting our minds at rest,' said Cora, 'and please thank Carol for the tea.'

'You're welcome, and I'm happy my mother has some friends, but please don't come back. I've got nothing more to say,' and he opened the front door.

'Goodbye' they chorused as they left.

'Oh by the way,' he called as they reached the pavement, 'how did you get my address?'

They pretended not to hear and with more goodbyes they hurried down the street.

Half an hour later, settled in a busy café with a toasted cheese and ham panini, a warm goat's cheese tart with salad, and a bowl of leek and potato soup with a crusty roll, they ate their lunch and pondered.

'It was mention of the police that got him riled,' Cora spoke through a mouthful of panini.

'Yeah,' Jackie stirred her soup, 'his manner changed as

soon as they were brought up.'

'Yes, and did you notice how he reacted when we asked him about the field—you know, the feathers and stuff?'

'He just sounded exasperated to me,' Jackie shrugged. 'I don't blame him either. If he's heard it all before, he's probably just fed up with her going on about witchcraft. We were the same, don't forget.'

'Yeah, you're right,' agreed Cora, 'and three strange women arriving out of nowhere and talking about the police, thinking about it now. He was quite calm, really.'

'We didn't get the chance to tell him we'd been to see Charlie,' Andrea cut into her tart.

'Probably for the best, really,' Jackie said. 'I get the feeling he wouldn't have been very pleased. Besides, I don't suppose Charlie will remember, so he'll probably never know, anyway.'

They finished eating in companionable silence, then pushing her plate to one side, Andrea said, 'what are we actually doing? We're wandering around asking questions of people we don't know, about something we don't even know has happened.'

'We're also having nice days out and lovely lunches,' Cora grinned. And they all laughed because it was true. That was exactly what they were doing.

They spent the afternoon wandering around the town, buying a few bits from the busy market and looking around the thirteenth century St. Denys' church, which boasts one of the oldest stone spires in the country. They decided to stroll over to the abandoned Bass Maltings, a group of eight disused malt houses now deserted and desolate. The huge brick buildings dominated the landscape and although the women had often seen them from the window of the train as it rushed past, this was the first time they had viewed them up close. The buildings stood sadly behind their fenced barrier, the only signs of life being the weeds and an occasional bird flying in through a broken window looking for a nesting site.

'Such an enormous empty place,' said Andrea, staring through the fence. 'Imagine being in there all alone.'

'Horrible, especially at night.' Cora shuddered.

'D'you think Kim is being kept somewhere like that?'

'What—you think she's been kidnapped, Jackie?' asked Andrea.

'Yeah, I mean I know no one's too worried about her, not the police or her son, but that's because no one believes the black magic bit, but what if she's been taken by someone and is being kept prisoner somewhere?'

'Hmmm, well I hope for her sake she hasn't,' Cora stared at the grim buildings, 'and I really hope she's not somewhere like that.'

26

The man unlocked the door and went inside. The woman did not move from where she lay.

It smells awful in here.

He placed the mug of tea and the bowl of cereal on the wooden chair, picked up the bucket from the corner and left, carefully bolting the door behind him. He couldn't afford to waste time. He had a busy day planned today.

27

Tuesday 11th February

Woodhall Spa is a pretty town, surrounded by expensive houses and boasting a delightful mix of independent shops and restaurants. Probably the most well-known thing about the town is the Kinema in the Woods. A short walk into the woods from the main road sits the pavilion cinema, opened in 1922 it's thought to be the only full-time cinema in the country still using rear projection and any film viewed there is a fun experience giving a feeling of going back in time to the golden age of movies. That's more or less what the guide-book says and Andrea, Cora, and Jackie wholeheartedly agreed and liked the little town a lot.

They had decided to have a day out in Woodhall Spa and go to the Kinema in the afternoon. During the morning, they intended to visit the magic shop that Kim had said she had visited to try to get some clue as to where Kim might be.

Cora drove, and having parked up, they soon found themselves having their usual lattes and cappuccino in the window of a warm coffee shop on the high street, looking out at the people passing by. It was a cold February day with a biting easterly wind and everyone was wrapped up in hats and scarves and bending into the wind as they walked.

'I hope it's warm in the Kinema this afternoon,' Cora cupped her hot coffee cup in her hands, 'I know sometimes it can be quite drafty.'

'It'll be fine,' Jackie reassured her, 'but first we need to find this magic shop. Anyone know where it is?'

'I do,' said Andrea as she sipped her coffee 'I've been in there once or twice buying incense sticks. I think I bought a crystal from there once too.'

'What are we going to say when we get there? That's what I want to know' asked Cora, 'I mean we can't just go in and say do you remember an odd woman who asked you about black feathers and thought there was a witches' coven on her land? Well guess what, now we think she's missing although she might just be on holiday, but we thought you'd know where she is.'

They laughed, but all agreed that would not be the right approach and so, as no one knew what to say, they went in and played it by ear.

They found the shop, A Witch's Brew, down a narrow side street. It was small and painted dark green inside, making it seem even smaller than it actually was. The shop was crammed with the usual shelves of incense sticks and wooden holders nestling alongside silver jewellery displayed on black velvet stands, necklaces with tiny skulls and bats dangling from them, heavy rings with big green stones and more skulls. There was a basket lined with red velvet full of differently shaped brass bells, and small glass bowls of colourful crystals: tiger's eye, rose quartz, red jasper and many more. There were boxes of candles in green, red and purple, and black lidded cauldrons standing on their three legs, arranged together in different sizes like family groups. In the window was a large resin sculpture of a black cat, back arched and claws drawn, surrounded by knobbly wooden wands of different sizes. At the back of the shop by the small counter were bundles of sage, bags of amber and frankincense, and tiny parchment scrolls rolled up and tied with red ribbons with a sign saying *Good Luck Spells*.

The shop was empty probably due to the dreadful weather, and Andrea went immediately to the crystals and began sorting out a couple to buy, when she looked up Jackie and Cora were at the counter talking to the tall thin man who was standing behind it. He was looking concerned and stroking his thin wispy beard with long, thin fingers.

'Oh yes, I remember her. How could I forget—is she a friend of yours?'

'No, not really a friend, more a colleague, we're looking for her and she mentioned she'd been in here a few times and knew you, so as we were passing we thought we'd pop in and see if you could help us.' Jackie beamed at the man.

'She came in many times last year, late summer, autumn time, I suppose. She seemed fine at first, interested in the shop, you know, eager to find out more about what I do here, asking questions and the like. I talked to her a lot, I told her about good luck talismans and crystals. I thought she wanted to learn about them, but then she started asking about local covens. I told her I didn't know anything about those. Later she started on about curses, dead birds, black feathers and black magic. Well, I don't get involved with black magic, that's not what I do here. I sell witchcraft supplies for people who are interested in what I call light magic. Nothing very heavy, you know.' The man fidgeted nervously with his wispy beard.

'Well, of course,' Jackie nodded encouragingly, and the thin man continued.

'I told her what I knew about black feathers. I said that although they're traditionally associated with mourning and death, they really represent change and she started getting hysterical, crying, you know.' The thin man was wringing his hands now, 'Well I didn't know what to do so I gave her a seat and made her a cup of tea. She calmed down a bit and told me someone had covered her land in black feathers and asked me if they were trying to kill her. Well, how did I know? I didn't know this woman and I certainly didn't want to get involved. I told her to go to the police if she was worried, but she said they wouldn't believe her. She said she thought it was the farmers next door who wanted her land and were trying to drive her away with curses and witchcraft and she wasn't going to go. She was hysterical, raving.'

'Oh, my goodness, what a thing for you to witness. Well, I should say you did the right thing by telling her to go to the police.' Jackie agreed. 'Did you see her again?'

'She came back about a week later and I'm ashamed to say I lied to her, I told her I was just closing for the day as I had an important appointment so she couldn't come in. It was awful as there were a couple of customers in the shop at the time and I had to ask them to leave too, but I just couldn't cope with her, she was so full on if you know what I mean.'

Jackie nodded and said she knew exactly what he meant.

'Then a few days later I was putting something in the window and happened to see her coming down the street so I quickly put up the closed sign, turned off the lights and hid behind the counter. The last time I saw her was just before Christmas when she came in, I couldn't get rid of her as there were lots of customers in, so I told her I was too busy to talk to her and she left. I haven't seen her since.' The thin man was twisting his wispy beard round and round his long fingers, getting more and more agitated as he thought of Kim.

This is the effect she has on lots of people, thought Cora.

'I see,' said Jackie, 'well you've been very helpful, thank you so much.'

Andrea stepped forward, 'I'll have these please,' she laid the two crystals on the counter and got out her purse. Andrea tried to pay with cash wherever she could, she believed in a 'use it or lose it' policy and thought the country would be a sadder place to live if all transactions were digital. 'Just one more thing if you don't mind, you don't happen to have a phone number for her, do you?'

The thin man took the money for the crystals and gave Andrea her change.

'D'you know I think I might. When she first came in, she ordered a book on witchcraft and gave me a contact number so I could ring her when it came in. I've probably still got it in the sales book somewhere.' He flicked back through a journal which lay open on his counter, where he kept a note of his daily sales. 'October, October… no, September ahh yes here it is.' He copied it down and gave Andrea the number.

With choruses of goodbye and thank you for your help, they left the thin man to his magic shop and went in search of lunch.

They decided to treat themselves today and found a nice-looking Italian restaurant on the main high street where they ordered spaghetti carbonara, a margarita pizza and grilled seabass with salad and sautéed potatoes, Jackie had also treated herself to a large glass of white wine as she wasn't driving but the other two stuck to coffee. Then they settled themselves down to review what they knew.

'Well, he wasn't very forthcoming was he,' Jackie sipped her wine happily.

'Oh, didn't you think so? I thought he was good, we learnt a lot. I knew she was on edge, but I had no idea she was that bad,' Cora said.

'Yes, she was really frightened, I feel bad now for not really taking her seriously,' Andrea gave a small sigh.

'None of us did though,' said Jackie 'I mean she did sound completely mad most of the time, even her son thought so.'

'True, and he knows her better than us,' agreed Andrea.

The food arrived, looking and smelling delicious. This was a good day out.

When they'd eaten, Andrea took out her phone and dialled the number the thin man had given her.

'Now we'll find out something. It's ringing.' She waited. 'It's gone straight to voicemail.' She put her phone away. 'Well, that's something anyway.'

'What d'you mean?' Jackie looked puzzled.

'Well, it means someone's been keeping the battery charged. If she'd been banged on the head or something, her phone would've been dropped, broken or thrown away and there would be the number unobtainable noise. As it is she's just not answering. Maybe she is on holiday after all.'

'Come on, we need to leave, or we'll be late for the film.' Cora stood up. 'We'll try again when we come out.'

The film was good, a murder mystery and they all enjoyed it, well Cora and Andrea enjoyed it, due to her large glass of wine at lunchtime Jackie had fallen asleep in the middle of it and at one point had to be nudged sharply by Cora when her snores became audible.

It was dark and heavy rain was falling when they emerged, so they decided their day out in Woodhall Spa was over and Cora drove them home. It was only when she was inside her cosy cottage and had given Nonsuch and Mrs Tim their much-anticipated dinner that Andrea remembered she had been going to try Kim's phone again. She rang the number, again it went straight to answer phone.

'Hi Kim, it's Andrea from the art studio. Just wondering if you're okay as you haven't come back to class. Maybe give me a call, hope to see you soon, bye.' Andrea rang off, there was nothing more they could do.

28

You have two new messages.

First message.

'Hi Mum, just checking in. We're all fine here. Just to let you know, three women came round yesterday, from your art classes they said. They were asking questions, wondering where you were, nosey I call it. Anyway, I said you were probably on holiday. Have a good time wherever you are. Talk soon. Bye.'

Beep.

To listen to the message again press one.

To keep the message press two.

To delete the message press three.

Beep. Message deleted.

Second new message.

'Hi Kim, it's Andrea from the art studio. Just wondering if you're okay as you haven't come back to class. Maybe give me a call, hope to see you soon, bye.'

The man pressed button two, laid the phone on the table and sat down. He needed to think.

The people from the art studio seem very interested in her whereabouts.

29

Wednesday 12th and Friday 14th February

Jackie set a plate of still warm blueberry muffins carefully on the coffee table and passed a mug of tea to Andrea.

'But what are we actually doing? It feels like we're getting nowhere at all. Help yourselves, girls. I mean, we know Kim was really frightened, and that she hasn't been home for a while, but she's charging her phone and could easily be on holiday. That's what Kevin believes anyway.'

Andrea didn't need to be asked twice and leant forward to help herself to a muffin. She'd had Jackie's homemade muffins plenty of times before and knew how delicious they were.

'Agreed. So perhaps the question is do we stop? Or if not, where do we go next?'

'That's two questions,' Cora grinned at the others as she also took a muffin from the plate.

It was late Wednesday afternoon and Andrea, having finished her pottery classes, had popped into Jackie's cottage to collect some shopping that Jackie had picked up for her and was surprised to see Cora, who had dropped by to return a book she'd borrowed, sitting in an armchair sipping a mug of tea.

'But just to play devil's advocate,' Cora continued, 'we are all assuming Kevin is telling the truth.'

'What? Why shouldn't he? D'you think he's hiding something?' Andrea took the last bite of her muffin and licked her finger. 'I hadn't thought of that.'

'What on earth would he be hiding?' asked Jackie, 'unless of course he knows where she is.'

'It's possible,' went on Cora, 'he got very cagey when the police were mentioned, although he may just think it's none of our business and he'd be right of course, but you never know, stranger things have happened.'

Andrea tried to get her head round this new train of thought. 'But he's her son, why would he do anything to his mum?'

'I don't know, I said I was playing devil's advocate, maybe it was visiting The Maltings the other day, it's put all sorts of weird ideas in my head.'

'Anyway, I don't feel we should stop, we're not doing any harm, we're just chatting to people, not really getting involved. Also, I quite like trying to solve the mystery, it's fun.' Andrea looked round at the other two for agreement.

'It wasn't fun when we entered her house illegally and thought we'd find a body.' Cora pointed out.

'No, that wasn't fun, you're right.'

Jackie drained her mug and set it down on the coffee table. 'Maybe we should go back to her house. Perhaps there's something we missed and now we know there's nobody and we know what to expect. We might find some clues.'

Neither Cora nor Andrea seemed very keen to visit Kim's house again so soon and said so.

'Well, how about we go to her land again then and

maybe talk to the farmers on the other sides. The magic shop man said the neighbours wanted her land. Perhaps there'd been a huge row, and she needed to get away.'

Andrea and Cora agreed, and it was arranged they would have another visit to Kim's land as soon as they could.

It was Friday before they were all free to go and bright and early, well muffled up against the unrelenting east wind, they climbed into Jackie's car and off they went to East Kime.

'I felt sorry for my postman this morning,' Cora said out of the blue.

'What? Why, what happened?' asked Andrea.

'He was carrying so many letters his poor little legs were buckling under him as he came up my path.'

'What?' Andrea was confused, 'you've lost me, why did he have so many?'

'He was delivering all my Valentines Day cards!' Cora shrieked with laughter and Andrea and Jackie laughed too, not so much at the joke as at Cora's reaction to it.

They parked by the wooden five bar gate and got out. The sheep were busily nibbling at the grass oblivious of the biting wind that couldn't permeate their thick fleeces.

Andrea looked at the sheep, they were nearer the gate this time and she could see them properly. *Those sheep are Lincolnshire Long Wool sheep, their fleeces will be in demand in the spring, to felt makers and crafters if no one else. I don't know the going rate for them, but they're excellent for felting. I wonder if Kim knows.*

'Come on, let's have a proper look at the building, we might as well now we're here' Cora leant over the gate and tried to open it. 'Oh, buggeration it's padlocked. Never mind we'll climb over,' and she climbed onto the bars of the gate, swung her legs over the top and landed with a thud in the field.

Andrea went next, then Jackie had a try, but she had been suffering from sciatica lately and although she managed to get up she couldn't get over the top. She had an electric pain running down her left leg.

'Oooh, I'm not going to make it. There's no way I can swing my leg over the top,' Jackie said.

'You mean you can't get your leg over?' Cora laughed.

'Not at the moment, no,' Jackie laughed too despite the searing pain in her leg, 'To be honest, I'm surprised you managed it. I thought that ship had sailed years ago.'

Andrea was laughed now as well.

'True,' Cora hooted, 'getting over that gate was the most action I've had for a long time.' They all screamed with laughter. It was always fun to be silly and act like schoolgirls, they never tired of it.

Leaving Jackie to recover a little and fetch some painkillers and a bottle of water from her car, Cora and Andrea went to have a look at the crumbling stone building. The sheep stopped their chewing for a moment to look up and watch them, then they slowly ambled away and began grazing again. The grey stone building such as it was, had only three walls, the fourth having fallen down in a heap, the roof sagged dangerously and many of the old slate tiles had fallen inwards. They walked round to the back and looked in through the gap where the wall had been. Weeds and nettles grew knee high through the earth floor and fallen masonry, but there was really nothing to see just a neglected animal shelter. Round at the front again, they were studying the CCTV camera and the one remaining security light which hung precariously on the corner facing the gate, when they heard voices. Looking up they saw

Jackie talking to an angry looking old man with a stick and very loud voice.

Hurrying back to the gate they heard Jackie's quiet voice gently reasoning with the irate man.

'Everything alright?' asked Cora as she scaled the gate.

'No, everything is not alright!' yelled the man. 'Who are you and what the hell do you think you're doing trespassing on this land?'

Andrea joined her and the three women stood together facing the furious onslaught.

'First of all, please don't shout at us, we might look old, but we're not deaf,' *well actually I am a bit*, 'and secondly, we're not trespassing this land belongs to a friend of ours and we have her permission to go onto it. Although I'm sure she'll be very grateful to hear that you're keeping such a good eye on it for her whilst she's away.' Jackie said this in such a calm, unflustered way that she completely took the wind out of the man's sails. *So, calm down, mate.*

The angry man visibly shrank down from his puffed-up, righteous position.

'Ahh, I see,' his voice changed, 'well, of course if you've got permission that's different. Only there's been a bit of activity round here lately and it's worrying all of us.'

'Of course, it must be very worrying for you, and I know Kim is very grateful for your vigilance,' Jackie continued, 'but I can assure you we are not vandals or intent on any kind of mischief, we are simply friends of hers who've come to have a look at what's been happening.'

'Hmm, friends of hers, eh?' The man looked them over, his piercing pale blue eyes studying them from under the peak of his hat.

'Yes, I'm Jackie and these ladies are Andrea and Cora.'

'Pleased to meet you ladies. I'm Dennis, but folk call me

Snowy on account of my surname, White.' His craggy face broke into a smile.

'Pleased to meet you Snowy, do you farm over there?' Andrea pointed to the left of Kim's fields.

'Yep, that's my land, and me brother's land is at the back o' this little strip.'

'You must know Kim quite well then, as you're close neighbours?' Jackie asked.

'Not that well. Don't see her much at all really. We've spoken a few times, but not for a while.' Snowy was relaxed now that he was sure the three women were not up to no good.

'We were looking for her actually,' Cora joined in. 'You haven't seen her around lately, have you?'

'No, but I wouldn't. She comes and goes without my noticing. I'm a busy man, you know.'

Snowy didn't seem very busy as he leaned against the gate and single-handedly fished in his pocket for a packet of cigarette papers and dextrously extracted one. Then still only using one hand, he removed an ancient brown rubber pouch from the inside pocket of his ancient brown coat and opening it separated a few long strands of tobacco which he laid on the paper and expertly rolled up into a very thin cigarette. Running it along his tongue, he rolled it round in his fingers and put it in his mouth. He returned the pouch to his pocket and brought out an old lighter, and it was only then that his other hand was employed to shield the flame against the weather as he lit the cigarette. Having returned the lighter to his pocket, he inhaled deeply. All of this had been carried out in the teeth of the biting easterly wind and Andrea, Jackie, and Cora watched mesmerised at the single-handed skill he had obviously honed over many years of practice.

Snowy looked like he was settling in for a good old chat,

so they decided to take advantage and find out what they could. After some talk about his land and what he planted and when, if he had any livestock and how long he'd been here, they had a good idea of the situation. Snowy farmed to the left of Kim's strip of land and his brother Eggy, farmed to the back. Yes, they had tried to buy the piece of land that Kim had acquired but had missed out due to Kim having paid a ridiculously over the top price for it. They wanted the strip so they could join their farms together, Eggy's son Young Eggy was now grown up and the three of them had planned to run the enlarged farm between them and increase the value, Young Eggy even had ideas around putting in a few yurts for glamping holidays. And no, they certainly didn't want a whole lot of trees planted on the land which would take up good farming acreage and remove any possibility of their ever getting hold of the strip in the future as once the Woodland Trust was involved the woodland would be protected.

Snowy smoked his roll-up down to the very end, and the three women wondered how he didn't burn his lips. When he eventually flicked the miniscule end to the ground and stood on it, he went through the whole cigarette rolling procedure again. They stood in silence, watching him. When he'd finished, he inhaled deeply, let out a long smoky breath, and said,

'She's a funny woman, your friend—can't say I take to her much.'

'Yes, she can be a bit odd at times,' Cora agreed. 'Can I ask why you came out to us, why you thought we might be damaging her land—has there been trouble before?'

'I heard a lot of loud voices and laughing and stuff and thought something was amiss, thought it was a lot of kids like before, don't often hear laughing round here we don't, so I came to have a look. Before Christmas, she thought someone had been on her land, damaging it and leaving stuff. She came round to the house and started shouting the odds about it being down to me and Eggy, that we wanted her off the land so we could have it. Accusing us of damaging her property, bloody mad she was, 'scuse my French. I told her I've seen a car a few times round by this gate, bloody kids, but she didn't care, she was ranting on at me saying she wasn't gonna leave no matter what me an' Eggy did, she was gonna have her woodland and we couldn't stop her. Well, she's right about one thing, we do want her off the land, but we don't go round trespassing and dumping stuff, we're just biding our time, she'll get bored soon. City types, you see. Don't understand the country, city types don't.' He took another big draft of his roll-up and let out a smoky sigh. 'Anyway ladies, you mustn't keep me standing about chatting. I've got work to do. I'm a very busy man.'

They said goodbye and were grateful to get out of the wind and back in the car. They drove away, leaving Snowy still leaning on the gate, smoking his roll-up.

'Stop the car,' Cora said suddenly, 'we need to go back. Quick turn the car round. I've just remembered something.'

Seconds later they were back at the gate and Cora jumped out, followed by Andrea and Jackie eager to know what Cora was doing. Snowy was still leaning on the gate where they'd left him moments before.

'Sorry Snowy,' said Cora, 'we forgot to ask about the car you saw. Do you remember when you saw it or anything about it?'

'Ah yes, the car, bloody kids causing trouble. I saw it a couple of times at night, parked up by this gate, headlamps off. It was young folk getting up to stuff in the back, if you know what I mean,' he winked at the women, 'then I saw a light in the field, bobbing about.'

'A light? Like someone walking about with a torch or something?' Cora asked.

'Could be. Though far as I could see, it was just bloody kids tramping about, trespassing. But it only happened a few times and then it stopped.'

'You didn't happen to see the car, did you—the make, the colour perhaps?' Andrea asked. *Stupid question. Even if he did, how would that help?*

'Well, funny you say that, but my house is up the lane a bit and I can see the field from my bedroom window. That's how I come to see the light in the first place. Anyway, I came downstairs to check the front door was bolted as we don't often see cars round here at night, and a car was using my front yard to turn round. I don't know if it was the same one, but as it reversed, I noticed a bit of the number. It was G L O. I remember it because that's what I called my late wife Gloria. God rest her.'

Snowy took a last heavy drag on his roll-up and flicked the minute end to the floor.

'I really need to get on now, ladies. I'm a very busy man.'

They thanked him and climbed back into the car, while Snowy, still leaning on the gate, reached into his pocket and pulled out his tobacco pouch.

30

Friday 14th and Saturday 15th February

Jackie's sciatica was no better. The painkillers had not had much of an effect and so for the first time, rather than find somewhere nice for lunch, they decided to go home. Andrea was secretly pleased as she knew she should be concentrating on her batik work for the upcoming exhibition.

Chatting together in the car on the way back, they mulled over what they knew. There seemed to be nothing amiss anywhere. They could find nothing wrong and no real cause for alarm. Everyone they had spoken to had found Kim odd. Some thought she was completely nuts, but no one seemed dangerous or resented her so much that they wanted to hurt her. Most were just happy to keep out of her way. The police were not interested and neither her husband nor her son were concerned, with Kevin believing she was on holiday. Assuming he was telling the truth, of course.

'So what now?' asked Andrea for the tenth time. 'We keep looking for clues and keep coming up with nothing. Should we just call it a day?'

'Yeah,' Jackie agreed, 'we've had a nosey about, had a chat with people, no one is bothered about her other than us and to be honest we're not actually too bothered ourselves, we don't really know her and only started nosing about for a little adventure. Yes, let's call it a day. Anyway, spring is on its way and my garden will soon be calling to me.' She laughed, and the others joined in.

'How about we have one last visit to her house like you said Jackie? You never know we might have missed something, she may even be back home again?' Cora suggested, 'we may as well, then if we've still got nothing, we'll forget it.'

'Good plan, and I can return her address book. Okay, one last trip to Bonkers Land. I hope she's there. It'll solve everything nicely,' agreed Andrea.

They all nodded, but no one really believed Kim would be there.

'We'll have to go tomorrow, otherwise it's next Tuesday. Will you be any better by then, Jackie?' asked Cora.

'I'll be fine, I'll do some gentle exercises when I get home and take some more painkillers and I'll be right as rain tomorrow.'

'Tomorrow it is, then. I'll drive, and our first stop will be The Trio of Fools for coffee.'

Back at her cottage after she'd had some lunch and fed her cats, Andrea went into her studio. She loved being in there alone, the smell of hot wax mixed with incense, her music or an audiobook playing in the background. She set the music on her phone to shuffle, and the voice of Boy George sang out.

'I'm a man without conviction. I'm a man who doesn't know...'

The lights were on, and it was warm, or as warm as it ever got in the afternoons, when the heat from the storage heaters faded. She laid her work out on the big table and looked at it, then she pinned it up on the wall to view it from a distance.

'You come and go, you come and go...' Andrea sang along. *'Karma, Karma, Karma, Karme, Karma Chameleon, you come and go...'* She was up and dancing now. *'Loving would be easy if your colours were like my dream...'* This was a good one, taking her back to her younger days when her life had been very different.

When the song finished, she sat down and looked at her painting. Properly looked at it. This was a vital part of the process for Andrea, and not just her. Most visual artists had similar routines. It allowed her to step back from her work and look with new eyes; she saw areas which needed attention, bringing forward or taking back. She could see where something wasn't working, or the balance was wrong. It was important for her to take this time to reflect on her next step.

Bang. Bang. Bang. Andrea nearly jumped out of her skin. *What the hell is that? Oh, someone's at the door. Thank goodness I'd stopped dancing about.* Walking to the door, she pulled back the bolt and opened it to find Ernest standing there laughing. *Oh, please no.*

'Andrea Bailey,'

'Ernest. Can I help you?'

'I want to see your art studio, Andrea Bailey. I looked through the window and saw you just sitting there daydreaming and thought I'd come in for a look around.' Ernest put a foot through the doorway but Andrea stopped him with the heavy door.

'I don't have visitors in my studio, and I wasn't daydreaming. I was actually working, so I'm sorry, but if you don't mind, I need to get on.'

Ernest let out a guffaw of laughter. 'Andrea Bailey, I think you are without doubt the stupidest person I know. You love rubbish, collecting it and photographing it and now I find you sitting about gazing into space and insisting you're working!' Out came the tissue to wipe his eyes.

'I have absolutely no interest in what you think. Now if you don't mind, I'm busy.' Andrea began to close the door, but Ernest's foot was still in the way. 'Please take your foot away.'

'Oh, Andrea Bailey, are you getting cross?' Ernest laughed, obviously ready for more taunting of the woman he didn't understand.

'No, I'm not cross,' Andrea spoke evenly. 'I'm just bored with you. I find you boring Ernest, very boring and I would be grateful if you didn't come here again and also in future if we meet in the lanes I would appreciate it if you continued with your walk without talking to me, as I intend to do with you. Now please remove your foot and allow me to get on.'

'Oh, Andrea Bailey, I do believe you're upset.' Ernest mocked, laughing again as he wiped his eyes on the tissue. 'So sorry to have upset you Andrea Bailey, I'll go now and leave you to your *work* I can see how *busy* you are.' Ernest emphasised the words with exaggerated seriousness, 'Oh and here's a little present for your collection.' He tossed his used tissue down in her doorway, and with more loud laughter, turned and walked away.

Andrea locked the door behind him, not wanting to touch the revolting tissue, got a dustpan and brush and swept it up. *Well, that was unexpected. From now on I'm going to blank him, he's just a ridiculous little man and I shan't let him drain any more of my energy.* And she went into the tiny kitchen to make herself a cup of green tea.

Late next morning, the three women were to be found nursing their coffees in The Trio of Fools, sitting at what was becoming their usual table, whilst a light February snow blew against the pub windows. The landlord remembered them from their last visit and added more logs to the fire, making the wood crackle as they sat gazing into the flames. It was cosy and warm and they were in no hurry to leave. A few Saturday morning regulars drifted in and leant against the bar, and other than the occasional burst of laughter, they were undisturbed.

'I've got a pen and my notebook, and I think we should have a review of what, if anything, we've got,' Jackie said delving into her bag, 'we may think of something we need to look for when we get inside.'

'Good idea. What do we know? Let's start from the beginning.' Andrea put down her coffee and looked at the others.

Jackie opened her notepad and wrote two headings, 'Kim's problems' and 'What we know'. And between them, they filled out what they knew or thought they knew.

Kim's problems.

Arguments with neighbouring farmers about her landTrue and explained

Neighbours trying to get her off her landTrue and explained

Ditch spoil dumped on her landTrue and explained

Bundles of grass placed around the edges of her land No proof.

Dead Crow nailed to buildingNo proof

Black feathers sticking out of the ground on her landTrue-but unexplained.

Holes made in her front gardenPhotos-unexplained

Naked people walking past her houseBad photos-no proof

Security light on land smashedTrue-poss'-Explained (wind)

Sheep are illPossibly true.

House broken into and signs on ceilingNo proof-Police involved

Strange scratches on car doorsTrue- poss. explained (bush)

What we know

Kim joined class in early September, came every week, seemed to enjoy it, and began to trust us all.

We've only known Kim for around four months.

Spoken to land neighbours, they don't like her. They don't want her there.

Snowy and Eggy White want her land. They are prepared to wait for her to get bored with it.

We've seen the black feathers in her garden. Is this proof?

We know Kim was scared.

Kim came to studio Xmas lunch and was keen to return to classes.

No confirmed sightings of Kim since 25th December.

Kim possibly left her house in a hurry.

Heating not turned off.

Kim has her phone and keys with her (car and house).

Kim has her car with her.

Kim is not abroad, her passport has expired.

Not answering phone, texts or emails, but phone is receiving calls.

Police are not interested.

Husband Charlie is no help.

Kevin saw her at Christmas and believes she's on holiday. Is this true?

Snowy saw person or people on her land – poss. courting couples.

Car reg no. GLO of poss. interest.

'Okay, what can we get from that?' Andrea asked. 'I think all we've got is that it looks like she left home in a rush although that's not proven as she may just hate housework. And no one's seen her since Christmas. She's got her phone, her car and her house keys and Kevin says she occasionally goes away on the spur of the moment, but then if Cora's theory is correct, he would say that, wouldn't he.'

'She's been out of touch for six weeks now, I suppose that's not very long really, lots of people go away for the winter months, I can't say I blame them,' Jackie said looking through the window at the swirling snow outside.

'Yes, but they usually go somewhere hot. We know she hasn't gone abroad and why did she leave old food lying around, leave the heating on, the vacuum cleaner plugged in, and the bins unemptied?' Cora took a sip of coffee. 'Although I suppose she could have gone somewhere in this country, The Lake District, or Scotland, holed up in a nice cosy cottage by a loch or something. Maybe that's what we should look for in her house, signs of her having taken some luggage with her.'

'You know what else we could do with seeing?' asked Andrea, 'The CCTV—we haven't even thought about that. She's got it on her land and by her front door. If we could look at that, it might tell us something.'

'How the hell do we do that? We'd need to access her laptop to see the film and for that we'd need her password,' Jackie pointed out.

'Well, that's another thing to look for, her password. Maybe she's got a book or a list or something with her passwords written down. You never know.' Cora drained her cup. 'Come on, let's go, we're the Studio Sleuths and we've got sleuthing to do.'

The pub had filled up whilst they were engrossed in their discussion, but despite the crowd, as they stood up to leave, the landlord called goodbye to them.

'This is such a friendly pub,' said Jackie. 'I really like it in here.'

They left the pub and drove round to Conker's Lane, parking opposite number 17. They were just getting out of the car when Cora suddenly pointed.

'Look at the car in front!'

'What about it? It's just a blue car.' The make meant nothing to Andrea. She looked at the colours only.

'Look at the registration number.'

'Oh, my goodness,' said Jackie. 'G L O.'

'Come on, that's too much of a coincidence. We need to find out who it belongs to.' Cora opened the car door and got out.

They looked up and down the street and then walked up the path to number 17. There was no one in sight, but as they reached the front door, it opened. The three of them drew back in surprise. Kevin was standing there, filling the doorway and looking furious.

31

The man unbolted the door and went into the room. He stood looking down at the woman as she lay on the bed, gazing up at the ceiling. He needed her for a while longer. He knew he couldn't stop yet or his plan would fail.

He took away the mug and the bowl. He would come back for the bucket. Carefully he bolted the door behind him.

Not long now.

32

Saturday 15th February

Kevin stood on the step, staring down furiously at the three women.

'What the hell do you three want?'

'We came to see if Kim was home.' Andrea smiled up at the angry young man.

'Well, she's not. Why are you so interested? You're just nosey busy bodies without enough to do. Join a knitting club or something, but just leave my family alone.'

'Please calm down Kevin, we only came to see if Kim was back yet.'

'I don't believe you,' Kevin was getting red in the face, 'I know you've been to see my dad. How dare you! He told me you'd been round there, cleaning up and buying him food, like we can't look after him ourselves. How bloody dare you! And you never even mentioned it when you came barging into my house and talking to my wife. Just who the hell do you think you are, asking questions? Mind your own bloody business, in fact, just sod off!'

Kevin went to shut the door, but Andrea put her foot out, stopping him. A ploy she'd picked up from Ernest.

'Hang on, Kevin, please let us in out of this horrible weather and we'll explain everything. I know it looks bad, but we can explain. Please, give us ten minutes. We're not trying to interfere, we're just worried for your mum and I think you are too.' The winning smile went unnoticed by Kevin, but he seemed to deflate, as if all the fight had gone out of him. He looked at them and saw three elderly ladies who were looking back at him with kindness and compassion, and slowly he pulled back the door and let them in.

They found the sitting room much as they'd left it when they had come before. They took off their coats and after moving a few piles of Kim's belongings from the chairs, they sat down and looked at Kevin. The young man flopped into an armchair and put his head in his hands. *That's exactly what Kim looked like when she came to the studio all those weeks ago. He's a man at the end of his tether.* Andrea looked at Kevin and her heart went out to him.

'Do you want to start, or shall we?' asked Jackie gently. She too, could see he was broken.

'I didn't mean it,' Kevin spoke quietly, his head still in hands. 'I only wanted a normal family. Just a normal family, that's all.' He began to cry. He sobbed into his hands. 'Sorry, I'm so sorry.'

'It's fine,' Andrea said very quietly, and they let the man cry.

After a few minutes, Kevin looked up, gazing at them through red-rimmed eyes, which he wiped on his hands.

'Here,' Cora handed him some tissues from her bag.

Jackie and Andrea sat in silence and Kevin wiped his eyes, but seemed unable to stop the tears. At last, he began to regain his composure a little.

'I'm really very sorry, ladies. I've had to be so strong lately. I think it's been building up for months now.'

'Please don't apologise,' Andrea said gently, 'we quite

understand. You have your family to look after and your dad too, and now you're worried about your mum. It must be very hard for you.'

'It is, and now I've done this terrible thing,' he put his head in hands and began to sob again.

Jackie, Andrea, and Cora exchanged glances.

'How about you start from the beginning—we're in no hurry—take your time and tell us what happened,' Jackie said softly. 'Maybe we can help.'

Kevin raised his head from his hands and looked at the three motherly women sitting quietly looking at him with gentle sympathy in their eyes. He took a deep breath and told them the whole story.

'I was an adult when mum and dad split up, but even so, it was hard for us all. Dad had lost his job, and being in his early fifties, found it impossible to get another. They were okay for money. Mum had a good job and was earning a good salary, but he took it badly and started to go to the pub every day. He would buy drinks for everyone just so he would have someone to drink with and he wouldn't have to go home and sit in an empty house all afternoon. His spending got out of hand and so did his drinking and mum had enough. They separated. She got dad a little flat and paid his rent for him, but he was unable to cope properly, and his drinking got worse and worse. She would go and see him and do some housework and shopping, but I could tell she hated it, hated seeing him like that. I started going each week to help her, but he wouldn't or couldn't stop drinking.

We got into a sort of routine between us, but then, as Maisie and Poppy came along, it became more difficult. Carol's parents live in Australia and although we Skype and try to visit, it's hard for the girls not having grandparents, at least not being a real part of their lives. When mum took early retirement and got her payout, I thought she'd be more hands on with her grandchildren and we'd be more like a proper family again. Okay, I knew mum and dad were probably past the point of getting back together, but there was still a part of me that thought if mum was around full-time, dad would be happy again and stop drinking. I know that's not how it happens, but I couldn't help hoping for some kind of miracle. I thought even if they didn't get back together, at least mum would move to Sleaford and live near us and be a part of my girls' lives, like a proper granny.' He held his fist to his chin.

'Then she went and bought this damn piece of land and said she was going to build on it and live there with a bloody woodland. It was like a slap in the face, as if she was saying she didn't want to be involved with us. I felt like I was spinning plates and couldn't stop, or they'd all come crashing down. I was looking after dad; I was angry with mum and trying to deal with the hurt, and I was working to support my family whilst trying to keep cheerful and always having to tell my girls that Granny was busy. It broke my heart to see their disappointed faces.'

Kevin stopped and wiped his eyes again. Andrea, Cora and Jackie said nothing. They were in no rush, and they knew Kevin needed to talk.

'I thought of a plan. I must have been mad. Maybe I was a little. Mum told me how the local farmers wanted her off the land and that gave me an idea. I thought if I could get her to sell her land, she might after all buy a house near us and everything would be alright. Mum had always had a weird interest in the occult, magical signs and witchy things, you know what I mean, so I decided to try to scare her into selling. She had told me about the problem with the ditches, it was obvious to me that John was doing her a favour clearing her ditches for her, but I thought I could use her paranoia, so I went over there one night and placed bundled up sheaves of grass around the edge of the field. I don't know why. I just thought they looked a bit pagan, a bit ritualistic. After that, I went again and nailed a dead crow to the old farm building. She rang me and told me about it. I told her to sell up and be done with it. By this time, she knew she wasn't going to get planning permission to build on it and the Forestry Commission was going to take years to get sorted. But she said she wasn't going to be beaten, and she was determined to stay put. She was so stubborn.

Around that time, my work took me to a farm factory over near Nottingham which plucks turkeys. They were gearing up for Christmas and when I was leaving, I saw massive bags of black turkey feathers waiting outside ready to be taken away to be made into fertiliser. They let me have one, didn't really ask me why I wanted it, they didn't care, so I waited for a windy night, and I took a huge builder's bag of feathers to her fields and emptied the lot into the gale. I wasn't sure what would happen, but I thought it might look strange, like something to do with the occult, the dark arts. They flew around everywhere, spiralling down and landing upright in the grass. I couldn't see exactly what they looked like as it was dark, but when mum rang me to tell me about it, she said it was like people had planted them on purpose. She was terrified. My plan had worked. But now I think maybe it worked too well. I haven't seen her since Christmas, and she's not answered my calls. At Christmas she told me how frightened she was and all I kept saying was sell up and come and live near us. I didn't really take notice of how scared she was and now she's disappeared and it's all my fault.' Kevin dropped his head again, but no tears came. He hadn't any left.

The room was silent. No one said anything. Kevin sat, head bent, exhausted with the effort.

Andrea who was sitting nearest to Kevin, reached out

and gently put her hand on his shoulder. 'It's been tough for you. We can see that. Everything you've done, you've done for your family. You're a good man.'

'I need to call Carol. Tell her I'll be a bit later than I said.' Kevin was trying to pull himself together.

'Good idea,' agreed Cora, 'you don't want her worrying where you are.'

'She knows I'm here, but I only came to see if mum was back.' He took out his phone to call his wife.

'While you gather yourself together, I'll see if I can make us some tea,' said Jackie as she quietly left the room, making sure she left the door open, as she didn't want to miss anything.

Because the bin had been emptied, the kitchen didn't smell as bad as when they had last visited, although the dirty plates were still in the sink and there was mess everywhere. Jackie found some tea bags, but of course there was no milk. She called to the others to let them know where she was going, then quickly popped next door and rang the neighbour's bell. Erin answered almost immediately.

'Hi, I don't know if you remem—' Jackie got no further.

'Yes, of course I do. You came before with two other ladies and took some cuttings from Kim's rose bush.'

The wind was bitterly cold and blowing the snow directly at the front door, so not wanting to keep Erin standing with her door open, Jackie quickly explained that they were inside with Kim's son Kevin and had forgotten to bring some milk. Erin was happy to supply some and invited her to step into the warmth to wait while she disappeared into her kitchen to fetch some. Jackie stood in the cluttered hallway looking at the photos on the wall of Erin's happy family groups on the beach in the sunshine, such a contrast to the here and now.

'Here you go,' Erin handed her a jug full of milk. 'Just let me have the jug back when you leave. No rush. So Kim's son is here, is he?' Erin obviously wanted to stand and chat, but Jackie wanted to get back and cut short the conversation.

'They'll be waiting for a cup of tea. Thank you so much Erin. Goodbye.'

33

Saturday 15th February

Andrea and Cora had followed Jackie into the kitchen to allow Kevin some privacy for his phone call home, still leaving the door open a little, just in case. While Jackie was gone, they began to tidy round and Cora, deciding to take the bull by the horns, rolled up her sleeves, filled the sink with hot water and began the washing up. Andrea located a drawer of clean tea towels and began to dry. Jackie returned from Erin's with a jug of milk and by the time Kevin had finished his call home and walked through to the kitchen, the dishes had been washed and put away and the room was looking a little better. The tea had been made and Jackie handed out the mugs.

'You're very kind, I'm sorry I was so rude before,' Kevin apologised, looking round at the three women.

'You weren't rude, you were upset, and you're very welcome.' Jackie smiled.

'If Kim is away on holiday, why didn't she turn the hot water off?' asked Cora as she pulled out the plug and wiped round the sink.

'There's a lot of unanswered questions,' Andrea said. 'Let's go back and sit down and we can tell Kevin what we know.'

They settled back in their chairs with their mugs of hot tea, and Jackie pulled out her notepad. 'Before we start with our list, Kevin, can I ask did you break the security light on Kim's land?'

'That was broken by the wind. Mum hadn't attached it properly.'

'Also did you dig holes in the front garden?'

'No, I didn't, but she told me about them and I said I thought it could have been squirrels. Mum had planted some tulips and crocuses earlier that week. Of course, she was having none of it and was still convinced it was someone persecuting her.'

'Ahh, of course, grey squirrels are notorious for digging up bulbs,' Jackie said. 'That would make sense. Now, do you know anything about the sheep being ill?'

'Yeah, she called a vet, and he gave them all a jab. Evidently they had an infection called Orf virus or scabby mouth, it's common in unvaccinated sheep. They're fine now, I believe.'

'Well, that's another thing explained then. Right, this is what we've got,' and Jackie began to read from the list. She listed Kim's worries and between them, they amended what they had.

Dead Crow nailed to animal shelterTrue and explained.

Bundles of grass placed around the edges of her landTrue and explained.

Black feathers sticking out of the ground on her landTrue and explained.

Security light on land smashedTrue and explained.
Sheep are illTrue and explained.
Holes dug in front gardenTrue and explained.

'So the only unexplained thing on Kim's list is the naked people walking past and there's no proof of these. If anyone did walk past it was November, why would they be naked? And anyway, they didn't stop, so what was the problem?'

'There's the house being broken into,' Andrea said, and they all looked up at the ceiling. They had forgotten to look for the signs scratched on the ceiling and remembered to do so now. There were a few very faint marks. They stood up to look, and Kevin climbed onto a chair for an even closer look.

'They just look like faint cracks in the plaster to me. I don't think anyone's scratched them on purpose.'

'So that remains as *no proof* and we think the scratches on the car doors are from a prickly shrub or something, agreed?'

'I can't say for certain, but due to my stupidity, mum was scared,' Kevin's voice broke, and he took a deep breath before continued. 'I think her fear developed into paranoia and these scratches or cracks, the so called naked people, the holes in the garden, these were all normal things that happen to everyone every day. I think she was so caught up in the whole black magic thing that she became paranoid about every little thing.' He wiped his eyes.

'I think you're right, I was thinking along similar lines,' Andrea put her hand on Kevin's shoulder again.

They were all agreed and so with the list of Kim's problems more or less explained and the unexplained things put down to paranoia, they began on the 'What we know' column and made a few amendments and one addition.

Kevin saw her at Christmas and no longer believes she's on holiday.

Snowy saw Kevin on the land.

Car reg no. GLO is Kevin's car.

Why did Kim leave her heating and hot water switched on?

So with Kevin up to date on what Andrea, Jackie and Cora had found out and them up to date on Kevin's information, they all knew as much as each other.

Kevin had regained his composure and was impressed at how much work Jackie, Cora and Andrea had put in to locating his mother, although they didn't see it as work, more like a puzzle with day trips, but they didn't tell Kevin that as he was obviously worried sick about his mum, and they didn't want to upset him.

'I've had a thought,' said Kevin as he sipped his tea, 'although mum isn't rich, she's certainly okay for money and if she did go away, she may have purposely left the heating and hot water switched on to stop the pipes from freezing if the weather turned. So I'm sorry, but I don't think that counts as unexplained.'

'Right. Well, that's certainly a good reason.' Jackie adjusted the list.

'What now?' asked Andrea. *That same question again. We must've asked it twenty times by now.*

'We were going to look for signs that she'd gone away, luggage etc,' Cora reminded them, 'and also it'd be good to have a look at the CCTV footage if possible. What d'you think, Kevin? Shall we carry on searching for Kim or would you rather we backed off and left you to it? We don't want to interfere.'

'No please continue, surely between us we can come up with something to give us a hint to where she might be.'

They decided to split up, Jackie and Andrea would search for suitcases or something that might tell them one way or another if she'd gone away, whilst Kevin with a bit of help from Cora, would have a look at Kim's laptop and see what they could find.

After searching Kim's bedroom and the spare room for suitcases and finding three, it was looking like Kim wasn't on holiday. It was difficult to know what if any clothes or shoes were missing, but there was no sign of anybody having packed a case or taken any toiletries, so unless Kim had two of everything including toothbrushes it was becoming more and more likely that she had not been planning on leaving. They went downstairs and found that Kevin and Cora had successfully managed to get into Kim's laptop. Kevin had tried two passwords that he knew his mother had used over the years and the second one had got them in.

They had accessed her emails and found nothing sinister or threatening, no one asking her to meet them or bring something somewhere, and now they had just located a file on the desktop named CCTV and were opening it. Andrea and Jackie stood behind them and looked down at the screen. Kevin opened a file titled Land Camera and found a list of dates for the previous weeks, dating back to October, when she first installed them.

'This is going to take some time, sifting through this lot,' he said, 'even if I put it on fast forward, it'll still take hours to look at it all. I'm going to take the laptop home and look through it there. I'll look at the Home Camera file too and let you know if it throws up anything of interest.'

They all agreed this was the best plan and insisted that Kevin made notes of everything unusual that he came across on the land CCTV and a list of everyone who visited the front door on the house CCTV, with times and dates, too. Kevin agreed. They swapped phone numbers and quickly made an instant messaging group of the four of them for easy communication, then after Kevin adjusted the timer for the hot water and the heating to come on just once a day for a couple of hours to save his mum some money, they collected their coats and went back out into the freezing weather.

34

Sunday 16th February

The next day was Sunday, Jackie was busy with her school garden project, there was some sort of meeting being held in the school hall to discuss the spring rotas, and Cora was attending church in the morning and helping with another church event all afternoon, something about books. Andrea had nothing arranged, but was looking forward to a long walk, a good stretch of her legs.

The weak morning sun was shining, but there was no heat in it and although yesterday's snow had not been heavy, it remained on the ground, giving everything a veiled appearance. Andrea crunched through the snow, walking on the spiked grass verges rather than the road to avoid slipping. Without really thinking where she was going she gravitated towards the river, the water was not iced over and the ducks were still swimming in groups. A pair of mute swans were there gliding gracefully and dipping their heads, and a line of white Chen geese standing on the opposite riverbank started honking loudly because she had the effrontery to walk by.

After a while Andrea found herself at the stile by the

bridge and decided to turn right and follow the lane to the place where the other day she had seen the square van and Ernest. As she approached the verge where it had been parked she was pleased to see it clear and rubbish free, but on closer inspection she realised that a double mattress lay hidden under the thin layer of snow surrounded by a couple of full black bin liners and a dismantled babies cot. *Oh no, what's going on round here?* Andrea took her phone from her pocket and photographed the scene. She sighed. She found it so depressing that people could do this to the countryside. To her mind, they didn't deserve to live in such a lovely place.

Andrea didn't enjoy making trouble for people and usually had a 'live and let live' attitude, but this was just too much. She understood it was difficult for people these days as many councils, having to juggle budgets, had decreased the opening hours of the local refuse tips. She knew their local one had shrunk from opening all week to just four days and she knew they had tightened up their rules on who could bring what and that businesses had to pay a fee to use the facility, unlike domestic users. She was aware this had led to people dumping their rubbish in lay-bys and on waste ground and in her view the new policy was shortsighted and unhelpful and might even be costing the councils more in sending out teams to deal with reported fly-tipping sites. It made her cross, and she tried not to jump on her soap box when the subject arose, but it pressed every button she had. She hated the throwaway society that seemed to prevail nowadays. No one wanted to mend anything or even pass things on. Everything needed to be bought new and to her mind it was madness and also very sad, with everyday skills of simple repairs being lost with each new generation.

Fly tipping was happening everywhere, she knew this, and that was out of her control, but it was a new occurrence in her neighbourhood, and she was determined to put a stop to it. If it was the square van, she would get proof and report him to the authorities, she wasn't going to let her precious countryside be spoiled by some selfish, greedy person who didn't give a fig for the wildlife whose homes and pathways were being ruined.

Andrea continued down the lane and was dismayed to find another load of fly-tipped rubbish a little further down. There were no houses in this quiet lane and with no street lighting, it was obviously perfect for dumping rubbish. She photographed the heap and walked on, only to find a third pile. Someone had had a field day, had taken advantage of the bad weather and off-loaded a ton of commercial waste when no one was around. *What a complete bastard. Whoever you are, I'll get you.*

Andrea finished her walk and went home. She sent her photos and reports through to Fix-my-Street and decided to go out again later as it was getting dark and see if she could see the van again.

The fly tipping had depressed her, and she went into her studio to work on her batik and try to forget the outside world. Soon the comforting smell of hot wax and incense filled the space, and she sat staring at her work trying to decide whether it was finished. She didn't want to overwork it; it was easy to do that, just to add a little bit more here and there until it was too late and it was spoiled. But her mind would not focus and she kept coming back to the fly tipping and to Kim. *I can't do anything about the fly tipping at the moment, so I need to forget about that, but what about Kim?* She went into the tiny studio kitchen and made herself a cup of green tea, then returned to the studio and sat gazing into space. *There must be something we're missing. I don't believe she's on holiday and now Kevin doesn't either. We don't suspect Kevin anymore, although I'm not sure we ever really did. The witchcraft malarky is explained so the answer must lie somewhere else, but where?* Her thoughts were going round and round and she could not settle to anything, so, as she hated wasting time, she returned to her cottage and reluctantly cleaned out her fridge.

Later that day, she went out for a second walk. It wasn't unusual, especially in the summer, for Andrea to walk two or three times a day, but she rarely did it during the winter when the days were shorter and she tried to avoid walking in the dark. She wasn't afraid of the dark, just of slipping over or falling in a ditch or worse still, the river and not being found till daylight when it would probably be too late.

Dusk had not yet arrived, but was on its way. A barn owl was flying low along the ditch looking for his supper. Ghostly, white, and silent with his heart-shaped head and sighing wings, he flew low along the bank searching for food. Andrea watched as he coasted soundlessly over the winter dead foliage looking for small mammals to take back for his nesting mate. She stood very still gazing at the beautiful bird and so intent on hunting was he that he seemed not to notice her until a few metres away at which point he wheeled round and upwards displaying his strong legs and taloned feet, flying up over the trees into the next field to continue his search undisturbed. Andrea smiled to herself. Sights like that were like a gift to her and she sent up a whispered thank you to the universe.

She continued along the riverbank again and at the stile turned left down the lane, reasoning that the lane to the right was probably full of rubbish by now and anybody dumping more would drive up a bit further. Dusk was settling in, but she wasn't too far from her home and was heading in the right direction so on she went. As she turned a bend in the lane, there ahead of her, tucked into the verge side by some trees, was the square brown van. The back door was open and a figure was just walking back from the trees to the vehicle. She braced herself and quickly walked towards it. As she approached the man, tall, heavyset and probably in his forties although it was hard to tell wrapped up as he was in his coat and beany hat, she called out,

'Excuse me, hey excuse me.'

He looked round and quickly shut the van doors. Andrea was up close now grasping her litter picking stick tightly.

'Hi, I walk these lanes a lot and have noticed an increase in the amount of rubbish being dumped on the side of the roads. You don't know anything about it, do you?' *I may as well just come out with it, no use dancing around the issue. What's the worst that can happen?*

'You accusing me of something? Mind your own business, I don't know anything,' his voice was gruff, and he had a strong Midlands accent. He turned his back on her and walked to the front of his van. Andrea followed.

'I'm not saying it's you, but I've seen your van around here a lot lately and wondered if you might have seen something or someone. I'm gathering evidence to try to get the person or people responsible prosecuted.' *I might just as well show him I mean business. If it is him, it might make him think twice and stop doing it.*

'You sound to me like a troublemaker. You wanna mind your own business, old woman.'

'I'm asking a civil question, and you sound to me like you've got something to hide.' *Okay, that's enough. Now stop and leave it alone. He's getting angry.*

The man was in his van now with the engine on. 'Do yourself a favour, grandma and mind your own fucking business.' He slammed the door and drove off.

Well, what did that achieve? He's just cross now, but he might stop now he knows I'm watching. Fat chance.

Andrea walked over to the trees and looked about, there just behind the tree line, were four big black bin liners, an open white builders sack full of broken plaster board and pieces of electrical wiring and a pile of broken tiles. *For heaven's sake, what a bastard. Well, that's proof it's him anyway and I've got his van number, but I think I need a photo of him actually dumping the stuff to get a prosecution.*

It was nearly dark now and after taking photos of the scene, Andrea turned down the lane again and began to walk home. There was no one around and apart from the square van, she hadn't seen a car all the time she'd been out. She had just turned from the narrow lane into the small road which would take her to the end of the lane where she lived when she heard a vehicle driving at speed behind her. None of the roads or lanes where she lived had streetlights and certainly there were no footpaths or pavements, so if there was no grass verge, pedestrians had to walk on the road. Andrea always made sure she walked approaching the oncoming traffic, but this sounded different to the usual traffic noise, faster and closer. She turned and was just in time to see a large, square van right behind her. Driving straight at her. She threw herself into the hedgerow and the van sped past.

35

Monday 17th & Tuesday 18th February

The following day was Monday and Andrea was usually in her studio at least an hour before the first class, tidying round, setting out everyone's work and turning on the wax pots, she liked to light an incense stick too so that it had finished burning before anyone arrived, but the scent remained. This morning was different. Andrea could hardly get out of bed, every muscle in her body ached and her right thigh was showing signs of a humdinger of a bruise. The van had missed her, but if she hadn't jumped out of the way and into the hedge, it would surely have hit her. *Clearly, he was trying to scare me, but would he have actually hit me? I think he would. He's a dangerous man.*

Luckily the women who came to the first class were all in the middle of their respective batik or felting projects and needed little help. Andrea wandered between them, giving a tip here or a helpful hint there, but mainly she was able to sit down and take it easy, only really getting up to make the drinks halfway through. The previous evening, she had taken a couple of painkillers and soaked in a hot bath before going to bed and that had helped a lot; she took some more painkillers now and by the time the first class had finished and the afternoon people had arrived; she was beginning to feel a little better.

Betty, Sal, Cora and Jackie were appalled when she told them what had happened.

'He's dangerous Andrea, maybe you should leave things alone for a while. Don't confront him again.' Sal looked worried.

'Tell the police,' said Betty, 'that's assault. He shouldn't be allowed to get away with it.'

'I went online last night and reported it, I added the photo of his van showing the reg number, but I don't think they'll do anything.' Andrea scrolled through her phone, 'The police website said, and I quote, *Our decision*—whether to proceed or not—*is based on four key factors. Vulnerability of the victim, e.g. is the victim in danger? seriousness of the crime, likelihood of solving it, and best use of our resources.* Well based on that criteria, I think the police will have better things to focus on and as I've got no proof and there were no witnesses, I don't suppose anything will come of it.'

'It's always good to report it,' insisted Betty. 'At least it's on record now. You never know, he may have done it to someone else.'

'True,' Andrea nodded slowly.

'Although you're probably right, nothing will happen, but it's a shame. Someone should know there's a maniac about,' said Betty. And the others agreed.

They all settled down and got on with their work. Their entries for the latest competition, "Musicals," were well under way, even though the judging wasn't until late June. Cora was taking her time with her Priscilla Queen of the Desert picture. She usually rushed her work and regretted it afterwards, so was determined to take more care this time. Betty was engaged on a batik of The Sound of Music and

Jackie was finishing a felted table runner as a present for her sister-in-law, but would soon be ready to begin her planned batik of the musical Chess for the competition. It would involve batiking a stylised knight, pawn and bishop. Jackie certainly didn't believe in making life easy for herself and enjoyed a challenge. She was in the process of rolling up the wet wool of the table runner whilst discussing with Andrea the best way to approach her next batik when three phones pinged at once. It was a group message from Kevin. Cora had her phone to hand and read it out.

I've looked at the CCTV, not much really, nothing on land camera except me and you three. House camera shows a few callers, nothing too suspicious. It falls, that's all. If you want to see for yourselves, I'll be at mum's tomorrow after 5. K.

'Nothing too suspicious,' said Cora, 'that's a shame. Shall we go, or not bother, what d'you think?'

'Oh, you should definitely go, if only to find out what *it falls* means,' said Sal, 'and you might spot something Kevin missed.'

'True,' Andrea agreed, 'and it will show Kevin we haven't given up on Kim. Any chance of you driving, Jackie? I think my leg will still be hurting.'

'Yes, I'll drive,' offered Jackie. 'You should rest your leg as long as possible.'

The class finished with Betty and Sal repeatedly telling Andrea not to confront angry men alone and in the dark, and everyone went home.

The next day Andrea's leg was feeling much better although her thigh was beginning to turn a wonderful blueish purple. She walked to the lane where all the rubbish had been dumped, taking with her a pair of rubber gloves, a couple of black bin liners and her trusty litter stick. The thin veil of snow had melted away and the piles of waste lay brazenly on the green verge. Andrea knew she couldn't move the large items, and she had faith that the council would come soon and take them away, but she wanted to pick up the smaller pieces and check for any danger that could hurt the wildlife, wood with nails sticking through, wiring, anything that could trap small creatures. One sad day she had been out walking after a heavy rain and had spotted a discarded crisp packet in the ditch, on retrieving it she discovered the swollen bodies of two small mice who having climbed inside tempted by the crumbs were unable to climb the slippery walls to get out and had drowned in the collected rainwater. People do not realise the harm they do, harm that could so easily be avoided. *Or maybe they do, and they just don't give a damn.*

She collected up the wiring, the pieces of broken tiles that had spilled. Picked up all the small pieces that she could, bits of plastic, pieces of steel angle beading bent out of shape and useless for protecting the edges of plaster board as intended but perfect for trapping the feet of small mammals or cutting the legs of Muntjac deer, although Andrea knew the deer wouldn't be foolish enough to come near the mess of humans. *But all the same, these are their tracks and pathways, and they live here.* When she had filled her black sacks with all the loose, dangerous pieces she could, Andrea tied knots in the tops and carefully left them together, trusting the council to take them very soon.

At twenty to five, Andrea walked down to Jackie's house, and finding Cora already aboard Jackie's car, they set off.

They arrived at Kim's house just after five and saw Kevin's car parked outside. Kevin had set up the laptop and lined up the footage and soon they were all sitting round looking at the screen.

'Here we go,' Kevin sped through CCTV footage of Kim's land. Slowing the film when a car drove past, but the only car that actually stopped was his own. The car number was obscured as the car had been parked at an angle and only part of the boot was caught but they now knew it had been Kevin. He sped up the footage again, slowing it to show Cora and Andrea climbing the gate and the subsequent conversation the three of them had with Snowy White. Nothing else of any interest happened at all.

'Well, that's all pretty straightforward. Nothing on there that's unexplained.' Jackie said, peering closely at the screen.

'Right, here's the house CCTV, there's not much here of interest either.' Kevin said.

The camera was set above the front door and showed the top of the front garden path and outside the front door. The film sped through and again Kevin slowed it when anyone came. Kim had set up the CCTV in early November and apart from Kim coming and going and the occasional delivery, there was not much to see. Kim didn't have many visitors. Kevin came a few weeks after the camera was installed. They watched him arrive and disappear from view as he went inside. According to the time in the lower right-hand corner, he stayed around three hours before leaving.

'I try to pop round each month or so. I was checking out her camera and asking her to come and stay for a few days at Christmas.' Kevin continued to speed through the film, 'This is odd though, look the camera angle shifts a little.'

On 21st December, the camera shifted position. They could see it had dropped and no longer had a view of the front path. It faced directly down showing just a small part of the front doorstep.

'Can you go back to see when it actually changes?' Cora asked.

Kevin went back and stopped the film exactly when the angle changed, he went back frame by frame and they saw a man delivering a long parcel, which seemed to accidentally knock the camera off-kilter.

'Well, would you look at that,' Kevin looked round at the others, 'When I looked through this at home, I thought it had slipped or it was the wind or something, but it was knocked. Was it on purpose, d'you think?'

'To be honest, it looked accidental, but what if someone did it on purpose? Why would they do it?' asked Andrea, peering over Kevin's shoulder at the grainy black and white film. 'It's not the highest quality film we could wish for—it's difficult to say. Who is the person, anyway?'

'Someone bringing a parcel. Could be any one of many delivery services. It was the week before Christmas there were deliveries everywhere. Could even have been a regular person. I can't make out a uniform or anything. Can't even make out a face because of the woollen hat. It could even have been a woman.'

'Hmmm, is it just a coincidence that it happened on the twenty-first?' mused Andrea. 'That was the date that Kim was concerned about, the Winter Solstice, the longest night or shortest day, whatever you want to call it.'

'So all we've got from that is yet another mystery. Let's see if we can get any more from the recording.'

Kevin continued to fast forward through the camera footage, but it was hard to make anything out now as they only saw feet coming and going.

But they could recognise Kim's boots. They watched the film and noted down dates and times and were able to work out that Kim left her house at three twenty on Saturday 28th December and as far they could see did not come back. They scrolled through the film slowing down each time any feet appeared on the step. It took them ages, but despite their vigilance they could find no sign of Kim's boots reappearing. She had not returned.

'Let's have a cup of tea,' suggested Cora, who had remembered to bring some milk this time.

'Ooh, I'd better pop round to Erin's and return her milk jug,' said Jackie standing up and walking into the kitchen. 'I won't be long. Get the kettle on Cora.'

Erin opened her front door and stood there smiling, her legs squeezed into colourful leggings and a red, gold and green wool hat pulled down, covering her hair.

'I'm so sorry we haven't returned this sooner, Erin,' began Jackie as she handed over the jug.

'Ahh no problem, thank you.' Erin smiled her huge smile. 'I'm glad you're all here and Kim's back safe and sound.'

'Hang on a minute, why do you think Kim is here?'

'Well, because she's back. Her car's parked outside and her son's here again. I saw him arrive.'

'What? Her car's back? Which one is it?'

'That red one there, the Astra,' Erin pointed to a car parked a little way down the street.

'When did she come back—do you know?'

'Well as I say, I haven't seen her, but her car's been there nearly a week now I think.'

36

Tuesday 18th & Wednesday 19th February

Kevin scanned the street.

'That's her car all right—I didn't even notice it. Well, where the hell is she? She's not answering my calls. Where is she?'

They sat in stunned silence. There seemed to be one mystery after another. If Kim's car was back, where was Kim? She obviously hadn't been home, although she could have come in the back way, as the CCTV would not have picked her up if she had. But there was no sign of her in the house and surely she would have tided up a bit or at least moved some things around. No, she definitely hadn't been home.

'Ooh! Hang on a minute,' Andrea began searching in her bag. 'Here it is, Kim's address book. I was bringing it back to return it, but in all the excitement I forgot. Anyhow when I was looking for Charlie and Kevin's numbers, I noticed the number for a mechanic.' She flicked through to the M's, 'here it is Mechanic—Tom, with a number and an address. Why don't we ring him and see if he knows anything? You never know, there's a slim chance.'

Jackie looked puzzled. 'Why would a mechanic know anything?'

'I don't know, really. I was just linking her car with anyone who might know where it's been for weeks. She's written him down as Tom. It sounds like she knows him. We've got nothing else to go on, have we?'

'Yeah, Okay. But he'll be closed by now,' Jackie glanced at her watch, 'how about we visit him tomorrow? We might get more information face to face.'

They arranged to go and see the mechanic the next afternoon as Andrea had her pottery classes earlier in the day and they thought a few more hours wouldn't matter much. Kevin would be at work of course, but they promised to keep him informed via their message group.

The following afternoon, Cora drove them onto the cluttered forecourt of Tom Thomas Motor Services. The three women trouped into the tiny office, rang the bell and waited. After a while a big man in his mid-sixties wearing old blue overalls walked in wiping his hands with a rag that looked like it was putting more oil on than it was taking off.

'Afternoon ladies, how can I help?' he spoke with a soft Welsh accent and smiled round at the three women muffled up against the cold.

'Hello, are you Tom?' Cora stepped forward.

'I am indeed, Tom Thomas, at your service,' Tom chuckled at his own joke.

'I'm Cora and this is Andrea and Jackie,' she waved a hand at the other two, 'we're friends of Kim Merchant. We believe she's a customer of yours.'

'Kim, yes, she is. Is she all right? I've been a bit worried about her.'

'Oh really? Can we ask why?'

Tom explained that he'd had Kim's car for some weeks and hadn't heard anything from her. They chatted with Tom for a while, giving him an edited version of their concerns and listening to his story of the saga of Kim's car.

Kim had booked her car in for a full service and, here Tom checked his book. On Saturday 28th December she'd brought it in and left the keys.

'Ahh yes, I remember now. She should have brought it in early in the morning, but it seems she forgot. She's always been a bit of a scatterbrain all the time I've known her.' Tom chuckled, 'I gave her a ring, asking where she was and she came rushing in, didn't even have a coat on. We were just having a tea break, so I made one for her to warm her up and then my mate Nish gave her a lift home.'

Tom told them Nish had worked for him for about six months, yes, he knew a bit about cars, he wasn't an apprentice or anything, just wanted a job around the same time that Tom decided he wasn't as young as he used to be and could do with a bit of help. Anyway, the next day was Sunday and Tom had gone down with severe food poisoning. After a few days of him getting worse and worse, he was taken into hospital, where he remained for two weeks. On his release, he was still weak and was advised to have a couple more weeks' rest at home. He managed one, but then despite his wife's protestations, had gone back to work.

In the meantime, Tom was pleased to say, Nish had kept things ticking over nicely, all that is except for the fact that it seems he had forgotten about Kim's car. There it was exactly where it had been left all those weeks before. Tom had rung Kim to explain, but it had gone straight to the answer phone, so he'd left a message and just got on with the service. A few days later, still unable to contact her by phone, he had driven the car round to Kim's house and knocked on the door. There was no reply, so he put the keys through the letterbox and rang Nish to come and pick him up.

That was all he could tell them. He still hadn't heard from Kim, but knew she'd pay him eventually as despite being a bit erratic about bill payments, she always settled up in the end. No, he wasn't unduly worried not to have heard from her as it wasn't unknown for her to decide to go away for a few weeks on the spur of the moment and he'd assumed that was what she'd done, what with the weather being cold and her having no car and all.

'Sorry to put you on the spot, but can you remember when you took Kim's car back? The date?' Andrea asked.

'No, not off the top of my head, but I know I needed to order a part, and it was delayed. Can't remember why now. I'll check my order book.' Tom flicked through his book and found the part had arrived early on Saturday 1st February. He had fitted it and taken the car back that afternoon.

'Thank you, Tom, you've helped us a lot.'

'No problem, ladies, I expect she'll turn up soon. There's nothing to worry about, I'm sure.' And whistling happily, Tom went back to work.

Half an hour later, Cora and Andrea were sitting in Jackie's comfortable sitting room drinking mugs of tea.

Jackie came in with a plate of chocolate brownies. 'Anyone want a brownie?' she handed round the plate and Andrea and Cora both took one.

Andrea took a bite. 'Delicious. Did you make them?'

'No, Ruby did. They're lovely, aren't they?' Ruby, Jackie's gardening buddy, enjoyed baking and often gave Jackie delicious treats.

'So, Tom brought the car back and still no one's seen Kim. Although now the last sighting is by Nish on Saturday 28th December, when he drove her home.' Andrea said, as she ate her brownie.

'Yes, and that agrees with the front door CCTV, such as it is,' agreed Cora.

'So, what about Nish?' asked Jackie. 'You don't think he could have done something, do you?'

'Done what?' Andrea looked at her, 'abducting her, you mean?'

'Possibly,' Jackie shrugged her shoulders, 'maybe even murdered her.'

'What!' Cora nearly choked on her brownie. 'Murder? Where did this come from? She's not dead. I thought we decided she was only missing, what with her phone still being charged and taking messages.'

'It's looking more and more like she's not coming back though, isn't it?' Jackie persisted, 'even when she's gone away before she was still in contact with Kevin albeit sporadically, and why hasn't she been concerned about her car, it was in the garage for weeks and she never bothered to even ring Tom to see what was happening. I call that very odd behaviour, even for Kim.'

'Maybe she's had an accident and lost her memory. Maybe she's in a hospital somewhere. We need to try the police again. Perhaps they'll take us a bit more seriously this time.' Andrea looked at the others and raised her eyebrows.

'Kevin should report her missing. He's her son, so should have more clout. They'll have to take him seriously.' Cora got out her phone and called Kevin.

With her phone on speaker, they updated Kevin between them. He agreed it was time to report his mother missing to the police and said he would do it immediately, so leaving him to it, the three women promised to keep in contact and wished him good luck.

'Going back to Nish,' Jackie said, 'Okay, Cora, forget about murder, but what if he is involved somehow? He's only been working for Tom for about six months and Tom didn't know him before. What does anyone know about him? He was the last person to see Kim that we know of, and he gave her a lift in his car. And to my mind, most suspicious of all, why did he just leave Kim's car alone when Tom was in hospital? Did he really just forget it? Although how he could forget a car I don't know, or did he not bother about it as he knew Kim wouldn't be needing it for a while?'

'You've got a point. It's very suspicious. Shall we go and have a chat with the mysterious Nish? Tomorrow?' Andrea drained her mug and stood up.

'I'm game, tomorrow it is, I'll collect you both from here at ten.' Cora stood up too. 'I'm off now, as well. Things to do. To paraphrase Snowy White, I'm a very busy woman.' She grinned and left.

37

You have one new message.

'Hello mum? Are you there? Where on earth are you? Your car's back outside your house and there's still no sign of you. I've reported you missing to the police. I had to. I'm so worried. Your friends from the art studio are helping me look for you too, talking to people and finding out what they can. People talk to them, maybe more so than to the police. Anyway, we're worried about you. If you get this message, please, please ring me. Love you mum.'

Beep.

End of message.

To listen to the message again, press one.

To keep the message press two.

To delete the message press three.

The man pressed button two.

Again the women from the art studio.

38

Thursday 20th February

'I've been thinking,' said Andrea as they drove to the garage the next day to talk to Nish. 'How come we didn't see the keys when we went to Kim's? If Tom put them through the letter box, we should have noticed them.'

'Or Kevin should have seen them when he went in. I'll message him and see what he says.' Jackie said, clicking on her phone to bring up the message group chat.

Hi Kevin, we're wondering if you saw Kim's car keys by the front door when you went in on Tuesday evening? Maybe on the door-mat? J.

No sorry, didn't notice any keys. K.

How did you get in? J.

Back door, the key's still in the frog. K.

Ahh, OK. J.

'Well, that explains that then,' Jackie put her phone back in her pocket, 'he came in the back way, he wouldn't have seen any keys.'

'Yes, but he opened the front door for us. We went in that way. How come he didn't notice them then, or stand on them or something?' Andrea asked.

'Don't forget, he was really angry with us. He may not have noticed,' Cora said as she turned onto Stickville High Street.

'If the keys were on the floor by the front door, they would have been seen, no matter how angry Kevin was he would have seen them, or surely one of us would have noticed them, stepped on them or kicked them or something.' Andrea persisted.

'You think someone's taken them? Kim?' Cora asked.

'I don't know, but if we could find out what's happened to the car keys, it may help us to track Kim down.' Andrea said.

Cora drove the car onto the forecourt of Tom Thomas Motor Services, and they piled out. Tom was working outside this time, bent over the open bonnet of a small car. He straightened up when he saw their car.

'Hello again ladies, back so soon?'

'Hello Tom,' said Jackie, 'yes sorry to disturb you again, we just wondered if we could have a word with Nish. Is he around?'

'Sorry Nish is away, compassionate leave. An uncle out in Spain has died, and he's gone over for the funeral. He was so good keeping this place going when I was laid up that I told him to take as long as he needs. I think he'll be away at least another week or so. Can I help?'

'Ahh, that's a shame, no it's alright, we just wanted to ask him about Kim, you know, how she was when he drove her home after she'd dropped her car off, if she said anything about going away, if there was anyone there with her. Any problems?'

'Can I just ask when Nish went away?' Andrea joined in.

'He heard about his uncle the weekend before last and went straight off on the Monday.'

'Does he live in the town?'

'Yeah, he rents a flat over one of the charity shops on the High Street. Why?'

'Oh, I just wondered.'

'Well, nice as it is to see you ladies, I have to get on. No rest for the wicked.' Tom gave them a wink and returned to the open bonnet of the small car.

'Right—round to Kim's house. We have to get to the bottom of this.' Jackie said, and she opened the door and got into Cora's car.

They entered by the back door. Everything looked as it had when they'd left on Wednesday evening. They went straight through to the hall and looked around. They saw the keys immediately, they were pushed right up against the wall by the front door, unnoticeable unless you were looking. Cora picked them up, two keys were attached to a plastic key ring with a picture of a smiling snowman on one side and *How does a snowman get around? He rides an icicle!* On the back.

'How did they get there?' Andrea looked around, 'Ahh, I see, when the door was opened it pushed them back against the wall.'

'Well, how come Kevin didn't see them?' asked Jackie. 'I'll go outside and post them through. We'll see where they land.'

Jackie went out the front door, and Andrea closed it behind her. The letterbox opened and the keys were dropped through. They fell on to the carpet immediately in front of the door, easy to see if anyone was looking but they could have been overlooked, say if someone was angry as Kevin had been. Andrea opened the door to let Jackie back inside and when the door was closed again, there were the keys pushed up against the wall once more.

'I think Kevin didn't see them because he was so angry, and they were pushed to the wall when he opened the front door to us.' Andrea said, 'I think that's probably a dead end.'

'Yes, but how about if Kevin didn't see them because they had already been pushed up against the wall? That would mean—' before Cora could finish, Jackie interrupted.

'Someone else has been here. And they came in through the front door. So, they had—' before Jackie could finish, Cora interrupted.

'Keys to the front door!'

'You two are like a double act,' laughed Andrea. 'But who came in? Who could have? We think it's unlikely to be Kim, so who was it? If we can find that out, I think we can solve this mystery.'

'I've just had a thought. Where's all the post? Why hasn't that been put through the letterbox?' Cora opened the front door again and went out. On the wall at the front of the house was a small post box with a keyhole. 'We need a key. It'll be a little one,' she called.

Andrea and Jackie looked about and on the tiny hall table was a china bowl and in it was a key. She passed it to Cora, who opened the post box and retrieved a handful of post. Back inside, they sorted through the pile; it was mainly flyers for pizza delivery or the Indian restaurant in the next town. There were no letters, nothing personal, just junk mail. Another dead end.

They had another look around the house, but found nothing had changed, no clues, so they took themselves off to The Trio of Fools for some much-needed coffee. The pub was cosy and welcoming as all ways and they sat in their usual place by the log fire warming their hands. The landlord came over bringing their coffees and bent to put another log on the fire.

'And how are you three ladies today?' he asked with a smile. 'You're becoming regulars in here, aren't you? Can I get you anything else?' he looked around. 'Are you staying for lunch? The kitchen has just opened.'

They looked at each other and nodded.

'Yes, I think we will,' said Jackie. 'we'll have a look at the menu in a minute. We'll have our coffee first, thank you.'

They sat for a while thinking everything through, then Andrea said, 'So we don't think it was Kim who came in the front door?'

'No,' replied Jackie, 'because if it had been, she would have picked up her car keys. It was someone who didn't know her car was back, and it was someone who had keys to the front door.'

'We need to see the CCTV footage from the fortnight between late afternoon on Saturday, the first of February when Tom returned the car to when Kevin arrived on Saturday the fifteenth. If it wasn't Kevin, then it's during that time someone else entered the house.'

The bar had filled up now with folk coming in for their lunches. Evidently the kitchen at The Trio of Fools was well known for good homemade food and Jackie, Cora and Andrea were glad they'd bagged a table before the rush. They decided to look at the menu and after choosing, Jackie went up to the bar to order their choices.

'I changed my mind,' Jackie said as she sat back down, 'decided against the soup and went for the steak and kidney pie instead.'

'Last minute decision? asked Cora.'

'Well, the bloke sitting at the bar behind us heard me ordering and said to try the pie instead, said it's very good.'

They all looked round at the good-looking young man sitting at the bar with a pint in his hand. He had dark hair, was clean shaven and was wearing a white tee shirt under a dark blue jacket. He smiled and raised his pint to them. They chatted some more and then the food arrived. Andrea and Cora had gone for the fish, chips and garden peas, which looked delicious, but Jackie's steak and kidney pie was truly a work of art. She beamed as she took possession of the culinary masterpiece and sighed as the mouthwatering smell drifted up from the plate.

'Hey, that does look good Jackie, good choice,' said Cora and they all three looked behind them again at the young man sitting on a stool at the bar, who again smiled and raised his glass to them.

They finished their lunch in near silence, especially Jackie, who was enjoying every succulent mouthful. Then Cora said, 'do you think we should ask about Kim in here? Maybe someone knows something. It is her local after all.'

'Can't do any harm,' agreed Jackie. 'Everyone seems very friendly so why not? We may learn something.'

The lunchtime rush seemed to be over and the amount of people in the bar thinned out. They waited until the landlord was less busy and then went up to the bar to pay.

'Did you enjoy your lunches, ladies?' he asked.

'Delicious,' Jackie grinned. 'I'll definitely be coming back for some more steak and kidney pie.'

'That's a house special and is on the menu every Thursday, Friday and Saturday. Our busiest days.' The landlord beamed at her.

He totalled up their individual bills on the till and as they paid Cora asked, 'I don't suppose you know a friend of ours, Kim Merchant, do you? She lives round here and this would be her local.'

'I'm afraid not, but I don't really bother with names too much. I might know her by sight. Does she come in often?'

'We don't know, we only know her from going to the same art classes. It's just that we haven't seen her for a while and wondered if she came in here. She's in her mid-fifties, about my height, dark hair cut in a bob, nothing to really make her stand out, I'm afraid. Never mind, just thought we'd ask.'

'Hey Mal, ever heard of a Kim, what was it Merchant?' the landlord called to the man sitting further up the bar who had recommended the pie. He turned back to the women and winked 'He may know her, he's a proper lady's man.'

'Nah, don't think so. Why?' Mal replied, turning on his bar stool and directing a dazzling smile at them.

'These ladies are friends of hers from their art classes and wondered if she comes in here. I don't recognise the name, but that means nothing.'

'What's she look like?'

Cora told him and Mal said he couldn't recall seeing anyone like that, but that didn't mean she hadn't been in. They all talked amicably for a few minutes. The landlord, whose name was Jimmy, a large friendly man in his fifties, chatted and smiled with his new customers. The younger man, Mal, who was probably mid-thirties, was charming, he was a regular and seemed to know everyone not just in the pub but in the town, except Kim unfortunately. Both men were very interested in the women's quest to find their missing friend.

'Wow, over six weeks, that's a long time to be away,' said Jimmy. 'have you notified the police?'

'Her son has,' Andrea told him, 'that reminds me,' she turned to Jackie and Cora, 'we must meet up with him again and find out if he's had any news.' She turned back to the men. 'Well, thanks anyway. If she does happen to come in, would you ask her to ring her son? He's worried.'

'Yes, of course,' said Jimmy. 'Now excuse me ladies, customers need serving. Another Hen in there, mate? I'm coming.' This last remark was to a customer further up the bar, who was waving an empty glass in his direction.

They gathered up their bags and coats and were turning to leave when Jackie spoke to Mal. 'I don't suppose you happen to know anyone called Nish, do you? He's a mechanic at Tom Thomas's garage. It seems he was the last person to see Kim.'

A look flickered across Mal's handsome face and as quickly it was gone, replaced by a smile. 'Nish, yeah, I know Nish. Good bloke. He comes in occasionally, doesn't really drink though, he comes in for the company.'

'I believe he lives in a flat over one of the charity shops?' Jackie phrased this as a question.

'Yeah, the Hospice shop, why? Is he missing too?' Mal smiled at them. And all three women were charmed.

'Not missing. Tom said he's in Spain for a funeral. We're just interested in where he lives, that's all.' Jackie said.

'Seems like you three are interested in lots of people's business. Are you private investigators or something?' Mal smiled again and they laughed.

'No, just friends of Kim and her son and wondering if we can help, that's all. Andrea here runs an art studio in Drayflot. That's where we all met. Kim hasn't been around since Christmas, and we can't get in touch with her, so we're just trying to find out where she might be.'

'Hmm,' said Mal, and he turned away. Then he turned back to them and said, 'as long as you're sure Nish really has gone to Spain, seems like you've only got Tom's word for it and really, if you think about it, Tom could have said anything.'

‘Why d’you say that?’ asked Andrea. ‘Why should Tom lie? And where’s Nish then?’

‘No reason, just a thought, that’s all. I dunno, I’m just messing about. Take no notice.’ Mal laughed and raised his empty glass to the landlord. ‘Another pint of Hen in there please Jim,’

Slightly confused, the women said goodbye and left.

39

Thursday 20th February

'Well, any luck with the police?' asked Andrea.

They met Kevin at Kim's house. He had contacted them to say he would be at his mother's house that evening at six and did they want to meet him there. They were all home when they'd got his message so had all trailed back again for six o'clock.

'I went into the local police station here in Stickville, I thought it would be best to report her missing at the same station where the other reports were made.'

Kevin went on to tell them how he'd spoken to Sergeant Potts, who had taken him seriously. He had been taken into a private room and had told the policeman everything. The sergeant made a note of everything Kevin said and seemed to understand his concerns, however he was very clear there was not very much they could do in matters like this as Kim was a functioning adult and there had been no sign of a break-in or a struggle. Kevin had asked if they could access Kim's bank account to see if there was activity, as obviously the bank couldn't tell him anything. The police sergeant had said this might be possible and he would look into it, he also said he would contact the local hospital to check if there were any admissions of patients with amnesia but didn't think there would be as it was the usual practice of hospitals to contact the police anyway in cases like that.

'So, there we are,' said Kevin, 'no further on, really.'

'At least the police are taking it seriously now, which is excellent,' Andrea pointed out. 'you never know, they may come up with something. In the meantime, we've found the car keys.'

'What—where were they?'

Cora produced them and gave them to Kevin. He turned them over in his hands and stared down at the smiling snowman.

'Maisie gave mum this key ring at Christmas,' he mumbled.

Cora leant forward and put her hand on his arm. 'She'll come back. We'll find your mum.'

Kevin seemed to pull himself together. 'So—come on, tell me where they were?'

They told him about finding the keys and asked if he could have missed seeing the keys when he opened the door to them. Kevin was adamant that he would have seen them had they been in front of the door. So they now had a time frame from when they were posted through the letterbox to when they were pushed up against the wall. Kevin agreed that this was a huge development, and they turned on Kim's laptop to find the corresponding CCTV footage for the time in question.

As before, the footage was grey, very grainy and jerky. There wasn't much to see due to the camera facing down and showing only part of the doorstep. No one had approached the door until the Saturday when they saw a foot. It stayed in shot for a while, then disappeared. This must have been Tom returning the car, ringing the doorbell a couple of times then giving up and posting the keys. Then nothing more for the whole of the two weeks until they themselves had arrived at the door and Kevin had let them in. They ran through the film again, still nothing.

'Well, that's it then, no one came in the front door,' Andrea said, 'and if they'd come in through the back why would they open the front door and if they did why didn't they see the keys on the doormat? It makes no sense.'

Kevin began to replay the footage again. 'There must be something on the film that we're missing,'

'There! What's that!' Cora pointed at the screen. 'Go back. Can you go frame by frame?'

Kevin went back, and they all stared at the screen as the grainy images jumped from one to the next.

'There, that's a foot!' Cora pointed at a blurred shape only just in shot.

They studied the film, going through it again and again until they were sure of what they'd seen. At 10.46 am on Wednesday the fifth of February a partial foot had arrived on the doorstep facing the door, where it had remained before quickly disappearing, then nothing for another three minutes or so, until it partially reappeared, briefly pointing away from the house.

'We've got him!' shouted Cora. 'We've got the bastard.'

Everyone laughed. It really felt like they had a tangible clue at last.

'We were right. Someone was in the house. It took them seconds to get in and they came out after about three minutes,' Jackie said. 'Why? What could they possibly do in just three minutes? D'you suppose Erin remembers seeing anyone? I'm going round to ask her.'

'Shall we come?' asked Kevin.

'No, probably best not to go mob handed.'

Andrea, Cora, and Kevin sat down in Kim's living room

and waited for Jackie to returned. They didn't have to wait long. A few minutes later, she was back.

'There's no answer. Maybe she's gone out. She probably didn't see anyone anyway.'

'What now?' Andrea asked, 'Unfortunately, we're still no closer to finding out what's happened to Kim.'

'Well, there's one thing we can do,' said Kevin standing up, 'put the bloody CCTV camera back in whack. At least if anyone comes back we'll be able to see who it is.'

Kevin left the room, and for want of something constructive to do, the three women trailed after him. It was dark now, and they were standing shivering on the front step watching Kevin angle the camera correctly when Erin appeared. She came up the front path, muffled in a thick coat and faux fur hat.

'Hello everyone,' she called brightly. 'I didn't expect to see a welcoming party when I came home from work. Is Kim back?'

'No, not yet,' said Kevin, 'we're just putting the CCTV camera back in its correct position, unfortunately it got a bit dislodged.'

'Ahh, so you can see who's coming and going. Good idea. You can see when Kim comes home.' Erin stood watching them, showing no signs of wanting to go inside and get warm.

'Oh, while you're here,' said Jackie casually, 'it's a long shot I know, but you didn't happen to notice anyone come or go on Wednesday the fifth did you, around 10.30 in the morning?'

'No Kim's had no visitors that I've seen. I usually watch TV in the front room most mornings until about eleven when I leave for work. I would have noticed someone coming up the path.'

'Are you sure? We wondered if someone had made a

quick visit? You know just for a minute or two. Posted something through the door or something?'

'I did see Tom walk up and put something through the letter box a few weeks ago. I couldn't see what though.'

'Yes, we know about that. It would have been a few days after Tom came. Oh well, never mind, it was just a thought.' Jackie smiled at her.

They said goodbye to Erin, and all trouped inside out of the cold.

'Well, I guess that's it for now,' said Andrea. 'I don't see what else we can do today.'

'This is awful. We get a clue and then it leads us nowhere. We get very excited and then realise we're no further forward to finding Kim than before.' Cora made a frustrated face.

'I'll get home now,' said Kevin, 'look ladies, I really appreciate what you're doing for mum, but I don't know what else we can do and now that the police are on the case, I'm sure it won't be long until this mystery is cleared up.'

Yeah, and pigs might fly, thought Andrea.

'Well, we're not giving up until she's back Kevin, so get used to it,' Jackie laughed.

There was a knock on the door and Cora went to open it. It was Erin. Cora brought her through to the sitting room where she stood in the middle of the room, staring round. The others had become used to the mess and clutter, the vacuum cleaner still standing in the middle of the floor, the piles of books and cushions stacked up, but Erin saw it through fresh eyes.

'Goodness, it's like the Marie Celeste, like she just walked out in the middle of doing her housework.'

'That's exactly what we think she did,' Jackie said. 'Anyway, can we help you? We were just gathering ourselves together to go home.'

'Well, I was thinking about what you said about that Wednesday morning and I remembered that I did see someone, don't know how I forgot, I even spoke to him,' she laughed, 'I can be a bit of a dozy cow at times,' she laughed again, 'my friend Sonia always said—Erin—I don't know how you manage to get through life sometimes, you can be such a dozy cow. She often says that.' Erin laughed again and beamed round at the four faces staring at her, mouths open, waiting.

'Who did you see?' asked Kevin impatiently. 'Tell us Erin, it could be important.'

'Oh, I'm sorry, I got carried away.' Erin was enjoying being the centre of attention and was wringing out every drop of drama that she could.

Just tell us, please.

They eventually got it out of her. It seemed that Erin had somehow missed the arrival of the person, but had seen him leaving. He was a delivery man, wearing a yellow high viz vest and a woollen hat pulled low over his head. No she wouldn't recognise him again as she hadn't seen his face, however he was carrying a parcel. She'd run out and called after him, offering to take the parcel in for Kim, but he had continued walking and said over his shoulder that he wouldn't leave it as it wasn't company policy, then he left. He drove off in a van. She thought it was odd because usually drivers are happy to leave parcels with neighbours. No, she didn't know what delivery company he was with, but the van was a big one, brown and squarish, and yes she had noticed the size of the parcel, it was a flat box about this by this, Erin indicated the size with her hands. It was roughly the size of a laptop.

They thanked Erin, telling her how much help she'd been, and ushered her out. Then they sat down and looked at each other.

'So, he came disguised as a delivery man carrying a parcel, very clever,' mused Jackie, 'so whatever he was after, he could have hidden in the parcel. In broad daylight too, he's certainly got a nerve, whoever he is.'

'Oh god, I've just seen the time!' Kevin glanced at his watch, 'I must get off now, Carol is out this evening and I'm on babysitting duties. Thanks for everything you're doing. Just pull the front door shut when you leave. Bye.'

Kevin grabbed his coat and ran from the house to a chorus of 'goodbye', 'we won't be long' and 'we're leaving now too.'

They were just gathering up their coats to follow Kevin when Cora spoke. 'Hang on a minute Jackie, you said he came disguised as a delivery man. What if he really was a delivery man? That could work. Think about it. What if he was delivering parcels one day and saw Kim? Maybe he knew her from somewhere, maybe he had a grudge or something?'

'Hmm, that's a thought. No one really notices delivery people. There are so many of them about these days. Everybody gets parcels, they go almost unnoticed,' Andrea said. 'Erin forgot about our one and she even spoke to him.'

'You mean he kidnapped Kim?' asked Jackie. 'But why, and how?'

'Well, we don't know, it's just a thought at the moment. Let's think about what we know. But first, how about we go back to the pub where it's warm? It's freezing here since Kevin turned the heating to timed. We can get a warm drink too.' Cora grabbed her coat and started for the door.

'Good idea.' And Jackie fished in her bag for her car keys.

40

Thursday 20th February Evening

The pub was warm and nearly empty as they were too early for the evening rush. There was no one sitting at the bar. Mal's usual stool at the bar stood empty and the only other people in were sitting at tables. The landlord was delighted to see them back again so soon and told them to sit down and he would bring the drinks over. When they were settled with a pot of tea, half of lager and half of cider, the talk turned to discussing their new theory.

As Jackie was digging her notebook out from the depths of her handbag, Andrea said, 'Something Erin said back at Kim's house. I think it might have been important, but I can't put my finger on what it was. Did either of you get that feeling?'

'No, only what she said about the delivery man,' said Cora.

'Yeah, maybe, but she said something else, I'm sure. Maybe it'll come back to me.'

They sifted through what they knew, what they didn't know and what they thought might have happened, and Jackie made notes in the notebook. Kim had disappeared.

No one had seen her since she had taken her car into Tom Thomas' garage on Saturday 28th December and Nish had taken her home again soon after. This was nearly eight weeks ago. Her house had been left in a state of untidiness and looked like Kim had been in the middle of housework and had expected to return very soon. There were no signs of a struggle, but it was clear she had not gone away of her own accord despite a reputation for taking off on the spur of the moment without letting anyone know. They now knew the dark happenings on her land were nothing to do with black magic and nothing to do with her disappearance. They were Kevin's way of trying to get his mother to sell up and move nearer to his family.

They knew the CCTV camera which Kim had set up over the front door had been dislodged from showing the whole path and everyone who came to the front door, to only showing only a small part of the doorstep. This had been done by a delivery man with a large parcel. They were unsure if it had been done deliberately or accidentally. They knew Kim's car had been in the garage for five weeks and no one had asked about it, and that Tom had returned the car on the first of February, posting the keys through the front door. They knew that someone, either a real delivery man or someone pretending to be one, had entered the house by the front door a few days later, pushing the keys up against the wall, and had left a few minutes later carrying a parcel.

'So, what's your theory, Cora?' asked Andrea.

'What if the man is a real delivery man, he could have known Kim in the past and come across her unexpectedly whilst doing his job, or he could have developed a grudge or something against her, I don't know, anyway he didn't like her.' Cora sat forward in her chair as she became more animated. 'He finds out where she lives and plans. First, he purposely knocks the security camera down to avoid being seen, then he manages to abduct her. I don't know how, but he's got a van. He could have knocked on her door and asked her to come out to the van to help him with a parcel and bundled her in. It could be easily done. There are no houses on the other side of the road and no one would notice.'

'Well, that would certainly explain the house being left as it was, the heating on, the vacuum cleaner plugged in, the full rubbish bin,' agreed Andrea.

'And also why Kim left her bag behind, but took her keys and her phone. She could have had her phone in her pocket and just grabbed her keys as she left in case the front door blew shut.' Cora continued.

'But the front door was shut,' Jackie said.

'He could have locked her in the van, then walked back to shut the door. Anyone looking would just think that Kim had been ahead of him. People don't notice deliveries. It's the perfect cover.'

'If that's true, he definitely had some nerve,' said Andrea, 'to abduct someone in broad daylight. Then to return weeks later to fetch something. He's certainly a cool customer.'

'True, but it may not have been broad daylight, it was late December, it's dark by three thirty or four and if the weather was bad, it could've been dark all day,' reasoned Cora.

'That's true, but if she had her phone, why didn't she phone for help?' asked Jackie.

'He could have knocked her out or taken it from her, anything really. I don't know the details. It's only a theory, but if he had her phone, that could explain how the battery was kept charged up.'

'It certainly explains a lot of things, but what could he have done with her?' asked Andrea.

'Well of course that's what we don't know. Any thoughts?'

'I don't like to say it, but you might be on to something, Cora.' Jackie chewed the end of her pen absent-mindedly. 'He could have killed her, either on purpose or unintentionally.'

'That's a possibility of course and if he has, there's nothing we can do, that's for the police, but if he's got her somewhere, then we have to continue to try to find her, but how I don't know. It's only a theory and I don't know that it really helps us that much.'

'I think it's a good theory. It answers all the unexplained questions.' Andrea reached for her bag. 'Another drink, anyone?'

'Why not,' said Jackie.

Andrea went to the bar to get the drinks. The pub had filled up a lot since they had arrived, and she had to wait to get to the bar. There were a couple of young men in front of her, local lads, larking about and one jokingly pushed the other, catching him off balance and he landed heavily against Andrea.

'Oi there Ben, careful mate, mind the lady,' it was Mal. He had arrived unnoticed as the bar had filled and was halfway through his first pint, but now he slipped off his bar stool and caught Andrea by the elbow, steadying her from the impact.

'Oh, sorry missus,' said Ben grinning sheepishly and turning back to the bar.

Mal guided Andrea to the bar and called to Jimmy, 'Hey Jim, service for the lady here when you're ready. She's just had a push from these two idiots.'

Jimmy finished serving and came over. 'Calm down you two, if you're gonna mess about upsetting my favourite customers,' he winked at Andrea, 'then you can go and play outside with the other bloody kids.'

The young lads laughed, 'Sorry Jim.'

'I'm alright,' said Andrea, 'no harm done. Can I have two halves of lager and a half of cider please.'

'Yes, you can. And these are on the house,' Jimmy beamed.

'Can we have ours on the house too, Jim?' asked the young lad called Ben.

'No, you bloody can't, idiot. You're nowhere near as beautiful as my favourite ladies.' Jimmy winked again and Andrea laughed at the good humoured banter.

Mal sipped his beer and nodding towards Jimmy said loudly, 'Watch him. He's looking for wife number four.'

'Number four!' Andrea laughed.

'I don't want another wife,' said Jimmy, putting down the two lagers and laughing too, 'can't bloody afford it. They've cleaned me out between them. That's why I have to work so hard putting up with daft pillocks like these,' he nodded towards the young lads, 'instead of lying on hot white sand in Barbados showing off my beach body.' He grinned, glancing down at his ample belly as he put down the half of cider. Andrea laughed again and went to pay.

'No, it's on the house, I said so.' He smiled.

'Oh, thanks very much,' said Andrea and she picked up two of the glasses.

'Here I'll bring this over,' Mal picked up the third glass and followed her back to the table.

'Hi Mal,' Jackie looked up and smiled at the young man, 'there was a lot of laughing going on at the bar. What have we missed?'

'Just the lads messing about. It's nice to see you all again. You're becoming regulars. Is it me or Jimmy you fancy?' Mal laughed.

'Whose Jimmy?' asked Cora.

'The landlord,' Andrea reminded her, 'and he's just given us these drinks on the house because a young lad accidentally fell into me.'

'This is certainly one of the friendliest pubs I've been in,' Jackie said, 'but as I don't often go into pubs, I've not got many to compare it to.'

'What brings you in here today, then?' asked Mal, his handsome face smiling at each of them in turn.

'We've just been round to our friend Kim's house again.' Jackie told him.

'Any news on your friend? Have you found her?'

'No, nothing. It's a real mystery. No one seems to have seen her since the end of December and we're in the middle of February now.'

Mal whistled. 'That's a long time for someone to be gone. So, what d'you think's happened?'

'Well, we've not really got any idea. That's what we're trying to find out.'

'We think she may have been kidnapped by a delivery man or someone dressed as a delivery man,' Cora added, and Jackie and Andrea glanced at each other both wondering if Cora should be expounding their theories around willy-nilly, especially in a pub full of people.

'Well, of course it's just an idea we have. We don't know anything. She's probably away on holiday,' Jackie said quickly, 'and it'll turn out to be nothing. We're just playing at solving a puzzle really, that's all.'

Cora looked confused and glanced at Andrea, who casually put her finger to lips, and Cora realising what she meant, nodded.

'Wow, ladies, you've really got your thinking caps on. Kidnapped, blimey, heavy stuff.' Mal looked round at the three women and slowly nodded his head. 'Well, any hints you want about the life of a delivery man just come to me. I've been doing it for five years now.' He grinned. 'We're an odd lot. We come from all walks of life. The company I work for, DTY, employs about six of us locally. Mainly young lads, students, lads between jobs or saving for gap years. I think there's only two of us who are what you'd call permanent. We use their vans and have our different rounds. Mine's Tattershall and Coningsby and the surrounding area, sometimes out to Sleaford if they're busy. It's a good life, I like it. Lots of free time if you want it. Anyway, I won't interrupt you ladies any more, I'll get back to my pint, it'll be missing me,' he laughed, 'see you later ladies, don't do anything silly now, we don't want you getting hurt.'

41

Monday 24th February

The following Monday afternoon, Betty and Sal were keen to hear the latest news.

'So do you think it could be Mal?' asked Betty, looking up from her batik. 'He's a delivery man and immediately told you he worked a different round even though he wasn't asked. Establishing his alibi, d'you think?'

'I don't think it's Mal,' said Cora as she painted dye onto her work. 'He doesn't seem like a kidnapper.'

'They never do,' Betty raised her eyebrows at her, 'that's how they fool everyone.' They laughed, but it was something to think about.

'I don't believe it's Mal either. He's too friendly,' said Andrea, 'I know it sounds daft, but there's something about him that's too kind to make him a kidnapper. Anyway, talking of deliveries, I'm expecting some glazes for the potters today. I hope they come soon. I need to get them mixed up and ready before Wednesday.'

Jackie finally finished her felted table runner, washing it in the sink and carefully wringing it out in a thick towel before laying it out on the table, then shaping the damp wool and teasing out the tassels on the ends. It looked lovely.

'That looks great Jackie,' Andrea gazed at the runner admiringly. 'Well done. All that hard work paid off.'

Jackie grinned and rubbed her aching shoulder. 'Yes, I'm very pleased with it. What now?'

'Take it home and let it dry flat and naturally and it'll be fine.'

Betty had also finished her project, The Sound of Music, and stood at the ironing board ironing off the wax from her batik painting. There was a lot of wax on the finished batik, as there always is, and it needed to be ironed off. Andrea had explained to them all that ironing is fine for paintings as there's always a little bit of wax left in the fibres, and this helps with framing as the fabric stays a bit stiff. If the batiked fabric is for wearing or a cushion or something that will need to be washed, then it has to be processed with hot water, washing soda and soap to remove all traces of wax. Betty stood at the old ironing board surrounded by sheets of paper. She placed the fabric between two sheets and began ironing. As she did so, the paper soaked up the wax. She then discarded the paper and replaced it with fresh and started again until no traces of wax came off on the paper.

'I always like the final ironing off as the batik is revealed, I like the drama,' Betty said, 'but I always forget how much actual ironing there is to do.' She ran an arm across her forehead in a dramatic gesture.

'Wow, look at that,' Andrea crossed the studio for a closer look, 'that's brilliant Betty, your best yet, I think.'

The batiked picture showing a novice nun standing on top of a hill with arms outstretched and with mountains in the background was certainly very good indeed.

Betty beamed, 'Yes, I'm happy with this one. It's not bad,

is it? I'll take it home and search out a frame for it. I think this one's a keeper.'

'The competition isn't for a few months yet,' Cora pointed out.

'I know, but I want to put this up on the wall until then. I know the perfect space.'

'Where are you thinking?' asked Sal.

'On the back wall by the doorway.'

'Ooh yes, it'll look lovely there, good idea.'

Cora and Sal were still working on their respective projects, but as there were only ten minutes left of the class, Jackie and Betty sat and chatted. There was no point starting something new until next week. Jackie had her chess idea lined up, but Betty hadn't got anything worked out yet and planned to have a think about it during the week.

'I might do some wet felting. I haven't done any for a while and Jackie's table runner has inspired me.'

Everyone began to pack away and organise themselves before going home. Betty rolled her finished batik up and put it by the door and Andrea gathered up the tea things, putting them on the tray, ready to take out.

'Where are my car keys?' Betty looked round wildly. 'Bloody things. I had them a minute ago.'

'Pocket?' Sal said and raised her eyebrows as Betty slapped her sides and found them.

They all drifted out, and Andrea locked the door after them. She turned off the wax pots at the switches on the wall and began to tidy round. She took the tea tray into the tiny kitchen, ready for taking back to the house, and returned to the studio to the sound of someone banging on the door. Glancing through the window, she saw a large dark van. *Great, my delivery's arrived, the potters will be pleased.*

'Ok I'm coming, hang on, let me unlock the door.' She

pulled back the bolt and opened the door. 'You? What the hell do you want?'

The next thing she knew, she was being pushed roughly back into the studio, a strong finger poking her hard in the chest, punctuating each word.

'Stay - out - of – my – fucking - business – if - you – know – what's – good – for – you. – You – interfering - old - woman.' He spoke quietly and calmly, pushing her back with each heavy poke.

'What the hell d'you think you're doing?' gasped Andrea as she staggered backwards. Her voice sounded strangely high pitched, and her heart was beating fast, the adrenaline pumping. 'Get out of my studio. I'll call the police.'

She was trapped against the wall now and the man's face was close to hers, his hot breath on her face smelling of stale cigarettes. She looked into his eyes and saw fury and hatred. Andrea was terrified. The man was mad. He was insane; she thought her heart would burst out of her chest. *He's going to kill me.*

He put a large hand round her throat and began to tighten his fingers. She felt her lungs begin to strain as she struggled to catch her breath. Frantically she pulled at his fingers, but he was too strong for her. Pulling back his other arm, he formed his hand into a fist.

'I can hurt you.' He breathed into her face with a slow smile.

'Oh no you can't!' a voice came from nowhere. It was Betty's.

There was a loud crash and Andrea felt hot splashes on her cheek. The face disappeared, and she watched the man slump to the floor. Then she fainted.

The next thing she knew, she was sitting in a chair. Sal had made her a cup of tea and handed it to her. She was shaking and felt very cold and could hardly hold the mug.

The studio seemed full of people. A policewoman was escorting the handcuffed man outside and Betty was talking to another policeman, telling him what had happened.

It seemed that in the confusion of losing her keys, Betty had forgotten her finished batik. Remembering halfway down the lane had turned the car round and returned to the studio to find a large square van outside. She had entered to hear a man threatening Andrea and on the point of punching her or worse, so in the moment she had picked up the nearest thing, the small wax pot, and hit him over the head with it. It hadn't really hurt him as it was quite light, but the wax, although no longer really scalding, was still very hot and the thick liquid had gone all over him. The surprise had caught him off balance and he had fallen, after which she'd sat on his chest and pinned his arms down with her knees. Sal now joined the conversation and added to the story. On seeing the van outside, she had followed Betty in and filmed the whole thing on her phone, then she had phoned the police.

The policeman viewed the phone footage and seemed satisfied with their version of events. He told them all to come down to the police station the next day at nine o'clock to make statements, then went outside to talk to the man.

'Oh, Betty, thank goodness you forgot your batik. It was the illegal fly tipper man. I don't know what he would have done. He was so angry.' Andrea was still shaking as she tried to sip her tea.

'He was furious. I think he's a dangerous man. He was going to hit you, no question.' Betty said. 'Well done, Sal for filming it, we've got absolute proof.'

'Yes, we have, he won't get out of it now,' agreed Sal. 'Good thing too, dangerous bastard.'

When the police had gone, Betty and Sal carefully locked the studio and took Andrea back to her cottage, where they busied around settling her in an armchair with a blanket and more tea. They fed Nonsuch and Mrs Tim, who were pleased to have company, especially company that fed them, and showed their gratitude by curling around Sal's feet as she filled their bowls.

'Are you sure you don't want something to eat?' Sal asked. 'You probably should, shock and everything. How about a piece of toast? A biscuit?'

'No thank you, I couldn't eat a thing. My stomach feels like a tight knot. This tea's fine.' Andrea sipped from her mug and then she began to cry. She could not stop. The tears fell from her eyes and ran down her cheeks onto her blanket. 'I'm sorry. I'm so sorry.'

'It's just the shock, it's a natural response,' said Betty. 'Let it out and you'll feel better.'

So Andrea sat and cried and Betty and Sal sat with her, sipping their tea and holding her hand and after about five minutes, Andrea began to feel better. They sat together quietly for another half an hour or so just talking it through.

'So that was the despicable square van man, the dumper of rubbish,' said Betty. 'What a piece of work. You must have really got under his skin Andrea, well done you. People like him need to be stood up to. What a complete bastard.'

Sal nodded. 'Hopefully he'll be prosecuted and that'll put a stop to his dumping habits, too.'

'That'll make it worth it,' Andrea gave a small grin. At least something good would have come from her frightening ordeal. 'Thank you both for staying, but you must get back to your dogs. They'll be wanting to go out. I'll be fine now. Don't worry about me.'

'We'll be going shortly, but you've had a shock. You shouldn't be alone tonight.' Sal said.

As if on cue, the doorbell rang. Betty went to open it, and

Jackie walked in, with a small bag on her arm and a smile on her face.

'Nurse Ratchet reporting for duty,' she laughed. 'What the hell have you been up to Andrea? Are you alright? Sal rang me and said you'd had a bit of trouble.'

Between them, they explained what had happened and then Betty and Sal said goodbye, having first arranged to come by in the morning to take Andrea to the police station with them to make their statements. Jackie had brought her nightwear and toothbrush and was staying the night and Andrea, overcome by the kindness of her friends, began to cry again.

Halfway down the lane Betty turned to Sal. 'Bugger, I forgot about my bloody batik again.'

42

Tuesday 25th February

Andrea felt much better the following day. Jackie had been upbeat and positive and had pointed out that Andrea had been through much worse. She was not trying to make light of Andrea's confrontation with the violent man, but it was over, finished and could be forgotten, and something positive would come from it. Jackie reminded her she had come through far worse and survived, they had both experienced worse that dreadful night when they had lived through the trauma of losing those they loved and remembering that terrible time always put everything else into perspective as that ordeal would never be finished for either of them.

When Betty and Sal dropped Andrea back home after they had all given their statements at the police station that morning, they stayed for a cup of tea. Jackie returned to hear what had happened and not wanting to miss anything, Cora popped in too. It appeared the violent fly-tipper was a man called Carl Briston, and he had indeed recently started up a local business. He advertised Commercial Waste Collection and was paid by his customers to legally dispose of their waste. Obviously, he didn't; he dumped it in quiet rural spots and so committed two crimes, illegal fly-tipping and fraud, to say nothing of dangerous driving, threatening behaviour and assault. The police told them that this kind of crime was taken very seriously and that Briston could expect a prison sentence of at least twelve months, but it could very easily be nearer to five years. The police had told Andrea that Briston knew she was on to his law-breaking activities and wanted to stop her from getting proof. He knew where she lived because he was the nephew of someone called Ernest Spite who it seems knew her, and he had suggested his nephew go and see Andrea to frighten her off, although it was unclear if Ernest had gone so far as to encourage him to physically attack her. The police would be talking to Mr Spite in due course.

'And I'm not going to be done for assault even though I clocked him with a wax pot,' Betty laughed, 'the police said I had just reason and acted on the spur of the moment to prevent further violence taking place. Though I'm sorry I didn't hurt him, I wish I'd used the heavy one,' and she hooted with laughter again.

Jackie disappeared into Andrea's kitchen and came back a few minutes later with mugs of tea for everyone and a carrot cake that Cora had thoughtfully brought along. They all sat in the pretty sitting room eating cake and silently thinking about recent events. Mrs Tim and Nonsuch were delighted to have company again and curled themselves around everyone's legs, assessing who would give them the most attention. Mrs Tim decided on Betty, and Nonsuch chose Cora and they tucked themselves onto the women's laps and received much chin tickling and ear stroking which both women managed despite the fact they each had a plate of cake,

Suddenly Betty gave a roar of laughter, 'I've just remembered, Sal never told you about her search for the pretty ceramic knobs she needs for her wooden cabinet, did she?'

Sal giggled. 'Oh Betty, I'd hoped you'd forgotten that.'

'Come on, tell us, we could do with a good laugh,' Cora stroked Nonsuch gently.

'Well, she was online looking for some and typed *small knobs* into the search engine!' Betty hooted again and Sal laughed. 'Well, you can just imagine what she saw.'

'I didn't know what would come up. Honestly, I was shocked, I've never seen anything like it before. Don't do it, girls.'

'We're not likely to do it,' laughed Andrea.

'No, and if we did, we wouldn't search for small ones,' Cora giggled.

'The daft thing was, when Sal told me what she'd done I told her to refine her search and make it more specific, I thought she'd add ceramic or pottery, but no, my sweet innocent Sal put in unusual! She certainly got more than she bargained for that time!' Betty roared again and Sal giggled and blushed.

When they had all stopped laughing and Jackie had made more tea, a companionable silence fell over them, five good friends, comfortable in each other's company.

After a while Sal said, 'you did a good thing there Andrea, without you Briston would be polluting the countryside all over the place, he would have eventually moved on and started dumping his crap further afield.'

'Yeah, well done,' said Cora. 'He's a dangerous man.'

Andrea looked a little embarrassed and said, 'I'm sure someone else would have reported him eventually.'

'Yes, but you stood up to him and to Ernest too, miserable little man, trying to intimidate you so you'd stop reporting everything,' said Jackie. 'And I know the wildlife will be pleased he's been stopped.' She laughed.

Andrea laughed at the lighthearted teasing. She said, 'I know you think I'm all hippy dippy, out there talking to the wind and the grass, and I don't care, someone has to stand up for the creatures that live here and I'm very happy to do it. Now let's change the subject to something more interesting. Is there any more carrot cake?'

They finished the cake, and the conversation shifted inevitably to Kim. They talked through every aspect of her mysterious disappearance they could think of. Could it be Mal? He was a delivery man and according to Cora's theory, perfectly placed to abduct Kim in his van whilst going virtually unnoticed by the general public. He had been very quick to let them know his round was not local, although they only had his word for that, but if he had taken Kim, why had he done it and where was he keeping her? Well, of course, they didn't know where he lived and even if they did, he probably wouldn't be keeping her there. He may even have a lock-up garage somewhere with Kim a prisoner inside. They wondered whether to inform the police of their theory but decided that as they had absolutely no proof, they would not, for the time being at least. Although they all agreed that the next time the three of them were in The Trio of Fools, they would study Mal a little more carefully.

'So what do you plan to do next?' asked Betty, 'is there anyone you haven't spoken to yet? Anyone who might have something to say or a clue that you haven't thought of yet?'

'I don't really know, I feel like we've spoken to everyone we can think of,' said Andrea, 'and of course it doesn't necessarily have to be someone local, she could have been taken by someone from her past who doesn't even live round here.'

'There's nothing we can do if that's the case, but assuming it isn't and it is someone local, we need to continue to try to work out where she could be.' Jackie said,

'If only Nish would come back. He was the last person to see Kim and could maybe tell us something. He could have seen someone waiting for her when he took her home or something. He wouldn't think anything about it at the time, of course, but in the light of what we believe might have happened—'

'That's certainly a thought,' Cora said, collecting up the empty cake plates and stacking them on the tray. 'How about we go to his flat? There's a tiny chance he's returned, but even so, at least we can see where he lives?'

'Well, as we don't know what else to do, I think it's a good idea,' Andrea agreed, 'and we can drop into The Trio of Fools while we're in Stickville and maybe chat some more with Mal.'

'And if we go Thursday, there will be steak and kidney pie on the menu,' Jackie laughed.

'Sorry Thursday's out for me,' said Cora. 'I've got an appointment at last. I've been waiting ages so don't want to cancel. Can we go Wednesday instead, after Andrea's finished her pottery class?'

'Oh Cora, I hope it's nothing serious.' Jackie looked concerned. 'I know it can take ages to see a doctor at the moment.'

'Who said anything about a doctor? It's an appointment with my hairdresser. She's been away on holiday for three weeks and I look like a shaggy dog.' Cora grinned round the room, and everyone laughed.

'Okay by me,' said Andrea and it was agreed they would go Wednesday afternoon. Jackie was disappointed about the pie, but she made the best of it.

Between them, they gathered up the mugs and Cora took the tray out to the kitchen. Mrs Tim and Nonsuch, having been temporarily dislodged nevertheless resigned themselves and as soon as Betty and Cora had vacated their seats, jumped back up and settled down again.

Betty and Sal were putting on their coats and Jackie was looking for her scarf, which had fallen down the side of her armchair when Andrea cleared her throat. 'Er hmm. Can I just say thank you to all of you for being so kind? I really appreciate it, you know.'

'And can I say a big thank you too, an even bigger and more important thank you than Andrea's' said Betty laughing, 'to Cora for bringing that delicious carrot cake!'

43

The man watched as the woman lay motionless on the bed, eyes open, staring. He wiped the bedposts, the wooden chair and the door handles both inside and out. He picked up the mug, the bowl, and the bucket and left the room. He unscrewed the bolt from the door and put it in his pocket. He removed his balaclava and washed the mug, the bowl, and the bucket, then after removing his surgical gloves, he left the building.

44

Wednesday 26th February

It was later than they planned when Cora, Andrea and Jackie drove round to the Hospice charity shop in Stickville High Street. There had been a disaster in the pottery room right at the end of the class. Someone had not put the lid on one of the buckets of liquid glaze properly and when they'd tried to replace it on the shelf, the whole lot had spilled everywhere. It was a huge mess, to say nothing of the wastage and Andrea wasn't best pleased as not only had it taken her over an hour to clear it up, it had also been a costly accident as glazes were expensive.

There was a blue door next to the shop which obviously led to the flat above. They knocked on it. No answer. They hadn't really expected an answer as they guessed Nish was probably still in Spain, but they thought they would try on the off chance that he didn't live alone.

'Let's just ask in the shop, seeing as it's still open and we're here.' Cora said as she walked in, 'come on, then.'

The shop was bright and warm, but empty of customers. A man in his late twenties, overweight and wearing a football shirt over a thick jumper, stood next to an older woman.

Long strands of grey hair escaped her pinned bun, and she wore a large pink cardigan over a long flowery skirt with four sets of wooden beads hanging round her neck. They were both behind the counter and the woman was doing something with a huge box of plastic coat hangers whilst the man watched her. They both looked up and smiled as the three women entered.

'Hello', the man smiled but could not make eye contact.

'Hello,' said Jackie. 'I wonder if you could help us?' she walked up to the counter and Cora followed. Andrea went off to look round the shop but stayed within earshot.

'We're looking for Nish, who lives upstairs. Do you know him?'

'I like Nish,' said the man gazing at a point near Jackie's elbow, 'he's funny.'

'I think he's away at the moment.' The woman looked up from the box of coat hangers. 'A family funeral, I think he said.'

'A funeral,' said the man to Jackie's bag, 'someone died. Poor Nish.'

'Yes, poor Nish,' agreed Jackie.

'I don't suppose you know when he's coming back, do you?' asked Cora.

'No, I'm afraid not,' the woman replied. 'We don't see much of him really, he just pops in occasionally to say hello or collect a parcel that's been left or something.'

'He says hello to me,' the man smiled at Cora's coat, 'he's my friend.'

'He sounds like a very nice man,' said Jackie.

'Oh, you don't know him then? I thought he was a friend of yours.' The woman looked concerned that she had inadvertently given away private information.

'Oh, it's fine,' Jackie explained. 'He mends my car, he's a mechanic at Tom Thomas's garage. I know him, but not very well. Tom told me he was away, but he didn't know when he would be back, so we thought we'd pop by and see if he'd returned. I need to ask him something.' *Oh well, there's some truth mixed in with the lies.*

'Nish mends cars. He's a nice man, he says hello to me, he does.' The man beamed round at them, although still not quite making eye contact. 'Nish is away. Someone died.'

'Yes, you're right, Dereck, but I expect he'll be back again soon.' The woman smiled at Dereck, then turning back to Jackie and Cora she said, 'We should really be closing it's gone half past four, is there anything else?'

'I'll take this please,' said Andrea, walking over and putting a pretty blue cut glass vase on the counter together with a five pound note.

'Of course. Dereck, can you put the money in the till and give the lady her change please while I wrap the vase in some newspaper. It's four pounds, so you need to give her one pound please.'

Dereck seemed delighted to have a job to do and carefully smoothed out the note before putting it neatly in the till and holding out a one pound coin to Andrea. There was a charity box on the counter for a local donkey sanctuary and Andrea said to put the change in the box. Dereck looked at the woman, who nodded and smiled, and then he carefully dropped the coin into the box.

'A charity box in a charity shop, that's nice,' said Andrea.

'Yes, Dereck loves the donkeys, so we have a box on the counter for any odd change that people don't want. Then every now and again we go to the sanctuary to pass the money on,' explained the woman.

'We go to help the donkeys,' Dereck smiled at the charity box. 'I love the donkeys and the donkeys love me.'

'I'm sure they do.'

‘Nish has a donkey upstairs,’ Dereck smiled up at the ceiling.

The woman looked fondly at Dereck. ‘Now Dereck, you remember Nish was joking. He doesn’t really have a donkey upstairs, he was joking.’

‘Nish is funny,’ Dereck was laughing now, ‘he said he has a donkey upstairs, but he was joking. He’s so funny. He said the noise was a donkey, it was a joke.’

‘The noise?’ Cora asked Dereck, ‘did you hear a noise?’

‘Yes, a noise like a donkey. Stamp, stamp, stamp. He came in the shop and told me he’d got a donkey. It was a joke. Nish is very funny.’ Dereck laughed loudly as he remembered Nish’s joke.

‘When was this Dereck?’ asked Andrea.

‘Today,’ the man laughed up at the ceiling.

‘No Dereck, you remember it was weeks ago, not today,’ the woman smiled affectionately at Dereck, then explained, ‘Nish had bought a new armchair and the noise was him getting it upstairs and then in the right place.’

‘It was weeks ago,’ Dereck shook his head. ‘Not today.’

‘Have you heard the donkey since then?’ asked Andrea.

‘It wasn’t a donkey, it was a joke. Nish is so funny.’ More laughing.

‘Have you heard the pretend donkey again?’ Andrea persisted.

The woman looked at her warily, wondering what was going on. Was she mocking her son?

‘The pretend donkey, hahaha,’ Dereck was delighted. ‘Today. I heard the pretend donkey today. Nish is very funny.’

‘I think we really must close now,’ the woman said firmly, walking from behind the counter towards the door. ‘I’m sorry to rush you, but we must get home.’

'Wait,' said Andrea, 'do you have a spare key for Nish's flat? For emergencies or the like?'

'Well yes, there's one kept in the drawer in case of burst pipes or leaks. Why?'

'I think there may be someone up there. I think the noise Dereck heard might be the woman we have spent the last eight weeks searching for.'

'You think Kim's up there?' Jackie said, amazed. 'Oh my goodness Andrea, you could be right! Kim could be upstairs. Please, can you get the key?' This last was to the woman who was looking between them, very confused.

'Certainly not,' she said. 'I'm not giving out Nish's key. It's his private flat and apart from anything else, with the greatest respect, I don't know you from Adam.'

'Our friend has been missing since Christmas and we've been looking for her. We know Nish was the last person to see her and we only have his word that he's gone to Spain.' Cora joined in.

'Nish has gone to a funeral.' Dereck said, still smiling.

As briefly as she could, Andrea explained their concerns for Kim and the woman stared at her wide eyed.

'Goodness gracious,' she said. 'I've never heard anything like it in my life. Well, if this is true, then the flat must be searched, but not by you. We have to get the police.'

'I completely agree,' said Cora, 'I've just rung them, they're on their way. I'm going to ring Kevin now.'

While they waited for the police to arrive the woman introduced herself as Marnie, she was Dereck's mother, and she managed the shop which was open four days a week from 10 to 4. She explained that they had stayed opened a little longer today due to having received a large, sealed box of donations at ten minutes to four and they needed to look inside to be sure there was nothing that needed dealing with immediately. It was not unknown for charity shops to receive donations containing a dead rat for instance, mixed in with the clothes, or a mouse nest if the box had come from a deceased estate for example, and these things needed to be dealt with sooner rather than later. Luckily today there had been no rotting rodents in the box, just old clothes, a few books and a lot of plastic coat hangers.

Marnie asked Dereck to see to the door sign, which he did with great care, turning the hanging Open sign round to display Closed. As he did so, a police car drew up outside and two police officers got out. Dereck stood there staring at the flashing blue light.

'Come over here Dereck,' said Marnie, 'let them come in.'

'But they can't come in,' Dereck pointed out, 'the sign says closed.'

'Just this once. It'll be fine.' Marnie smiled fondly at Dereck and Dereck laughed loudly at the rule breaking.

The police officers came into the shop, a young policewoman and their old friend Sergeant Potts. *The young one doesn't look old enough to drive, let alone arrest anyone*, thought Andrea. *Oh god, I'm getting so old.*

Sergeant Potts was aware of the situation from Kevin's report of Kim having been missing for weeks. Between them, the three women told the police officers why they thought she might be in Nish's flat and they agreed it was worth a look. Marnie gave them the keys and the police left the shop, with Andrea, Cora and Jackie following, while Marnie and Dereck stayed behind.

'You three go back and wait inside,' said Sergeant Potts sternly, 'this could be a crime scene and we don't need you lot messing it up.' Reluctantly the three women trailed back inside the shop.

They could hear the police clumping up the uncarpeted stairs and walking across the floor above.

‘It’s Nish’s donkey!’ Dereck laughed.

After what seemed like an age but in reality was only about ten minutes, they heard footsteps on the stairs again, slower this time, and hushed voices. The policewoman passed the shop window and came into the shop, her arm round the waist of a hunched figure wrapped in a blanket. Gently guiding the figure to a chair, she nodded at the little group, who were staring in amazement. It was Kim.

45

Friday 28th February & Monday 3rd March

Jackie, Cora and Andrea arrived at the hospital and headed up to the third floor, ward 3B.

'Only two visitors at a time, I'm afraid,' said a nurse at the desk. 'Mrs Merchant has one already. Her son is here. You can wait in there.' She pointed to a doorway off to the left.

'Thanks,' said Cora to the nurse. 'You go first Andrea, and we'll wait in there. When you come out, you can swap with us. We'll take it in turns.'

'Alright, shall I take the grapes?' Andrea took the bag and went into the ward.

Kim was in a small private room with a window which overlooked the car park. She was sitting propped up in bed, looking very thin and fragile, lost in a blue hospital nightie that swamped her. A drip was fixed to the back of her hand, attached to a half empty pouch of clear liquid suspended above the bed. Her pale face was almost ghostly and there were big purple bags under her sunken eyes, but she was smiling at Kevin, who was sitting next to the bed holding her hand.

‘Sorry to intrude,’ said Andrea. ‘I just wanted to see how the patient was.’

‘Andrea, come in, sit here. I’ll get another chair,’ Kevin jumped up.

‘No, you stay put. I’ll get a chair.’ Andrea drew up a chair next to Kevin’s and sat down. ‘Well Kim, how are you? It’s good to see you.’

Kim began to cry.

‘It’s okay mum, it’s all over now, you’re safe.’ Kevin squeezed her hand.

‘I’m sorry, shall I go? Come back another time, maybe—when you’re feeling stronger?’ Andrea went to stand.

‘No,’ said Kim, her voice a whisper, ‘I’m fine. It’s all just a bit overwhelming, that’s all.’

‘It’s been a lot for mum to take in,’ Kevin said. ‘It seems she was drugged for the whole time, almost nine weeks, kept in one room. She was dehydrated, and she’s a bit weak and still a little confused. But you’re safe now, aren’t you mum, and everything’s going to be alright.’

‘Thanks to you both,’ said Kim, looking at Kevin and Andrea through watery eyes.

‘Not only us by any means, but it was also a joint effort between the four of us,’ Andrea smiled at Kim. ‘Cora and Jackie are outside, hoping to pop in and say hello.’

‘I’ll go and let one of the others in,’ said Kevin, ‘I’ll be back in a little while, mum.’ He bent over and kissed her forehead.

Cora came in and joined Andrea. ‘Good to see you Kim, ’she said, gently patting Kim’s bony hand.

After a few minutes, Andrea left and Jackie went in. Between them, the three women stayed only about ten minutes as Kim was very tired and they didn’t want to keep mother and son apart for too long. They said goodbye, with promises to come back soon, and went down the stairs to the café in the hospital foyer. Seated by the window with their coffees they looked at each other and grinned.

'Wow,' said Cora, 'a job well done, I think.'

The following Monday at the textiles class, Betty and Sal were agog to hear the news of Kim's safe return and how she had been found in Nish's flat. Andrea, Cora and Jackie had a few more details now as Kevin had phoned them with an update. The hospital had told Kevin that Kim had been drugged slowly over a period of weeks, administered in her drinks. It had built up quickly and after a few days, Kim had become completely passive and malleable. The police still did not know for sure why she had been abducted but had established that during the time of her captivity she had bought an extremely expensive car—a brand new Porche for around one hundred and sixty thousand pounds. It had been delivered to an address in East Kime. It seems the car had been immediately resold to a cash buyer and was now owned by a collector in the south of England. All very legal. However, there was no sign of the money which amounted to just over one hundred and twenty thousand pounds, the car having been resold at a lower price. The police were still looking for Nish as the most obvious suspect, even though it seems that the kidnapper had kept a mask on the whole time and wiped down the surfaces in the room where Kim had been locked up, removing most of the fingerprints, although a few remained that had yet to be identified.

'So he wanted her money,' said Betty, 'her lump sum payout. But I don't know how he thought he'd get away with it. Keeping her in his own flat, that wasn't very clever.'

'I agree, but I guess he wasn't thinking properly and had nowhere else to keep her,' said Jackie.

‘It’s weird that he wiped away his fingerprints though, isn’t it?’ Andrea mused, ‘I mean if he lives there, what’s the point?’

‘I don’t understand how he could have bought the car with her money, I mean banks are so strict these days about their customers spending large amounts. Why didn’t they check?’ asked Sal.

‘Kevin said they did. The police checked with her bank and they had verified the payment after speaking directly to Kim on the phone. They said she had sounded normal and had answered all the security questions correctly so they could find no reason not to authorise the transaction.’ Andrea explained.

‘Where’s Nish now?’ asked Sal. ‘Haven’t the police got him?’

‘No, not yet, but it’s only a matter of time before they catch up with him. I’m sure we’ll hear from Kevin as soon as they do.’ Andrea crossed the studio to where Cora was unrolling her batiked silk scarf which had been kept on the shelf from the previous week. ‘Anyway Cora, how’s your scarf looking?’

‘It’s ready for ironing and then washing. I hope it doesn’t lose all the colour when it’s washed.’

‘Well, it’ll lose some as you know, the silk fibres are thin and only hold so much dye and this is Ponge silk, very light and delicate so the colours won’t be strong, but it’ll be lovely, I know it.’

Andrea was right, she usually was about fabrics and dyes, and Cora’s scarf, despite a lot of excess colour coming out in the wash which made Cora panic, turned out beautifully. It was a pretty turquoise blue with tiny raspberry pink flowers and acid green leaves at either end. It really was lovely.

'Oooh, that's gorgeous Cora,' said Sal, as Cora proudly held it up, 'well done, one of your best, I think.'

'Wow, that's stunning,' Jackie agreed. 'It'll look fabulous on summer evenings.'

Cora laughed as she let the fine silk run through her fingers. 'I'm not waiting till the summer. I'm going to wear it now.'

'Silk is great for keeping warm,' Andrea pointed out, 'despite it being so flimsy and looking insubstantial it works like magic, keeping you warm in winter and cool in summer, and it's not heavy or itchy, it'll make a good winter warmer. That's why a lot of people wear silk underwear.'

'There you go Cora, your next project can be making silk pants,' Betty laughed. 'You can keep your bits cosy and look sexy at the same time.'

Cora screeched with laughter, 'My bits are quite cosy enough thanks and as for sexy, well, I wouldn't want to be responsible for driving the innocent men of Drayflot out of their minds with lust and desire.'

Everyone laughed and Cora grinned.

Cora could not settle down to anything else that day. This often happened when someone finished a project. They needed a bit of breathing space before starting on the next one, so she sat admiring her delicate scarf and chatting to Sal as she worked on her wooden cabinet.

Ping.

A message came through from Kevin.

I'm going to ring you, I have news is it convenient? K

Yes, of course. C.

. . .

'Kevin's got news he's going to ring in a minute,' Cora announced. 'I expect they've got Nish.'

'Well put him on loudspeaker when he does,' said Jackie and the others agreed.

The phone rang almost immediately, and Kevin's voice was heard. Cora told him he was on speakerphone and they were all there, Betty and Sal too, and asked if that was okay. Kevin said it was fine and yes, the news was about Nish.

The police had been in touch and had told Kevin that Nish had returned and had a watertight alibi. He had definitely been in Spain for the funeral of a relative. His passport showed the dates when he left England and returned a month later. There was absolutely no doubt that Nish knew nothing about Kim being held in his flat. They said he hadn't given his keys to anyone, and he had no idea who could have used his flat while he was away. The police had taken Nish's fingerprints for elimination purposes and discovered the prints they had found in the flat that hadn't been wiped away, unsurprisingly belonged to Nish. The person or persons who had abducted and held Kim hostage for over eight weeks were still unknown, and there was still no sign of the money.

The police had asked Kevin if he knew of anyone with a grudge against his mother and he had told them no, he didn't. They told him they were giving full priority to catching the abductor or abductors, but as the stolen money was cash and the transaction was legal, and as Kim could remember nothing at all, and due to limited funds and resources and the spate of burglaries that was rife in the area, they were overstretched and there was not much they could do. They told Kevin they were glad Kim had suffered no lasting harm and should she remember anything else, she or Kevin was to get in touch immediately.

'So it sounds like they're giving up,' said Cora. 'Or at

least not making finding him a priority, despite what they say.'

'How d'you feel about that, Kevin?' asked Andrea.

'Well, obviously I think the bastard should be found and soon too, but to be honest at the moment I'm so grateful that mum's been found safe and sound, well sort of anyway, that I can't think about anything else.'

'How's she getting on?' asked Jackie, 'is she on the mend?'

'Yes, she's doing well. I think the hospital will be letting her go home in a few days or so.'

'Doesn't she remember anything at all? I know the police will have asked, but surely she must remember something.'

'She says she remembers nothing and doesn't want to talk about it. She just wants to forget about it as it's over and done with now, as it's only money after all.'

'Only money, ha!' said Cora, 'only one hundred and sixty thousand pounds!'

'I know, but that's how she feels, so I'm going to respect her feelings. I'm just so grateful she's safe.'

Kevin went on to explain that Kim didn't want to stay on her own in Stickville and would be coming to stay with him and Carol in Sleaford for a while to convalesce. He told them he was hoping that when she was completely better, they could persuade her to sell her land and house and buy a place in Sleaford near to them. Then the conversation ended and after many expressions of 'that's great news' and 'the best outcome' and lots of 'goodbye's and a few 'speak soon's, Cora hung up. The women looked at each other and shrugged. Kim had been found, but the mystery remained unanswered.

46

Tuesday 4th March.

The three women were sitting in Cora's living room looking out through the French windows at her neat little garden. It was Tuesday morning, and they had planned to go to The Point for coffee and a walk, but Jackie had seen a post on social media saying it would be closed for a few days as they were having a problem with their electrics.

'It's such a shame, I was looking forward to walking on the beach in the sunshine,' said Andrea taking a sip from her mug, 'and to some nice coffee too.' She made a face and laughed as Cora told her to be grateful that she'd got instant.

'I agree, but rather than sit here complaining, let's go somewhere else. How about we pop over to Stickville?' Jackie suggested. 'We might find a new walk. You never know, we've never really looked for public footpaths—there could be some lovely walks around there.'

'Why not?' Cora stood up from her chair, sending Ollie, who had been snuggled on her lap, flying, 'Oh sorry Ollie, I forgot you were there. We can go to the pub and have lunch and maybe Mal will be in there, possibly even Nish. You never know.'

So it was decided and three hours later they found themselves in The Trio of Fools ordering lunch, as Jackie had said, 'It would be rude not to despite it being a Tuesday and therefore no steak and kidney pie on the menu.'

They had found a nice walk at the edge of the town, a signpost pointing over a stile led them on a circular track around fields, across a stream, through a little wood and back to where they started. It was lovely. Taking a couple of hours, it had been perfect and although sadly there were no views of the sea, they had seen yellow coltsfoot and primroses flowering along the banks of the stream; the daffodils were in full bud ready to burst into colour very soon and there were signs of the bluebells yet to come in the small woodland. Spring was definitely here at last.

The pub was reasonably busy, but they quickly spotted their usual table by the fire was free. Andrea ran to grab it, nodding as she did so to Mal, who was sitting at the bar. She felt like a regular having a usual table and being on nodding terms with other regulars. Jackie and Cora went to the bar and ordered two jacket potatoes, one with chilli and cheese and one with prawns in Marie-Rose sauce, and one ham, egg and chips, then they went to join Andrea by the fire. Although it was early spring, there was still a nip in the air and the fire was very welcome after their walk. As soon as they were settled the conversation as usual turned to Kim's kidnapping.

'So Nish is innocent,' said Andrea, 'well who on earth kidnapped Kim then?'

'Just when we thought the mystery was solved it goes and does this to us.' Cora nodded. 'Who knew that Nish's flat would be empty whilst he was away? That's the question now.'

'Yes, and who could get hold of a key to it?'

There were a lot of people who knew Nish was away and they made a list. Heading the list were obviously Marnie and Dereck from the Hospice charity shop, although they discounted them immediately, if by any strange chance they had been responsible it was fairly certain that Dereck would not have been able to keep it a secret for over eight weeks. Next on the list was Nish's employer Tom Thomas, then came Mal, Jimmy the landlord of The Trio of Fools, and every one of the regulars in the pub. It wasn't a secret. In fact, there were probably many more people who had heard he was away at a funeral.

'Well, that's got us precisely nowhere,' said Jackie. 'We can't go talking to all the regulars in here it would take forever and even if we did, they're hardly going to 'fess up to kidnapping Kim and keeping her in Nish's flat.'

The waitress brought over the plates of food and the conversation stopped as they got stuck in. They were hungrier than they had realised, and as usual, it was delicious. When they were finished a different waitress came over to collect their empty plates. It was Erin.

'Hello, I thought it was you, that's why I said I'd come and get your dirties,' Erin said as she smiled round at them.

'Erin,' said Cora, 'What are you doing here? We haven't seen you here before.'

Erin laughed. 'I work here. I've been part time now since Christmas, just a few hours every day except Sundays, helping with the lunches in the kitchen. I don't often come out barside except when it's empty or they're short staffed and I'm needed. I've worked in pubs before, so I know how to pull a pint.' She laughed again.

'Do you like it?' asked Andrea, 'working in the kitchen, I mean.'

'It's fine, nice staff and very warm too. The perfect place

to work in the cold weather, not like my last job. It was freezing in the winter there. I also get to take home any left-overs, which is great as it saves me cooking when I get back. Anyway, better get these dirties back to the kitchen and washed up or I'll be in trouble,' she laughed again and began to stack the plates.

'You'll have heard about Kim,' said Jackie, 'being found in Nish's flat and everything?'

'Yes, how awful, poor Kim. I believe she's still in hospital recovering from starvation.' Erin balanced the plates on her tray.

'Well yes, sort of, but her son told us she's getting on well and will be home soon. I don't suppose you know who in here knew Nish was going to Spain, do you?'

'No, as I say, I'm usually in the kitchen. You should maybe ask Mal,' she nodded behind them to where Mal sat at the bar with his back to them. 'He knows everything that goes on in here and outside too. These delivery men get around and know everyone's business.' She laughed again, and picking up the tray loaded with the stacked plates, made her way back to the kitchen.

'Did someone say my name?' Mal turned on his bar stool and directed his handsome smile at the three women. 'Was Erin talking about me? Whatever she's said don't believe it.' They all laughed.

'We were just wondering who knew that Nish was going to Spain,' said Jackie.

'Ha, everyone knew, Nish came in here the evening before he went and told us all he was going to the funeral, said his uncle had died. He said he wasn't too upset as he didn't really know the old feller, probably wouldn't have gone if Tom hadn't been so grateful to him for keeping the garage going while he was in hospital and giving him the time off, but he was really looking forward to seeing all his cousins again. Seems like he's got loads of them and there was going to be some serious partying.' Mal laughed again. 'It's alright for some, getting paid to go and party. Why d'you want to know anyway? I know you love asking questions. What d'you think happened?'

'We don't know,' replied Jackie, 'we only know what the police have told us, which isn't very much, that Kim was kept in Nish's flat while he was away.'

'So, you're wondering who knew it was empty? I see, well, the answer's everyone.' Mal laughed again. 'You're going to have to read some more detective stories to work this one out, aren't you ladies?' he smiled and winked. 'How's your friend anyway? I hear she was rich and kidnapped for her money. She was starved wasn't she?'

'Well, not quite,' said Cora, 'but she was definitely not in the best of health when she was found. Anyway, she's recovering well and will be coming out of hospital in a few days, so that's good news.'

'Good news for sure,' smiled Mal, and he turned back to the bar and his pint.

'That's just reminded me,' said Andrea quietly to Cora and Jackie, 'as Kim's due out soon. How about we go round and tidy her house up a bit before she comes home?'

'What? You hate housework. What's come over you?' laughed Jackie.

'I know, but it's less boring with the three of us and it'll be nice for her not to come back to a mess.'

'I think it's a good idea,' said Cora, 'but she's not going back to her house. She's going to be staying with Kevin and Carol at least for a while.'

'I know, but I assume she'll be popping back first to collect some essentials, so she'll see all the mess and it could be really depressing for her, you know taking her mind back to the day it all happened,' Andrea reasoned, 'at least if it's tidy it won't be so bad.'

'Yes, of course, it's a nice idea. Let's do it. I'll message Kevin and check it's okay for us to go in,' and Jackie got out her phone.

The afternoon was getting late, and it was time for them to leave, so they finished their drinks and were just gathering their coats to go home when Kevin came back to them. He was at the hospital and Kim was much improved. She would be coming out Thursday or Friday, he thought it was a very kind offer of theirs to go in and tidy round and it would be much appreciated as yes, he would be taking her back there first to collect some clothes and toiletries before going on to Sleaford.

So it was all arranged. Tomorrow afternoon after Andrea had finished her pottery classes, they would go round to Kim's house and give it a bit of a tidy up.

47

Wednesday 5th March

Cora, Jackie, and Andrea went in through Kim's back door. The days were getting longer, although it was still a few weeks before the clocks changed to British Summer Time and gave them an extra hour of daylight in the evenings. They shut the back door behind them and put their essential supplies of cakes and biscuits on the counter and the milk in the fridge.

'Now then, where to begin?' said Cora taking off her coat and hanging it with the others in the hallway. 'How about we start in the kitchen?'

They rolled up their sleeves and got down to work. Normally all three of them would have shied away from housework, only really doing their own out of necessity, and they certainly couldn't have imagined ever volunteering to do anyone else's. But doing this for Kim felt like closure, they had visited her a couple more times in hospital, but they knew they probably wouldn't be seeing much of her again once she moved to Sleaford and that was fine as although they'd become quite fond of Kevin they had never really been close friends with Kim. It had been the mystery of her disappearance that they had enjoyed and now that she had been found this felt like a good way to end it.

They began work on the kitchen. They had washed up and emptied the rubbish bin on a previous visit so it was just a matter of wiping down the counter and giving the floor a quick wash, after all they were only making the house look tidy for Kim's brief return not doing a deep clean. The sitting room was next, and they began by tidying the clutter from the surfaces and wiping away the months of dust. They polished and cleaned; they chatted and sang and laughed, and the time passed quickly. Andrea began to clear the papers lying in a disordered heap on the table and noticed the old passport had gone.

'I expect Kevin took it when he was here last.' Jackie said.

'Why would he take an out-of-date passport?' asked Cora.

'He probably wanted to send it off to get his mum a new one. That's obviously what she was doing before she was interrupted. Maybe he's planning a holiday for them all.' Jackie had it all worked out.

Before returning the vacuum cleaner to its proper home in the cupboard under the stairs, they had a small ceremony, raising their mugs of tea in a toast to the hoover that had stood faithful sentry in the centre of the room for nearly nine weeks. They then immediately realised they still needed it and had to retrieve it from the cupboard again whilst falling about laughing. They were surprised at how quickly the time went and actually how much more fun housework was when they did it together.

It had taken longer than they had thought it would to sort out the sitting room and time was getting on, but as none of them had any plans for the evening, they soldiered on. After giving the front hall a quick going over, they went upstairs to sort out the bedrooms and give the bathroom a wipe round, although to be fair to Kim, it didn't need much.

Another cup of tea and a few biscuits later and they were all upstairs in Kim's bedroom, the main room at the front. The duvet was still across the orthopaedic pillow, which no longer looked like a hunched figure, and they laughed as they remembered their fear all those weeks ago when they thought they had stumbled across Kim's dead body.

It was beginning to get dark, and Cora had just switched on the light when Andrea put her hand to her ear.

'Shhh,' she said quietly, 'what's that noise?'

'What noise, I can't hear anything,' said Jackie.

'Me neither,' said Cora.

'Shhh!' Andrea whispered urgently, 'be quiet, I think there's somebody trying to get in.'

'What! Are you sure?' Jackie's hearing wasn't the best.

'Yes, I can hear the front door being opened. Quick Cora, turn the light off. Whoever it is may not come upstairs and if we keep quiet, they might go away.'

Cora reached for the switch and turned off the light. 'Could it be Kevin?'

'Don't see why,' Andrea whispered. 'He knows we're here and would have called out.' But Jackie quickly sent a message to Kevin.

Kevin, are you in Kim's house? J.

Kevin replied instantly

No, I'm still at work. Why? K.

We're in Kim's house cleaning up, ready for her return, and someone else is here. J.

An intruder? K.

Yes. J.

Get out quick. Don't hang about, get out! K.
Don't think we can. J.

They stood very still listening, hearts beating fast. The bedroom door was very slightly ajar and in the dark silence, they heard the front door being slowly pushed open and then very quietly closed. They held their breath as they waited to hear what the intruder would do, go into the living room or come upstairs. Then they heard the soft tread of footsteps slowly coming up the stairs. They looked frantically around for something to arm themselves with and motioned to each other to spread out around the room, Jackie by the front window, Andrea in the middle by the wardrobe, and Cora back behind the door. The carpeted steps came nearer and nearer, echoing the thumping of their hearts. *Oh my god, who the hell is it?* Andrea's heart was beating so fast she thought she'd faint and looking round at the other two, she could see they looked to be in a similar state. The footsteps stopped at the top of the stairs, and then the door opened slowly, and a torch shone on the floor. *Oh god! What if he's armed!* The torch light flashed round the room and immediately lit up Jackie and Andrea.

'What the hell!' the muffled voice was that of a man. 'Get over there. I've got a knife.' He motioned for Andrea to join Jackie and get into the far corner by the window.

Dazzled by the torch light neither woman could properly make out the figure and couldn't see if he had a knife or not, but they were taking no chances, so they did as they were told and stood together in the corner he had indicated with his torch. The man moved towards them and as he did so Cora jumped out from behind the door, and using a picture she'd grabbed from off the wall, smashed it over his head. She then quickly turned on the light at the switch on the wall. The picture glass broke into pieces but didn't hurt the man who they could now see was wearing a thick woollen hat. He turned and grabbed Cora by the arm, pushing her roughly into the far corner of the room with the other two. The women stood looking at him; he was tall and dressed all in black. He wore gloves and had a scarf pulled up over the lower part of his face and his hat pulled down. All that was visible were his eyes.

I've seen those eyes before. Where have I seen them? 'Who are you? What do you want?' asked Andrea in a shaky voice.

'Shut up!' growled the man through the scarf.

'I think you should know we've called the police,' said Cora. *It's worth a try.*

'No, you haven't. Now get on the floor and keep quiet and maybe you won't get hurt.'

They got down on the floor. They were trapped in the corner of the room furthest from the door between the bed and the wall, with the burglar blocking the way past. There was no way out.

'It's not easy for me to get on the floor you know,' said Jackie. 'I've got sciatica.'

'Just do it,' growled the man again.

'Well, just so you know, I'll need help to get back up again.'

The man turned to Kim's dresser which was in the bay of the window next to where the three women were crouched and began pulling out the drawers and looking through them. He seemed to know what he was doing, working from the bottom to the top, saving time by not having to close them again. From one drawer, he pulled out a small wooden box, he opened it and tipped all the contents out onto the top of the dresser, then scooped them up and put them into his pocket. The three women couldn't see properly from their position on the floor, but from the sound of it, he had discovered Kim's jewellery. He continued to rifle through the drawers, turning over the contents with his gloved hands.

'Hey, be careful,' said Cora, 'we've been tidying up.' She winked and motioned to Andrea and Jackie, who caught her meaning began to harass the man.

'Yes,' said Andrea, 'watch what you're doing. We've just sorted all that out.'

'You're making a hell of a mess, you know,' Jackie joined in.

'Shut up!'

'Perhaps we can help you. What is it you're looking for?' continued Jackie. 'Save you making more mess than necessary.'

'Yes, can we help?' asked Andrea sweetly, 'are you looking for valuables? Well, I suppose that's a silly question really. What else would you be looking for?'

'Of course he's looking for valuables,' answered Jackie. 'Don't be daft. What else would he be doing here?'

'Yes, of course, he's a burglar, you're right that's what they do isn't it, burglars look for valuables.' Andrea went on. 'Anyway, we can't help as we don't know if Kim even has any valuables, let alone where they might be.'

'That's very true. We have no idea at all if she has any valuables here, and like my friend says, we wouldn't know where she kept them if we did know.'

'Will you shut up!' the man growled, 'or I'll have to shut you up.'

'Oh, indeed,' said Jackie, 'how will you do that? There's three of us. It'll be difficult.'

'Yes, very difficult, there being only one of you.'

'Yes, three against one is not very good odds, is it?'

'Not good at all,'

'No, we completely outnumber you.'

'Yes, in fact, we outnumber you three to one.'

'Oh, for god's sake just SHUT UP!' the man turned to Cora, who was the nearest to him, but as he tried to take a step, he toppled and fell against the bed.

While the others had been distracting him, Cora had crawled a little closer to his legs and having silently removed her beautiful turquoise silk scarf from around her neck, she had managed to tie it round his ankles. The Ponge silk was so light and delicate he hadn't felt a thing, but when he'd tried to take a step he had lost his balance and fallen. The three women immediately pounced on him. Actually Andrea and Cora pounced. Jackie took longer, as she hadn't been joking about needing help to get up. They dragged him down onto the floor and then following the example that Betty had shown with the studio intruder, Andrea sat on his chest, straddling him and pinning his arms down with her knees, while Cora sat on his legs. Jackie, having managed to get up with the help of the bedside cabinet, strode round to his head and grabbing his hat and scarf ripped them off. There lying on the floor looking up at them, was Mal.

The police arrived shortly after, having been alerted by Kevin. Andrea heard the car and saw the blue lights flashing through the upstairs window and while she and Cora remained sitting on Mal, Jackie went downstairs to let them in.

As Mal was led away, hands cuffed behind his back, he looked at the women and smiled his dazzling smile. 'Well done, ladies,' and he winked.

'Goodbye Mal,' and they waved.

48

Thursday 6th & Friday 7th March

The next day Andrea drove them all to the police station where they were to make their statements about the happenings of the previous evening. She felt like an old hand after having so recently made a police statement regarding the assault by Carl Briston, the illegal fly-tipper, but for Cora and Jackie, it was their first time.

That afternoon, Andrea went back into her studio to finish framing her batiks. The Massey Hall exhibition was getting nearer, and stretching and framing her work always took her longer than expected. There was no dancing for her this time, no upbeat music making her want to jig about. Oh no, she had to focus. There was no room for error today. Searching her phone, she found some gentle Chopin piano music, perfect for background listening.

Carefully she cut and glued the wood and clamped it to the edge of her table to allow it to dry correctly. If she didn't take care and do it properly, the finished frame would be buckled and the picture would not hang true. Andrea didn't use glass on her larger pictures. She made a wooden frame and stretched the batiked fabric over it, securing it with a staple gun. Another wooden frame was made to fit snugly around the edge of the first, hiding the staples and finishing the piece off nicely. It all took time, as she had to wait for the glue to dry fully before stretching the fabric.

Working with the wood had engrossed her, but now as she stood waiting for the glue to dry, her mind wandered back to the mystery of who had kidnapped Kim. Mal had confessed to all the burglaries that had been taking place in the local area but had categorically denied having known Kim's whereabouts, and there was absolutely nothing to link him to the kidnapping. He was now off their list of possibles, but there were still one or two unanswered questions to ask. She messaged Jackie and Cora.

Anyone up for another trip to Stickville? Catch up on the gossip and maybe go back to the garage and have a chat with Nish? A.

Definitely—was just thinking the same. C.

Tomorrow? J.

So, Friday found them yet again back in The Trio of Fools. Due to a local outbreak of early spring flu, the pub was short staffed and Erin was behind the bar, having been brought out from the kitchen to cover for the morning. The three women were keen to hear all the local gossip about Mal, and Jackie was just as keen to sample the steak and kidney pie again. The few regulars that were propping up the bar were talking about Mal's arrest and his secret burglary career. No one had suspected him, and it had come as a great shock to them all to think that the handsome, charming and friendly Mal had been a criminal, responsible for the spate of burglaries working the area for months.

The local police had told Cora, Andrea and Jackie that with his job as a delivery man and his charismatic manner, when the recipients were not in, and Mal left their parcels with neighbours he would chat and find out all the local news about who was away and when they'd be back. With the hope of a shorter sentence, Mal had told them everything.

Apparently he had acquired some of his information from listening in to Jackie, Andrea and Cora's conversations in the pub and had actually been inside Kim's house before. He had knocked the CCTV camera out of whack accidentally whilst legitimately delivering a parcel, but when it happened, he decided to leave it as he thought it might be useful one day, then when he heard that Kim was away and not taken her passport he decided to burgle her house the first time. Among his many burgling skills was lock picking and he could open standard Yale locks in seconds, explaining how he got into Kim's house and why the car keys had been pushed to the wall. Having overheard their conversation in the pub, he knew that Kim had left her out-of-date passport lying on the table and he had gone straight to the dining table and stolen it. This seemed to be a common occurrence in other houses too, passports were taken among other things, and it turned out he had a lucrative market for the stolen documents and could sell them on for a lot of money.

He always carried an empty parcel for cover in case he was stopped and which he could also use to remove anything that wouldn't fit in a pocket. When he had recently discovered Kim had been kidnapped because she was wealthy, and when he'd then overheard the three women say she was still in hospital, although she would be back soon, he thought he'd have another quick look round and see what pickings there were upstairs in the way of cash or jewellery. But he had not bargained on the three women being there and panicked when he saw them.

Andrea, Cora, and Jackie ordered their coffees from the bar and chatted to Erin while they waited.

'Who would've thought it, eh? Our lovely Mal, sitting there good as gold,' Erin nodded at the empty bar stool that he had usually occupied, 'a hardened criminal.'

'Well, perhaps not such a hardened criminal, but certainly a habitual burglar who seems to have fooled everyone,' said Jackie.

'And you three ladies being attacked by him and then taking him on single-handed,' Erin put a large cappuccino down on the bar.

Andrea, Cora, and Jackie glanced at each other and smiled at Erin's dramatic interpretation.

'Everything's been going on here lately. There must be something in the water, what with Kim's kidnapping and Mal and everything. I hear so much more working here. I'm glad I lost my previous job. It wasn't anywhere near as exciting as learning all the gossip and news.' Erin put down the two large lattes.

'Where were you working before?' Andrea asked idly as she picked up her coffee, ready to walk to a table.

'Oh, I worked for Tom at the garage for years. I cleaned for a few hours each morning. I don't know how I stood it so long, rundown house that it was. It was impossible to get clean, no matter how hard I worked. And it was freezing in the winter. Tight old git didn't have central heating and would only light the fire in the evening after I'd gone home. And the pay was rubbish too.'

Andrea put down her coffee. 'You worked for Tom and his wife?'

'I worked for Tom. His wife had gone by the time I started. Another Hen in there Sid?' Erin took the empty pint glass from an old man sitting further along the bar and began to fill it with draught Old Hen's Piddle, the local ale.

'Hang on, his wife had gone? Gone where?' asked Cora.

'Oh, she left him years ago. That's when I started cleaning for him. That's why he needed me. Couldn't look after himself. Took most of their money and disappeared she did. Don't blame her either. All those cars he kept buying, it was like he couldn't help himself. He should've gone to car buyers anonymous,' Erin laughed at her joke and gave Sid his pint.

'He told us his wife still lived with him,' said Andrea.

'Between you and me,' Erin lowered her voice although no one else was listening, 'I think Tom went a bit doolally after she went. Anyway, he told me she'd come back and brought the money back too. That's why he didn't want me to come anymore, so I left at Christmas. Christmas I ask you, what a time to lose my job, such as it was. I was so lucky to get this, and it's turned out to be much better. Every cloud, as they say.' Erin laughed and moved up the bar to help another customer to a pint of the local ale.

They remained standing at the bar sipping their coffees, waiting for Erin to finish serving and come back.

'Have you seen Tom's wife since her return? What's her name, by the way?' asked Jackie.

'Joan. I always laughed, Tom and Joan. D'you see Tom Joan? It's like Tom Jones, get it?' Erin laughed. 'No, I haven't seen her. I heard her though not long after she came back.'

'What happened Erin?' asked Andrea.

'Well, Tom still owed me some money, wages you know, only twenty quid, but I wanted it what with Christmas having been expensive and all and as he hadn't given it to me and it looked like he'd forgotten, I went round to the garage to ask for it. Lucky, I did as he was sick not long after and went into hospital. He wasn't on the forecourt or in the garage, so I knocked on the door of the house. I could hear banging and shouting, a woman's voice. I knocked louder, and the shouting stopped. Then Tom opened the door a little and looked out. I asked him for my money, and he gave me two tenners from his trouser pocket and shut the door in my face. Well, that was it really. I'd got my money, so I was happy.'

'How d'you know it was Joan?' asked Andrea.

'Well, who else would it be? And anyway, Nish said Joan was back, he was talking in the pub one night, everyone knew.'

This was interesting new information and when they finished their coffees, they drove round to Tom's garage to see if they could find out more.

The garage was open but there was no sign of Tom, instead a younger man was working on the forecourt dressed in similar blue overalls to those Tom had been wearing on their previous visit. The man was bent over the open bonnet of a car. It was Nish. A radio was playing loudly, and they got very close before he noticed them. They introduced themselves and as he straightened up; they saw a lean man in his mid-thirties with a neatly trimmed beard and jet black hair held back from his face by a red bandana. Nish was not handsome in the conventional way, but his irregular features gave him an attractiveness that was enhanced by his warm, open manner.

Reaching down, he turned off the radio then he looked at them steadily taking in the three older ladies standing before him muffled up in their coats and scarves despite the slightly warmer weather they were all experiencing lately.

He smiled, then wiping his hands on a rag from his pocket, he said, 'How can I help you?'

'Is Tom around?' asked Jackie.

'No, he's taking a bit of a holiday. I'm Nish, I'm running the place, will I do?' He smiled at the three women.

They explained who they were and how they knew Kim Merchant and her son Kevin and asked if they could ask him some questions.

'I'm happy to answer your questions if I can. I've had to answer so many from the police since I came back. I won't notice a few more.' Nish laughed good naturedly, dazzling them with his perfect white teeth.

'She was kept in your flat wasn't she? It must have been awful for you to return to a crime scene.' This was more of a statement from Cora than a question.

'Well, it was certainly a surprise, that's for sure,' Nish nodded. 'I didn't know what was going on when the police met me at the airport.'

'Oh, they met you off the plane. Goodness me, you must have been surprised, to say the least.'

'They were fine. It was obvious I had nothing to do with it, but they needed to speak to me and put me in a B&B for a night while they processed the flat, dusting for fingerprints and whatever else they do. Anyway, I'm back in now and it's fine.' Nish smiled his perfect smile again.

'Where was she kept, do you know?' asked Jackie.

'It's a two-bedroom flat, although neither are very big, and it seems she was kept in the smaller of the two bedrooms. It's a rented flat and I rent it furnished, but there's only the essentials, just a single bed and a chair in that room. I never go in there to be fair, never have call to use it.'

'I wonder why no one heard her,' mused Andrea. 'I know she was drugged, but I understand the drug took a few days to subdue her properly. She must have tried to escape, banging on the window or the walls, or even if she was tied up, she might have shouted. Why didn't the neighbours hear?'

'Well, of course I don't know, but there are no neighbours. The rooms above the shops either side to the Hospice shop are used as store rooms, no one lives there.'

'Ahh, well, that would explain that then.' Jackie changed tack. 'Do you mind if we ask what happened when you drove Kim home from here on the 28th of December? We understand you were the last person to see her before her abduction.'

Nish looked confused. 'Sorry, but I really don't think I was the last person to see Mrs Merchant before she went missing.'

'Well, can you tell us when you did last see Kim? Can you remember Nish?'

'Now you're asking. The police asked me this and I'll tell you what I told them. I can't remember. Simple as that.' Nish looked into the distance, trying to remember, 'It was a long time ago and I've been away, you understand? Hmm, no I really can't remember, sorry.'

'Fair enough,' said Cora, 'but can you remember taking Kim home in your car the day she dropped her car off here for a service? It was the Saturday after Christmas, if that helps.'

'No, I didn't do that, I remember that because I was working on an oil change and couldn't stop as the customer wanted his car by the end of the day, he needed it to drive to a family birthday party on the Sunday. I guess Tom took her back.'

'Interesting. Tom said it was you.'

Nish laughed. 'He probably got mixed up. I probably took someone else back home that morning and he got confused. I didn't take her back. I didn't even know she was here.'

‘Can we ask if Tom’s wife is back, do you know?’ Andrea changed the subject. She had a good feeling about this young man. He was so relaxed and easy to talk to.

‘Well, I think she came back at Christmas,’ Nish answered. ‘Why d’you want to know? What’s it got to do with Mrs Merchant?’

‘We’re not sure really, just trying to get an overall picture, that’s all.’ *Being downright nosey, really, that’s all.*

‘So Joan came back at Christmas?’ said Jackie. ‘Did you see her?’

‘No, I never saw her. I heard her a couple of times, but she stayed indoors. Tom said she had a bad chest and couldn’t go outside in the cold.’

‘What did you hear?’

‘Just raised voices a couple of times, Tom and Joan were having a bit of an argument. I guess it was nothing, didn’t last. Then Tom got food poisoning and went into hospital and Joan went to stay with a friend near to the hospital so she could visit him easily. When he came home, I found out my uncle had died and Tom suggested I go to Spain for a month for my uncle’s funeral, and now they’re away on holiday in Wales for a couple of weeks and I’m looking after things.’

‘So, it was Tom’s idea that you went to the funeral?’ Jackie asked.

‘Oh yes, he’s a good bloke Tom, he said as I’d run the garage for him when he was ill. He’d pay me a bit of a bonus to help with the airfare. I couldn’t have gone otherwise.’

‘Thank you, Nish, you’ve been very helpful. We’re sorry to have bothered you.’ Andrea smiled at the young man, ‘goodbye.’

‘You’re welcome. Sorry I can’t tell you more,’ Nish smiled at the three women, nodded goodbye and bent down to turn up the radio.

49

Friday 7th March & Saturday 8th March

They were back in the pub, back in their usual place, waiting for their lunch order to arrive. They had hurried there after speaking to Nish and were all very excited at what they'd discovered.

'We have to go to the police with this,' said Cora. 'Don't you see? It was Tom who kidnapped Kim.'

'You're right,' agreed Andrea, 'it's got to be Tom.'

'Hang on, hang on, let's get this straight. We might think it's Tom who kidnapped Kim, but we can't just go accusing him. We need proof.' Jackie was the voice of reason.

'But it's got to be Tom,' insisted Cora, 'it all fits. Let's go through how it happened.'

They began at the beginning using Jackie's notebook for reference to dates and tried to remember all the clues they had.

'So, Tom's wife left him some years ago and took all the money.' Cora began. 'He seemed to go off the rails a bit when she went.'

'*A bit doolally,* as Erin said.' Andrea chipped in.

'Indeed, and she left him because of his penchant for

spending large amounts of money on new fast cars. At Christmas, he sacked Erin from her cleaning job, telling her that his wife had come back and brought the money back. That's very unlikely and we think it's probably a lie.'

'Yes, so we think it could have been a cover for his having kidnapped Kim and he was keeping her prisoner in his house.' Andrea said. 'He could have drugged the tea he gave her when she dropped her car off and bundled her into his house so Nish wouldn't see her. He'd expected her to arrive in the morning when she was supposed to, when Nish was out dropping another customer home, but that plan went wrong, so he had to improvise.'

'What about if he didn't really go into hospital but stayed holed up in the house slowly drugging Kim to get her subdued?' Cora leant forward in her seat. She was really getting into her theory now.

Jackie nodded. 'We have no proof he had food poisoning, so that's possible, but how would he survive for a couple of weeks?'

'He'd stockpiled supplies. Don't forget he planned this. Then when Kim was completely compliant, he came home from hospital.' Cora indicated speech marks with her fingers. 'When Nish told him about his uncle having died, Tom seized his chance to get Kim out of his house. He gave Nish the time off to go to Spain, telling him to take as much time as he needed, giving him a bonus for the airfare and continuing to pay his wages too, from what Mal told us.'

'Yes, and from what Erin said about him being so tight with money, that was very out of character.'

'Definitely. He then transferred Kim to Nish's flat. He could easily have got the key from Nish, either telling him he'd keep an eye on it or pinching it from his pocket one day and making a copy before returning it. He then kept Kim there until the car sale was completed. Don't forget, he knows about fast cars and no doubt knows people, collectors who would be in the market for a bargain. When he'd done the deal, he wiped away his fingerprints and left Kim to recover alone, knowing that Nish would be blamed, at least for a time while the police investigated, allowing him time to get away.'

'That's it, it all fits perfectly.' Jackie agreed. 'It explains her car not being mended. He could have told Nish not to touch it as he'd take care of it. He probably took it back to Kim's to muddy the waters further. Maybe he heard our phone messages and wanted to confuse us. I wonder why he picked on Kim, though?'

'I imagine the police will be able to find that out, but perhaps in his confused mind he mixed up Kim with his wife, maybe they looked similar, and he began to hate her instead, a kind of transference,' Andrea mused, 'you know, where someone redirects their feelings for one person onto an entirely different person. It's not uncommon. Kim could have told him about the huge payout she'd received, and he decided to get back what he thought his wife had taken from him. Who knows, we'll never know. So, what should we do? Go to the police now?'

'Let's have our lunch and then decide,' Jackie sat back in her chair just as the waitress came over with a tray.

Cora had decided to join Jackie in having the steak and kidney pie and was very glad she did. Andrea, not really keen on red meat, opted for the cheese and leek quiche with chips and salad. The food as usual, was delicious, and they took their time enjoying their meals.

'That was absolutely delicious,' sighed Cora, 'the best pie I've ever had.'

'Yes indeed,' Jackie leant back in her chair and grinned, 'I forgive Mal for scaring us that night. He recommended the pie and anyone that appreciates a good pie can't be all bad.' They laughed and sipped their drinks.

At the police station later that afternoon, the young policewoman on the desk looked up and smiled as they came in.

'Hello, it's the three ladies who located Mrs Merchant, isn't it.'

Cora marched up to the front desk. 'Hello Constable. Sorry, we don't know your name.'

'Copper. Constable Copper,' she grinned, 'I know,' she sighed, 'I've heard all the jokes. So what can I do for you?'

'We'd like to speak to Sergeant Potts if we can, please.'

'You're in luck. He's here, I'll get him for you.' She left the room.

'Good afternoon. How can I help you today?' Sergeant Potts followed Constable Copper into the front office a few minutes later, but when he saw the women, his face fell. *Oh, hell it's those three women again. What madness have they got into their heads now?*

'Now we know it's not up to us to put forward theories...' began Cora.

Too bloody right it's not. Just leave us to do our work.

'But we think Tom Thomas kidnapped Kim Merchant. All the facts fit, you see.'

'We've talked it through and think we've worked out how he did it,' Andrea added, and Jackie nodded her agreement.

'So you think you're cleverer than the police, do you?' Sergeant Potts raised his eyebrows. *They're all mad as hatters, but I'd better hear what they've got to say.*

'No, not at all,' said Jackie quickly. 'It's just that we've been talking to people, Kim's neighbour Erin, and Nish and they've told us bits and pieces that we've put together.'

'And what makes you think we haven't spoken to them?' asked the sergeant. 'we do try to do our job, you know. We don't just sit about waiting for you three to stumble across things. Ok, tell me what you've come up with.' *Let's get this over with.* 'Come into the interview room.'

They followed the sergeant through the door and squeezed into a tiny room where between them they told him what they knew and what they'd worked out, and Sergeant Potts dutifully made notes, sighing occasionally. When they'd finished, he put down his pen and looked from one to another with the same smug smile on his face that he'd worn before when addressing them, a sort of patronising I know better than you, smile.

'Well ladies, that's quite a theory you have there, well done for coming up with it and I have to agree it fits all the facts.' He gazed round at their eager faces. 'Apart from one major stumbling block,' here the sergeant paused for dramatic effect, 'in the course of doing our job properly,' he raised an eyebrow sarcastically, 'we checked with the hospital and Tom was definitely admitted with severe food poisoning and was kept in for two weeks.'

Hahaha gotcha.

As the sergeant saw the women off the premises he said, 'Now I suggest you three ladies stop worrying yourselves about this, your friend has been found, yes, I know you found her but she wasn't locked in and would have got out herself the next day anyway. Leave it to us, as you're not helping anyone by turning up here with your off the wall theories about innocent people and wasting police time. You can't go around accusing people, you know, just leave it to us. Join a knitting club or something if you haven't got enough to do. There are lots of things for the elderly to do nowadays. Volunteer in a charity shop if you want to feel useful.'

Jackie started to speak but Andrea quickly put her hand on her arm, no sense in making things worse.

Andrea went walking early the next morning. It was still cold despite the early March sun. The ditches were yellow with marsh marigolds and coltsfoot and along the river bank common daisies dotted the footpath. She breathed the fresh air and looked about her, smiling as she picked up a tissue with her stick and put it in her litter bag. Probably someone had dropped it accidentally. This was the level of littering she was dealing with now, and it was fine. The large-scale dumping had ceased, the constant mocking from Ernest had stopped. Her everyday walking was back to normal, and she was enjoying every second she was out in the countryside. Tiny footprints in the damp earth showed the trails of the little muntjak deer no longer having to detour around piles of waste and she smiled. Life was good.

That afternoon found Andrea and Cora in Jackie's cottage, sipping mugs of tea in her sitting room and nibbling on digestive biscuits and more of Ruby's delicious chocolate brownies.

'I was sure we'd solved it,' said Cora, 'I was positive it was Tom.' She held her mug and absent-mindedly dipped a digestive biscuit into her tea, holding it there just a bit too long until it broke off. 'Oh, bugger it.'

'Yes, bugger it is right,' Jackie agreed, not noticing the biscuit accident, 'and the patronising Sergent Potts thinks we're interfering old biddies with not enough to do, so now we'll probably never know who abducted Kim.'

'Never mind, we've had some fun trying to find out. I've enjoyed having a puzzle to solve and going out on trips, talking to new people and having lovely lunches,' Cora smiled round at the others, 'even if we haven't solved it, it's been interesting, I'll miss it.'

'Me too,' agreed Andrea, 'although I would like to have some sort of ending. Still, I can properly concentrate on the upcoming exhibition now. I'll have to finish off my batiks, help set it up, do my share of invigilating for four weeks, and help with the take down, so actually, what with my classes I wouldn't have much time for any more sleuthing anyway.'

'The Studio Sleuths will hang up their notebook,' laughed Cora.

'Yeah, it's a shame though. We're a good team.' Jackie sighed, and they all agreed, yes it was a shame.

Just then, all their phones pinged together. It was a message from Kevin.

Are you free? Mum and I are at her house collecting a few bits. Wondered if you wanted to pop over and see her. No problem if you're busy, but I've had an update from the police, I can fill you in. K.

We're free, see you in 30. J.

They sat looking at Kim. She was much better, actually she looked better than they had expected. Her colour had returned, but she still showed the telltale signs of the ordeal she had undergone by the dark circles round her eyes and the drawn cheeks. She was still very thin, and Jackie was glad she had brought the remainder of the chocolate brownies, which they were all enjoying now, with a cup of tea in the now tidy sitting room.

'We've had an update from the police,' Kevin swallowed the last of his brownie, 'and thought you'd want to know. They've spoken to all the locals, Tom and Nish included and are now convinced mum was abducted by someone from her past and not a local person at all.'

Andrea glanced over at Kim, and she shrugged. She seemed resigned to the fact her kidnapper might go free.

'They don't know how the person or persons unknown knew about Nish's flat being empty,' continued Kevin, 'but think as it was common knowledge in the pub the kidnapper heard about it and made a last-minute decision to move her there to cover his or her tracks. With the spare key to the flat being kept in a drawer behind the counter at the Hospice shop, again, anyone could have taken it. They're keeping the case open but have stopped questioning the locals.'

'Ahh, I see, well it's very unsatisfactory, but I suppose that's it then,' sighed Andrea, reaching for another brownie.

Jackie leant forward and put her hand on Kim's arm. 'What happened Kim? Can you remember anything at all?'

'The last thing I remember was when my phone rang on the Saturday after Christmas. I was in the middle of my housework. It was Tom from the garage saying I'd forgotten to take my car in. I just grabbed my keys and ran out of the house. I thought I'd be back in twenty minutes, didn't even take a coat. Little did I know it would be months before I was back here again.' She looked round the room, now thankfully tidy, as she shook her head and tears welled up in her eyes.

'It's okay mum, don't worry, it's all over now.' Kevin stood up. 'Mum's staying with us for a bit while she decides what to do. Maisie and Poppy are doubling up and Mum's in

Maisie's room. Shall we grab some bits and pieces that you'll need for a week or two at ours and get going?'

Kim wiped her eyes and nodded.

'Just one thing though,' Andrea looked at Kim, 'haven't you any idea at all who it was that abducted you?'

'The police have asked her that already and mum can't remember anything.'

Andrea could see that Kevin was very protective of his mother and didn't pursue the question, but Kim spoke.

'I remember driving to the garage and handing my car keys over to Tom, and that's all. I think I had a quick cup of tea with Tom but honestly, after that, it's all a blank. Maybe not a complete blank. There are some bits I sort of remember, but I don't know if they were real or I dreamt them. Just a shadowy figure.' Kim shuddered.

'Come on mum, you've told the police everything you can, now let's go home.'

Kim was looking tired, and the women decided it was time to go and leave mother and son together. They were pleased to see Kim safe and sound, but they knew this was probably the last time they would see her. They knew she wasn't coming back to the studio. So, with many 'goodbyes' and 'good lucks,' they left.

50

Monday 10th March

The following day was Monday, and the afternoon textiles class was well underway. The studio was warm and smelt of hot wax despite a window being open to let in some much-needed sunshine. A delivery van drew up outside the studio and a young man in an orange high vis vest jacket got out with two parcels. Andrea went to the door to meet him and he stood on the threshold looking round at everyone. The delivery man smiled and the women all smiled back.

'I've got one for you and one for next door. Can you take it in?' the man gave Andrea her parcel and snapped a photo, then offered her the other one.

'Yes sure, no problem,' Andrea took it from him and was snapped once again.

'I knocked but no reply. Are they away?' the delivery man smiled again, a charming smile.

'Sorry, I've no idea, but probably not. They never go away. They're probably just out.'

When the man had left, Jackie laughed, 'Haha, you didn't fall for the lovely smile. You know they're away for a fortnight.'

'I know, it's just that after Mal, I'm not going to tell anyone anything anymore. I'm sure he was innocently asking, but you never know where it can lead.'

Andrea's parcel contained supplies for the studio, a length of Ponge silk, a length of Habotai silk and a selection of dyes to top up the existing stock, and everyone was keen to see if any new colours were in the box. The usual quantity of yellow was there, they got through more yellow than any other colour, so Andrea had stocked up on both lemon and golden, but in with the scarlet, magenta red, cobalt blue, olive green, turquoise and more, were a couple of new ones, duck egg blue and warm black. They had had warm black a few years ago and everyone had loved it. When used on silk and put over another colour, it gave it a silvery iridescence which was beautiful, and when painted over yellow, it turned it gold. It seemed to be a magical dye, giving an uplift whenever it was used. Andrea hadn't been able to get it for ages, but it had now come back on the market, and everyone was excited.

'Oh, this is good news, the return of warm black,' Jackie said happily.

Andrea was putting the silks away and Cora helped by putting the dyes on the shelf and moving the pots of ready mixed dyes to make room.

'Be careful Cora, don't get dye on your jumper, maybe you should put an apron on.' Andrea said.

'We've had a lot of mysteries lately, but one of the biggest unexplained mysteries is why you wear good clothes to come here,' Jackie laughed.

'I'm going on somewhere. You forget I have a life,' Cora giggled, 'and before you say it, yes, I know I should have brought something else and changed here, but I forgot, okay. I can't remember everything, I'm not Superwoman.'

'If you were, your super power would be clumsiness, and

dyes would be your Kryptonite,' chortled Betty. 'Anyway, fill us in on the news from Stickville. Sal and I are dying to know.'

'Dying to know! Very good,' laughed Sal, and the others grinned.

Jackie repeated what Erin had told them, telling them about her thoughts on Mal's sentence and Tom and Joan's move.

'So, Mal may not even serve three years. That's preposterous. He threatened you three with a knife! That's armed robbery.' Betty was outraged.

'Actually, he didn't have a knife,' said Cora. 'He just said he did. He panicked when he saw us. I think he was as scared as we were. He was never going to hurt us. He just wanted Kim's jewellery, and we got in the way.'

'But that doesn't matter. Surely it's still armed robbery. He threatened you with a knife and you weren't to know if he had one or not.' Betty was incensed.

'Well, to be honest we didn't tell anyone,' Andrea explained, 'none of us mentioned the threat in our statements and as Mal didn't say anything either, no one knew about it, so he was just charged with burglary.'

Betty made a noise like a burst tyre and rolled her eyes.

'He's still a burglar,' said Sal. 'He deserves to be in prison, knife or no knife.'

'I totally agree,' Cora nodded, 'but I think three years with possible time off for good behaviour is probably fair. He'll learn his lesson, I'm sure.'

'You actually still like him, don't you?' Betty shook her head in disbelief. 'He scared the life out of you and you still like him. I don't understand that at all.'

'I know,' said Cora with a grin, 'but he was essentially a very likeable man, wasn't he?' she looked at Jackie and Andrea and they both nodded in agreement.

'But he stole people's passports.' Betty wasn't giving up. 'That's really bad. He should have got an extra two years for that alone.'

'Yeah, I know it's not good, but that was obviously taken into account at his trial. Why d'you think he should have got more?' Andrea asked.

'Because it's a bloody pain in the arse to get a new passport, that's why, and it costs a bloody fortune nowadays, too.'

They laughed. They knew it wasn't funny that people had had their homes broken into and their belongings stolen, but they were laughing at Betty's outrage, not at the crimes.

'Oh my goodness, of course, I think that's it Betty!' Andrea stopped laughing and looked round at the others. 'Is it obvious? Have we sort of known all along?'

'What are you talking about, Andrea?' asked Jackie, 'What have we sort of known?'

Andrea screwed her face up as she tried to get her thoughts in order. 'We know Nish and Mal knew each other, right? Mal told us that.'

'Yes, Mal said Nish used to go in the pub now and again, but so what?'

'Then it has to have been Nish who kidnapped Kim.' Andrea began to explain. 'It's been bugging me. Everything has pointed to him all along. It was his flat that was used, and he had the opportunity, but his alibi was so strong he was thought to be innocent. If that's disproved, it could put a new light on everything.'

'Ahh, I think I know what you're getting at Andrea,' Cora nodded slowly. 'It all hinges on Nish's alibi. Oh, very clever, Nish, very clever.'

'What? What are you thinking?' Sal looked round as the realisation slowly appeared on Cora's face.

'Ahh I'm beginning to see now too,' Jackie smiled at

Andrea, 'if he wasn't in Spain at the funeral he could easily have been here keeping Kim prisoner.'

'But he was in Spain. The police have checked,' Sal was getting animated now, 'will someone please explain what you think you've discovered?'

'Mal stole passports, right? We know that much, then he sold them on for cash. Now although I don't know anything about stuff like that, I assume by association he knew people who made false passports.'

'Ahh, I see.' Sal looked between the women. 'Mal got Nish a false passport.'

'Yes. He could have gone out to Spain on his real one, returned immediately on the false one, worked on Kim to get her money, then flown back to Spain on his false passport and then come home using his real one. The police would check his real one and find he'd been in Spain for a month.'

'The perfect alibi.' Betty nodded, 'It's a good theory.'

'But what about the fingerprints—why were they wiped away?' asked Sal. 'It was his own flat so they would be expected to be there.'

'I think that's why he only wiped away some, those in the room where Kim was kept, I think he wanted to make it look like someone else had been there who had cleaned up after themselves. He wanted to bamboozle the police,' Cora grinned, 'and if it's true he certainly did, he bamboozled everyone.'

'It's a strong theory. Will you go to the police with it?' Betty asked.

'I'm not sure we should after last time. What if we're wrong again? Sergeant Potts told us to go away and stop interfering.' Andrea looked round at Jackie and Cora and raised her eyebrows in a question.

'I think we have to,' said Cora. 'What's the worst he can say? He'll just tell us to go away. We can cope with that.'

'Ha! Go and see Sergeant Potts once more?' Jackie chuckled. 'That would make his day, give him the opportunity to say we're being interfering busy bodies again after our Tom theory.'

'Yeah, even so, we have to go and tell him what we think. I think we've got it right this time.'

Cora, Jackie and Andrea grinned, Betty smiled to herself, and Sal beaming round at the others, and suddenly exclaimed, 'Look out!' but it was too late, Cora had caught the small pot of freshly mixed magenta red with her elbow and knocked it over. The bright red splashes on her jumper looked like cherries in a bowl of custard.

'Oh buggeration!' said Cora, 'why am I so clumsy?'

'And why the hell are you wearing yellow?' laughed Jackie.

51

Sunday 26th April

A month later they were back in The Trio of Fools, it was definitely spring now and the late April weather was warm enough for a few hardy folk to sit outside in the pretty beer garden at the back, and the friends decided to join them. Andrea was having the delicious fish and chips, but Jackie and Cora had wanted to sample the steak and kidney pie again as they would have no need to come to Stickville so often now that Kim had been found.

They had finished their lunch and were sitting back looking around, taking in the unfamiliar surroundings of the colourful hanging baskets and tubs of ornamental shrubs that decorated the small patio area, and remembering the many times during the winter they had sat cosily inside with the log fire blazing. Today Jimmy the landlord had been as welcoming as ever and told them not to be strangers. They assured him they wouldn't be.

'Well, I didn't think I'd be seeing you three again,' the voice came before the person. 'I've come for your dirties. How are you all?'

‘Hi Erin,’ Andrea looked up and smiled, ‘we’re fine thanks, and you?’

‘Haha, nothing stops me. What are you doing here? Not more investigating?’ Erin laughed loudly at her joke and a couple of the locals looked round.

‘No, it’s the steak and kidney pie that’s brought us this time.’ Jackie grinned. ‘It was delicious.’

‘Any news?’ asked Cora, ‘We drove past Kim’s house on the way here and saw the sold sign up in the garden. Has Kim gone then?’

‘Yes, she never really came back, moved in with her son temporarily, and put the house on the market. It was snapped up straight away. I think she’s buying another, too many horrible memories with this one, I suppose.’

‘Yes, of course, she wouldn’t want to go back there. I don’t blame her.’

‘Have you met your new neighbours yet?’ asked Jackie.

‘Yes, they’re fine. An old couple about your age, quite sweet, really. I don’t suppose they’ll complain about my ciggy ends in the flower beds, probably won’t be able to see them.’ Erin laughed again, but this time the locals ignored her.

‘Oh, they sound nice,’ said Jackie ignoring a snorting sound coming from Cora, ‘anything else happened of interest?’

‘No, I don’t think so. Oh yes, I heard Mal got sentenced to three years in a category C prison in Nottingham, but I guess you’ll know all about that being witnesses and all.’

‘Yeah, we did know, although we weren’t at court for the hearing,’ Andrea explained, ‘we wrote out statements and didn’t need to be there in person.’

‘I expect he’ll charm his way to an early release,’ Erin continued. ‘Oh, and Tom and Joan have decided to sell their garage and retire to the south coast of Wales. They say they want to spend more time together. Ha, I'll give them a year before they're back arguing again.' That laugh again.

'What happened with Nish?' Andrea asked innocently. 'What about his job there?'

'Nish? Oh, haven't you heard? He was arrested, that was one of the reasons Tom decided to retire, said he couldn't continue single-handed and couldn't afford anyone else. Seems Nish worked for a pittance. I've no idea why.'

The three women looked at each other.

'Arrested?'

'Yes, he kidnapped Kim. It was him all along, tricked everyone he did, police and everyone. Something about pretending to be in Spain. Right, I must get these dirties back to the kitchen. Nice seeing you ladies again, take care,' and Erin and the dirties tripped back across the patio and disappeared inside.

The women stared at each other.

'Well, that's good news, but you'd think Sergeant Potts might have told us. After all, it was our theory that made him look for Nish's false passport.'

'Probably pretended he'd thought of it himself. Never mind, it's good to know we were right.' Cora grinned, 'What with us being Studio Sleuths.'

Just then their phones pinged simultaneously. It was Kevin. Cora answered.

Can you talk? I've got news. K.

Yes. C.

They turned away from the bright sunlight and watched as Kevin's face appeared on the small screen.

‘Hi Kevin. Good to see you again,’ Jackie spoke for them all.

‘Hello ladies, lovely to see you too. Are you all well?’

‘Yes, we’re fine, thank you. We can see you are. Where are you?’

Kevin laughed. ‘We’re in Italy. We’re having a real family holiday and it’s wonderful. Everyone’s here and they want to say hello.’

He turned his phone round, and the friends saw a sea of happy smiling faces in front of a whitewashed villa in the Italian sunshine. Kim was there looking tanned and healthy with her arms round the shoulders of two happy little girls in bathing suits and Carol was behind, smiling and looking relaxed.

‘Hi there everyone,’ they called into the phone and waved.

‘Thank you again for all your help and support.’ Kim smiled, ‘I think you know my gorgeous daughter-in-law,’ Carol nodded and waved, ‘and these are my beautiful grand-daughters, Masie and Poppy, say hello girls.’

‘Hello,’ they chorused, then ‘come on nana, let’s go back in the pool, come on.’ The little girls tugged at a laughing Kim.

‘Sorry I’m wanted, Kevin will fill you in on the news.’ and with a final wave at the camera she allowed herself to be pulled away towards the water. This was a new Kim the women watched, calm and contented, and it was delightful to see.

Kevin turned the phone back, laughing. ‘They’re spending every minute they can together. Mum has a new lease on life. It’s lovely.’

‘That’s great, we’re so pleased for you all,’ Andrea said.

‘I thought you might want to know the latest.’ Kevin continued.

'Yes, we do, go on.'

'Well, first of all, mum has sold her land at last. Snowy and Eggy White bought it from her, cash buyers. Everyone's happy. Now they can join their two farms together and put their expansion plans with Young Eggy into place. They were so pleased mum decided to sell to them that they gave her what she paid for it, and they've kept the few sheep on too, so as I say everyone's happy.' Kevin smiled into the camera, and they could see how delighted he was. The three women smiled back. 'And mum has sold her house, too.'

'Oh yes, we've just seen Erin, and she told us she has new neighbours.' Jackie said. 'I expect you're pleased.'

'Yes, it was a quick sale, no chain, so that was excellent. And Mum has had her offer accepted on a nice little cottage in Sleaford, just round the corner to us and it should go through in the next few weeks. She's really excited about being near the grandchildren. As you saw, they've developed a lovely bond now.'

It was good to see Kevin clearly so happy; it was hard to believe that this cheery, smiling face before them was the same one that a few short months ago was broken down and sobbing with worry about his family.

'Have you heard any more from the police?' asked Jackie. She glanced at Andrea and Cora. 'We heard Nish has been arrested.'

'Well, that was really why I was ringing,' Kevin's face broke into a smile. 'Yes, the police have caught him. They've charged him with kidnap and extortion. He's in prison on remand at the moment. He's due in court later this year, but we've been told there's absolutely no doubt he did it. They found the money hidden in his flat.'

'What? They've even got the money back. You must be so pleased.'

'Well, most of it, a hundred and twenty thousand, that's

what Nish sold the car for, but mum is really happy. She'd resigned herself to not seeing any of it again.'

'So what happened?' Jackie asked, although the three women already knew.

'It seems he had a false passport and flew out on his real one to establish an alibi, then flew back on the false one.' Kevin went on to explain what the women had already guessed.

'How did the police come up with that idea?' Cora asked innocently.

'They didn't say. I expect they just worked it out, but they spoke to Mal, who admitted to getting a false passport for Nish. He said he had no idea why he wanted it and wouldn't have done it if he'd known what Nish planned to do. What with them finding the money and Mal's evidence, he'll be put away for a very long time.'

'Do they know why he did it?' asked Andrea.

'It seems he had a weird grudge against mum. He'd worked at Avere on the production line and had applied for a training programme which he didn't get chosen for, so when the company amalgamated, he was let go. He blamed mum although it wasn't her fault.'

'Why on earth did he blame her? She was in H.R.'

'The department choosing who would go onto the training programme asked H.R. for details on all the applicants as a matter of course. Just the usual stuff, you know, how long everyone had worked there, their work record, etc., nothing incriminating or bad. But when Nish went for the interview and wasn't chosen, he somehow got it into his head that it was down to what H.R. had said about him and as mum was head of that department, he blamed her.' Kevin shrugged. 'There's sometimes no understanding what people get into their heads.'

'Heavens above,' Cora shook her head in disbelief, 'Poor Kim. But how did he find her? Had he been looking?'

'No, not really, but he bore the grudge against her.' Kevin continued. 'As we understand it, Mal had worked at Avere too and met Nish in the pub when he moved to Stickville and they got chatting. Mal happened to mention that he'd seen someone else from Avere in the town and told him about mum. It seems Mal had delivered some parcels to her and had recognised her name. So, when he just happened to mention it in conversation, Nish seized on it and all his misplaced hatred for her resurfaced.'

'Wow, what a chance series of events,' said Jackie. Andrea and Cora nodded in agreement.

'But that's excellent news. We're really happy for you and Kim, in fact, for all of you. Life will be fun now you're all together.'

'Yes, we're a proper family at last,' Kevin beamed. 'Anyway, I just thought you'd like to know it has all ended happily. Once again, I can't thank you enough for all the work you put into finding mum and the support you gave me when I was so low, I'll never forget it. Goodbye.'

'Goodbye Kevin.' And the phone line went dead.

The women sat back in their chairs and looked at each other.

'This calls for more tea. I'll be back in a minute.' Jackie left the table and went inside.

A few minutes later, she was back with a tray of tea and a plate of homemade shortbread biscuits that Jimmy had given them on the house.

Andrea took a biscuit and nibbled it as she pondered what they'd learnt from Kevin.

'So, Mal did know Kim after all. He lied to us in the pub when we asked if he knew her. I wonder why?'

'I expect he didn't want to get involved. He wouldn't

want the police asking him questions, would he? Not when he was in the middle of a burglary spree.' Jackie sipped her tea.

'No, I guess not,' Cora agreed, 'but I thought he was a bit shifty at the time, didn't you? Anyway, it's all over now and Kim is back in the bosom of her family.'

'I wish we could have found Kim sooner, though.' Andrea mused. 'I mean yes, we found her, but Nish had already stopped drugging her and she had always been able to move physically. The drug just slowed her mind down, making her compliant and amenable. It was wearing off when we did find her. She wasn't locked in, and like Sergeant Potts said, she would have found her own way out soon, anyway. So really all we did was shave a possible day or two off her captivity, not much to be proud of really seeing as she was there for nearly nine weeks.'

'You're right,' agreed Cora, 'we didn't actually achieve very much despite our expert sleuthing over the last few months,' she grinned, 'but it was fun being a studio sleuth. I enjoyed it.'

'Well, I disagree, I think we achieved a lot between us,' Jackie said, 'for a start we gave sergeant Potts the idea about the false passport so he could catch Nish, and Kim even got her money back. Then we kept Kevin going. We gave him someone to talk to when he had no one and was really low, and to my mind, that counts for a lot. We discovered that Mal was the burglar and stopped him from burgling even more houses, and Andrea has cleaned up the countryside and put a dangerous man in prison. Even if we didn't find Kim until the end, I think we should be very proud of ourselves.'

'Well, that's true and now you put it like that. I think we did well for three novice sleuths.' Andrea lent back in her chair, 'D'you know what I'm most delighted about? Apart from Kim's safe return, of course.' She looked round at the others. 'Getting bloody Ernest off my back. Now the police have had a word he's been keeping out of my way.'

Jackie smiled. 'Well, for me the best thing is discovering the finest steak and kidney pie in Lincolnshire.'

'I agree.' Cora raised her glass, 'and also this lovely pub, here's to the Trio of Fools.'

Printed in Great Britain
by Amazon

59875998R00173